CW00879799

TRANSCENDENT

TRANSCENDENT

PATRICK GALLAGHER

Orion

ORION CHILDREN'S BOOKS

First published in Great Britain in 2024 by Hodder & Stoughton

1 3 5 7 9 10 8 6 4 2

Text copyright © Patrick Gallagher, 2024
Illustration copyright © Teo Skaffa, 2024

The moral rights of the author have been asserted.

*All characters and events in this publication, other than those
clearly in the public domain, are fictitious and any resemblance
to real persons, living or dead, is purely coincidental.*

All rights reserved.
No part of this publication may be reproduced, stored in a retrieval
system, or transmitted, in any form or by any means, without the
prior permission in writing of the publisher, nor be otherwise circulated
in any form of binding or cover other than that in which it is
published and without a similar condition including this condition
being imposed on the subsequent purchaser.

A CIP catalogue record for this book is available from the British Library.

ISBN 978 1 510 11242 1

Typeset in Sabon Palimpsest Book Production Limited, Falkirk,
Stirlingshire

Printed and bound in Great Britain by Clays Ltd, Elcograf S.p.A.

The paper and board used in this book are made
from wood from responsible sources.

Orion Children's Books
An imprint of Hachette Children's Group
Part of Hodder & Stoughton Limited
Carmelite House
50 Victoria Embankment
London EC4Y 0DZ

An Hachette UK Company
www.hachette.co.uk

www.hachettechildrens.co.uk

For Eunata, my grandma

CHAPTER ONE

The town of Jinja, Uganda, was an explosion of sound and vivid colour, its smell a pungent mix of car fumes, market spices and body odour. Car horns blared. Market sellers shouted. Dirt was heavy in the air. It coated everything from the dented bonnets of the cars to the fruit and vegetables in the stalls. Crouched in the alleyway, Kira Flynn could feel it mingling with the sweat on her skin. The sun was so hot that she could not stay in the same place for too long. She winced and shifted her back along the rough brickwork.

Kira's piercing eyes of electric blue peered into Wanyama Road. The facades of the buildings, originally painted in bright colours, had dulled over time beneath the burning African sun. Market stalls lined the red soil on either side of the afternoon traffic, which was at a standstill. A policeman in the middle of the street blew his whistle and pointed but nothing moved. Kira could see a black Jeep Cherokee parked next to him. The car was gigantic. It dominated the road and all the cars around it looked little more than toys. Its windows were tinted so they were just as black as its bodywork. Something about the car made Kira uneasy. It took her a moment to work out what that was.

The Cherokee was gleaming. There was not a speck of dirt on it. It obviously had not been in Uganda long and people who came to town in that sort of car were rarely up to anything good. Kira pulled out her RanaPhone, scrolled until she found the contact named ORANGUTAN and began to type. A bead of sweat curved its way through the grimy layer from her frizzy hair to her temple. When she was finished, she tapped SEND.

ORANGUTAN!

The word blared from Jacob Flynn's own RanaPhone in the sound of Kira's voice. Jacob grimaced. He really needed to stop Kira changing his text alert. Ian turned and looked at him, eyebrows raised. Jacob pulled his RanaPhone out of the back pocket of his jeans. He switched it to silent, put it back and waved in apology.

'My bad. Do continue.'

Jacob and his best friends, Ian and Zachary, were squeezed into the sweltering basement of Ian's mother's drapery shop on Wanyama Road, less than a hundred feet from the alleyway where Kira was crouching. Fabrics were stacked against the walls. High on one side, a barred window looked out to street level, letting in not just light but the sounds and smells of Jinja. Jacob could see ankles and feet walking past. He did his best to ignore all of that and focus on the video they were supposed to be recording.

'Actually, Captain Cosmic,' said Ian, scowling at the RanaPhone which Zachary was holding up to film them, 'it's your turn to speak.'

Zachary swivelled to point the RanaPhone at Jacob and gestured impatiently with his other hand.

'Oh, right! Thank you, Spaceman,' exclaimed Jacob. He pointed at an old gas lantern on the floor in front of him. Joined to the lantern by a rubber pipe was a contraption that looked like a heavily modified electric microwave. The contraption began to splutter and spark violently.

'Get a good shot of it before it catches fire!' Jacob beckoned to Zachary before straightening to face the camera and speak excitedly.

'In the middle of Jinja, we are surrounded by engines, guzzling fuel and coughing up carbon dioxide into the atmosphere. My twin sister and I have created this atmospheric converter to recycle that carbon dioxide into fuel for this gas lantern. It works by reducing the carbon dioxide into carbon monoxide and then combining it with hydrogen to—'

ORANGUTAN!

Both Ian and Zachary looked at Jacob this time. He had switched his RanaPhone to silent! How did she do that?

'Apologies, Spaceman. We're going to have to cut today's video short.' Jacob hurried towards the basement door and past the atmospheric converter, which was producing a lot of smoke. Zachary stopped recording and lowered his RanaPhone.

'Jacob, that's the third video your sister has ruined.'

'She does it on purpose,' Ian pouted.

'The last time Kira texted me more than once, she'd flooded and set fire to our kitchen at the same time,' said Jacob. 'I really need to go.'

'Before you do,' said Ian, using one of his mother's drapes to fan away the smoke, 'Double M's uploaded a new video. Looks like a good one.'

'I'll watch it tonight,' said Jacob. 'See you later.'

He jogged up the steps that led onto Wanyama Road. It had been hot underneath the drapery shop but stepping outside was like stepping inside an oven. Sweat crawled from the fade of Jacob's close-cropped hair. His T-shirt and jeans clung to his body. Making his way along the crowded footpath beside the road, he stood on the tips of his toes to look over the heads rushing past to the other side of the street. Where was Kira?

Jacob stopped. His electric blue eyes narrowed.

Kira's text had been right. That Jeep Cherokee was definitely too clean.

The driver's door of the Cherokee opened and Jacob retreated under the shade of a market stall, keeping his eyes fixed on the parked car. A man stepped out. Just like his car, he was a colossal figure, clad completely in black. More than six feet tall, his broad shoulders towered over the other shoppers, who made sure to step aside as he stalked onto the footpath. The man was wearing a bomber jacket and sunglasses. His bald head was taut with muscle and his face contorted into a permanent scowl. Both sleeves were rolled up to reveal an expensive watch on his tattooed left wrist.

ORANGUTAN! ORANGUTAN! ORANGUTAN!

Kira was calling him now. Jacob frowned and pulled his RanaPhone out of his pocket, answering the call. Bomber Jacket was bending to speak to a street seller and had his back to Jacob. He seemed to be arguing over the price of a bottle of water.

'I don't like him,' said Kira on the other end of the line.

'Where are you?' Jacob muttered, looking frantically around. 'Also, how did you change my text and call alerts to the sound of your own voice? There's not even an option for that!'

'Clock the boy,' said Kira, ignoring the questions.

Jacob turned again. A little down Wanyama Road, a

boy no older than ten was creeping along the footpath by the road and away from the other shoppers. He was wearing a faded T-shirt that hung to his knees. There was something on the boy's neck. Even from a distance, Jacob could see it was the blue tattoo of a spider.

Spider's eyes were fixed on Bomber Jacket's watch.

Spider ran, his naked feet slapping the road. He held his hand out, aiming to rip the watch from Bomber Jacket's wrist. Bomber Jacket was ready. He turned with alarming speed away from the street seller and grabbed the front of Spider's T-shirt, hauling up the boy so he was dangling in front of him. Spider struggled and kicked with his feet. Bomber Jacket's face was twisted in fury, like a towel being wrung. He raised the other hand. It was the size of a dinner plate. He was going to strike the boy across the face.

'Yeah, I really don't like him,' said Kira.

'Kira. Don't,' said Jacob.

'Too late.'

There was the scream of an engine. It was Kira, racing a red Yamaha DT125 motorcycle down the far side of the street in the narrow gap between the cars and the footpath. People yelled and threw themselves out of the way. Just before she reached Bomber Jacket, Kira hurled herself from the bike and grabbed Spider. They collapsed onto the footpath in a heap at Bomber Jacket's feet. The bike crashed onto its side and skidded in a six-foot arc until it rested, smoking, at the feet of some tourists, who had dodged it just in time. Bomber Jacket looked down at Kira in shock while still holding his hand up to strike Spider. The rear wheel spun in the air.

'Pick on someone your own size,' panted Kira, heaving herself to her feet. She straightened to her full, fourteen-year-old height and only then seemed to realise the top of her head barely reached Bomber Jacket's barrel of a chest.

'Kira!' Jacob shouted. He fought his way through the crowd and onto the road. The traffic had just started moving again. Jacob ignored the car horns and dodged the hot, metal bonnets that were slowly beginning to roll forward. The Cherokee was still parked in the middle of the road with its driver's door wide open. The other cars beeped as they manoeuvred around it. Jacob placed himself between Kira and Bomber Jacket.

'Back off, mister. Or I'll make you back off,' Jacob said.

Bomber Jacket's eyes were wide, his face screwed into an expression of flabbergasted surprise. He seemed unable to speak.

Kira mouthed a bemused, 'Mister?' at Jacob then ran to the Yamaha, hauled it upright and jumped back on. For a moment, Bomber Jacket looked as if he were finally about to say something but Jacob turned his back on him to face Kira.

'What do you think you're doing?' Jacob demanded. 'I could have stopped him hitting the kid.'

'From across the road?' she asked in return. 'I know you've got the freakishly long arms of an orangutan but—'

'No, I mean, what do you think you're doing *now*? Get off the bike. I'm driving.'

'Why? Because I'm a girl?'

'No! Well, yeah.'

'What's the point? You can probably reach the handlebars from over there.'

'Kira, you're wasting time!'

Jacob looked back at Bomber Jacket, who was starting to look less and less surprised and more and more angry. His hands were curling into fists the size of plump market chickens.

'OK. Off we go,' said Jacob.

He darted to the Yamaha but Spider had already hopped onto the back, thin arms wrapped snugly around Kira's waist. Jacob could see the hairy body of the tattooed spider nestled on the boy's neck. Two of its eight legs crept up to his ear.

'He's coming too, is he?' asked Jacob in exasperation.

'Do you want to leave him here?'

The boy blinked mutely up at Jacob, who glanced back at Bomber Jacket.

'Good point. Let's go.'

Jacob had just enough time to leap on and put his arms around Spider and Kira before his sister released the throttle and kicked the Yamaha into third gear. The 123cc engine screeched. The back wheel spun, spraying dirt. They sped down the road. Hot air rushed over them. Jacob's shirt hugged his chest and rippled across his back. Sweat that had been creeping vertically down his face slowly turned horizontal. Pedestrians, cars and market stalls hurtled past in a blur, inches away on either side. A dog yowled and dashed out of their path.

'Kira, slow down!' yelled Jacob over the bellow of the engine and the howl of the wind.

'Do you really want me to do that?' Kira yelled back.

Squinting to keep the biting dust out of his eyes, Jacob twisted round to look back down the road. His stomach wrenched itself into a knot.

The Cherokee was following them. Its gigantic, black form could be seen over the tops of the other cars. The traffic was flowing much faster and there were large enough gaps between vehicles for the Cherokee to navigate its way around them to keep up with the Yamaha.

'Speed up! Speed up! Speed up!' Jacob shouted, facing forward again.

Kira was forced to do the opposite. Spider had also seen the Cherokee and appeared to have decided he had more of a chance of escaping Bomber Jacket on foot than he did on wheels. He squirmed on the seat. The Yamaha rocked dangerously and Kira had to jerk the front brake. The front wheel of the Yamaha screamed to a halt. The back wheel skidded and cut another arc into the footpath with the sound of tearing paper. A cloud of red dirt billowed around them. Stones scattered across soil. As soon as the Yamaha was stationary, Spider attempted to spring from it like a leaping frog. Jacob saw a glint of something in the sunlight.

'Wait!' Jacob's hand closed around the boy's wrist, hauling him back. Incredibly, Spider was wearing Bomber Jacket's watch. The black leather strap was far too big for him and slid up and down his spindly arm.

'That doesn't belong to you,' said Jacob.

Spider tried to wrench his hand out of Jacob's. As the two of them struggled, both pairs of eyes fell on the back of the round watch face and the logo engraved upon it.

It was an R in the middle of a golden crown. The RanaTech logo.

Both Jacob and Spider stared at the logo and then each other. Then Spider finally tore his hand free and, with nothing but a toothy grin, slipped from the Yamaha and vanished into the crowd that had gathered around them.

Jacob looked back at the oncoming Cherokee. It was less than twenty feet away and the gap was closing fast.

Either Bomber Jacket had not seen Spider escape or he did not care. It appeared to be Jacob and Kira he was interested in now. Even though Jacob could not see anything through its tinted windows, he could imagine Bomber Jacket's huge form hunched over the steering wheel, black leather boot pushing ever further down on the accelerator.

'Time to go.' Kira twisted the throttle.

'Wait!' Jacob gripped Kira's hand to stop her releasing it completely.

'What are you doing?' Kira cried.

Jacob was muttering under his breath. 'If we take a left by Ico Computers then a right by Dheyongera Electronics that will bring us onto Tororo Road and we can lose him by Mukobe Homestay and if acceleration is the rate of change, that means it's a derivative of velocity so the speed differential will be less than . . . I got it. Go that way!'

Jacob pointed through the crowd towards an alleyway five feet in width. Kira did not question him. She wrenched the handlebars. Onlookers scattered as the bike careered into the alleyway and away from Wanyama Road. Flashing past them on one side was a rugged brick wall and, on the other, a corrugated metal fence, behind which the concrete skeleton of a high-rise loomed. Hot air and stinging dust buffeted them. Up ahead, construction workers milled around the alleyway, staring up at a stack of blue water pipes on a pallet the size of a small car. It was being hoisted precariously to the upper floors by a rope winch.

'Is he following us?' Kira shouted over her shoulder.

'I don't know! I can't see him,' Jacob shouted back.

With feline agility, Kira twisted herself around so she was facing Jacob. She pulled her legs up and rested her dirty trainers on the saddle.

'Get off! Get off! Get off!' Jacob pulled his face away from the filthy knees of Kira's jeans. He reached around her to grab the handlebars. The Yamaha swerved alarmingly. Tufts of grass whipped at the spokes.

The construction workers shouted, scrambling out of the way as Jacob and Kira roared past. The shadow of the water pipes swept over them. Kira reached into her back pocket and pulled out a slingshot, along with a stone that had been sharpened to a vicious point. She loaded the stone, pulled back the elastic sling and then it was her turn to mutter under her breath.

'Multiply the spring constant by the distance to find the magnitude of the force and use the kinetic energy of the projectile to find the horizontal and vertical velocity so the trajectory will be . . .'

Kira stuck her tongue out between her teeth and let fly with the slingshot. The stone whistled through the air, slicing the rope. It frayed. The water pipes jerked violently. Their shadow swayed over the alley. The construction workers pulled each other out from underneath it, yelling and gesticulating after the Yamaha. Kira waited until the workers were clear, loaded another stone and let fly again. The rope snapped cleanly. The pipes plunged downward. There was a shattering discord as they struck the rough gravel of the road, bouncing, quivering and rolling along the ground. A cloud of red dust filled the alleyway.

'Let's see him bully his way through those.' Kira grinned and twisted herself back to take the handlebars. She slowed the Yamaha and steered it out of the alley and onto the main road.

'There was no need to do that,' said Jacob. 'I'd already thought of a shortcut.'

'It was an amazing shot, though, wasn't it?'

'There's something very wrong with you,' Jacob sighed.

'Yeah? Then why didn't I miss?'

Cars honked as Kira weaved the bike past them to reach the other side before following Tororo Road out of Jinja. Jacob loosened his grip and leaned back on the saddle. He looked down at Bomber Jacket's watch, which he had managed to pull from Spider's wrist before the thief had escaped. The golden RanaTech logo glinted in the sunlight.

'Kira, that man worked for RanaTech.'

'RanaTech? The biggest technology conglomerate in

the world?' Kira sounded surprised. 'Did you forget to pay your phone bill?'

'What if he comes looking for us?' Jacob asked.

'He won't come looking for us, Jacob. That kid stole his watch so he went after him. It had nothing to do with us.'

Jacob craned his neck back around to watch Jinja shrink behind them. There was no tarmac outside of town, and the Yamaha lurched along the red dirt track, belching smoke.

'I don't know,' he said nervously. 'It looked a lot like he was gunning for the two of us back there.'

'Don't worry yourself, Jacob.' Kira laughed. 'I bet you five thousand shillings we never see that guy again.'

CHAPTER
TWO

Mbale was two hours east of Jinja, connected by Tirinyi Road.

The sky began to streak with oranges and purples as the echoing bellow of the Yamaha rolled across the fields. Jacob and Kira dipped into a valley where the air was cooler. The breeze was a balm on their sticky skin. The setting sun was a simmering, red disc, slowly sinking beneath the hilltops. The fields, once a lush green, were a burnt ochre, cut into the hills and stacked on top of each other like steps on a staircase. There was the smell of burning, too, from the bonfires, red glimmers in the distance that cast long shadows across the grass. There were women working in the fields. They looked up and watched as the bike screeched past. One of them, standing by the red dirt road, leaned on her hoe and waved in greeting. Jacob waved back. The woman smiled. A baby bound to her back peered from behind her. Further along, a group of men sat in plastic chairs by the side of the road.

'Mzungus!'

Laughing children were running along a ridge high above. Jacob could see their thin forms silhouetted against the darkening sky.

Mzungu. 'White' in Swahili.

It was only half true but that far out of town, anything different was an attraction. Jacob and Kira's blue eyes and light skin – the result of being the twins of a Ugandan mother and English father – were enough to cause everyone to look up from their warm bottle of Nile Special. Jacob could not see Kira's face but felt her body stiffen.

'Ignore them,' he said, just loud enough to be heard over the bike.

Before returning to their business, the children, women and men of the valley watched the small but noisy shape of the Yamaha diminish into the dying light.

The only light came from the red flames of a fire rustling in front of the porch. There was the fragrant smell of burning logs. Creaking banana trees lined the Flynns' wood-panelled cabin and garage, which sat amongst a vast patchwork of paddy fields that stretched in all directions into the darkness. Mount Elgon stood on the horizon. At just over fourteen thousand feet, it was the seventeenth highest mountain in Africa and straddled the border of Uganda and Kenya. Now, it was merely a reassuring, black shape in the distance, obstructing the inky glow of the night sky. An endless sea of glistening, white specks spun overhead, spiralling from the shimmering aurora of the Milky Way. Sitting on the porch and rocking backward and forward on the swing seat, Eunata Flynn heard her children coming before she saw them.

There was the distant squall of an engine and a tiny headlight flickered into existence in the darkness, like the flame of a candle. The light grew until Jacob and Kira finally chugged into view on the back of a filthy, red motorcycle, following the winding lane up to the house. The bike struggled to a halt. Kira swung off elegantly. Jacob, less so.

'What time do you call this?' asked Eunata, trying to sound angrier than she was. 'I thought you were just going to Jinja for the afternoon.'

'We went for Jacob's jerk jamboree,' said Kira, striding towards the house.

'It was not a jerk jamboree!' Jacob cried. 'It was another really important video I needed to shoot with Ian and Zachary, and Kira ruined it – again!'

'Fine,' said Eunata. 'Make sure the boda boda goes into the garage tonight.'

The porch shuddered as Jacob stomped up the two

steps and into the house. Wind chimes tinkled as he opened and closed the door. Kira jumped onto the swing next to Eunata. It swung back and forth before Kira settled it, dragging her trainers on the worn, wooden decking.

'Did you two get up to anything unusual in Jinja, mtoto?' Eunata asked.

Kira thought for a moment. 'Honestly? Not really.'

'Are you hungry?'

'No. We picked up a rolex in Nabweyo.'

'I was up the mountain with Sunny today,' said Eunata, 'and you will never guess what.'

She removed her RanaPhone from her pocket. Kira leaned forward to see a photograph of a patch of grass. At first, Kira thought a large circle had been cut into it, leaving only exposed red soil. Then she realised that something large, circular and extremely heavy had been pressed into the grass, crushing it into the earth.

'Is that . . .' Kira breathed.

Eunata nodded. 'Elephant tracks.'

Eunata looked at her daughter. Face bathed in the red glow of the fire, the light of the screen glinted in Kira's shining blue eyes. It was not just those she had inherited from her father. The expression of childish delight and zeal at the new, the dangerous and the unexplored was something Eunata had seen on Henry's face many a time. Kira was the same size as Jacob, more because he was small for a fourteen-year-old boy than because she was large for a fourteen-year-old girl. Though both pairs of cheeks were dotted with freckles, Jacob's face was longer and more serious. Kira's was heart-shaped, smaller and brighter. Her hair was tied back into French plaits in the same way Eunata's was, just frizzier and without the traces of grey.

'In Uganda?' Kira said excitedly. 'I thought the elephants kept to the Kenyan side of the mountain these days.'

'I thought so, too,' said Eunata, putting her RanaPhone back into her pocket. 'Sunny and I found these tracks leading to Wagagai Cave. Something is causing the elephants to stray from their usual territory. We are going out tomorrow to investigate. Do you want to lend a hand?'

'Sure! I'll ask Jacob.' Kira leaped from the seat, causing it to rock back and forth and the porch to shudder.

'I want that boda boda in the garage tonight!' Eunata called after her.

Kira had already disappeared inside the house. The door slammed. The wind chimes tinkled. A bird cried in the distance. Eunata instantly recognised it as the eastern bronze-naped pigeon and smiled. The thoughts of a bored environmental conservationist.

'They truly are your children, aren't they, Henry?' she sighed.

It was already starting to get cold. Eunata rubbed her shoulders over the body warmer she always wore with her sleeves rolled to the elbows. She was a small but athletic woman and easily used the swing to propel herself onto her feet. Eunata walked to the edge of the porch and looked up at the stars again. They twinkled reassuringly. At no point in her thirty-eight years had the view gotten old and she doubted it ever would.

'Goodnight, my love,' Eunata said.

She walked back to the house and closed the door quietly behind her.

Jacob threw his RanaPhone onto his desk with a clatter and then himself onto his bed with a heavy sigh. The springs of the mattress creaked as he bounced a few times before settling. He stared up at the white shroud of the mosquito net that dangled above the bed.

ORANGUTAN!

Kira's voice, muffled yet still infuriatingly loud in the enclosed space of Jacob's bedroom, emanated from the discarded RanaPhone.

Jacob groaned. The springs creaked again as he sat up and looked around his cramped bedroom. It smelled of slight damp covered up by cheap deodorant. There was a vintage poster on one wall for *Star Wars: Episode IV – A New Hope*. Like the floor, shelves and most of the other flat surfaces, the desk was piled with Alex

Rider books and Spider-Man comics. Jacob swung his legs off the bed and walked over to the cluttered desk. Scouring the desk for the RanaPhone, Jacob's eyes fell on something else.

On top of a pile of old paperbacks was a small, spreadeagled action figure, an astronaut in a crimson and gold spacesuit. It was so well-used that it was covered in white marks where the paint had been scratched off. Jacob picked it up. The astronaut's face was wearing an expression of boyish determination. Jacob's father had bought him the action figure from Mbale Central Market when he was five. Jacob had named the figure Captain Cosmic. It was one of the last things his father had done for him. He had died a few months later.

Jacob picked up Captain Cosmic, enjoying the familiar feel of the plastic figure in his hands. Memories of running around the cabin, clasping the action figure and soaring through space to fight imaginary alien beasts, ran sunnily through his head like an old Super 8 film. Jacob tossed Captain Cosmic onto his bed and spotted the RanaPhone, tucked underneath the cover of a battered copy of *Dune*. He picked it up. Kira's voice alert had not been heralding another text from her. It was from Zachary.

> *Bro watch double m's new video right now*

Underneath the text was a link. Jacob dived onto the bed, scrambling back to lean against the headboard. When it came to online conspiracy theorists, Double M was the real deal. Jacob's own video channel, which he hosted alongside Ian under their own pseudonyms, Captain Cosmic and Spaceman, could never hope to compete. Their videos mostly centred around Jacob and Kira's inventions and received around a dozen views each time – usually from Ian's mother, as well as some loyal customers of her drapery shop.

Jacob opened the link. For a moment, his eyes hovered enviously over Double M's subscriber count. It was in the millions. He found Double M's latest video. The tip of his thumb hovered over the screen, about to press PLAY.

There was a loud knock on the door. Jacob threw the RanaPhone in surprise. It clattered onto the hardwood floor.

'What do you want, Kira?' he asked, hoping he had not cracked the screen.

'I just wanted to say sorry,' said Kira through the door. 'For today. If I freaked you out. And for interrupting your video.'

Jacob paused.

'It's fine,' he said eventually.

'You sure?'

'Yeah. Honestly.'

'OK. Well, we need to help Mama up the mountain tomorrow. I thought I might try out my model rocket again. I think I've found a way to fix the cooling cycle so there are no more hairline fractures.'

'Sure.'

'OK.'

Kira pranced down the corridor and into her bedroom. Jacob heard the door closing behind her. He picked up his RanaPhone in the corner of the room, next to a pile of more books: Harry Potter and His Dark Materials. No cracks. Getting back into bed, he untied the mosquito net from the railing on the ceiling and folded it around every corner of the mattress. Jacob leaned back against the headboard and, holding the RanaPhone extremely close to his face, finally played the video.

All the screen showed was a dark and featureless figure sitting inside a dark and featureless room. Shrouded in shadow, the figure of Double M was huge and took up most of the screen. The pale light of a single lightbulb hanging behind them illuminated a bowed head, concealed inside a black hoodie and the outline of two hulking shoulders. Whoever Double M was, they were incredibly physically imposing. It was easy to imagine them as an ex-military type, one who had turned their hand to uncovering the secrets of the wealthiest and most powerful people in the world.

Jacob's excitement flared, his hands clammy. He

remembered a previous video which had exposed an oil company that had been dumping waste in the Peruvian Amazon. Another had successfully predicted the downfall of a member of the British royal family after some unpleasant habits had come to light. Of course, Double M had never been acknowledged by any legitimate news channel. More often than not, however, when a scandalous story hit global headlines, it was preceded by a video from Double M with more than a million views. If the curtain needed to be pulled aside on a global mystery or plot, Double M was always going to be the one with their hand on the cord.

Double M spoke three words.

'THEY ARE COMING.'

The voice was a low, genderless rumble, clearly digitally altered to hide Double M's identity. Their breathing was loud and echoey, as if they were using a gas mask.

'THEY ARE COMING, CREEPING OUT OF THE DARK SPACE IN THE SHADOWS BEYOND THE STARS. WE HAVE ALWAYS KNOWN THEY WOULD COME. AND NOW THEY ARE ON THEIR WAY. THEY ARE SO VERY FAR AWAY NOW, TINY, A SPECK IN THE NIGHT SKY. BUT THAT SPECK IS GROWING LIKE A BLACK STAIN. AND THEY ARE GETTING CLOSER.'

Jacob stared at the RanaPhone, blue eyes wide. He

was numb. If his heart was still beating, he could no longer feel it.

'THEY ARE CALLED THE OTHERS,' Double M boomed. 'OR, AT LEAST, THAT IS WHAT RANATECH CALLS THEM. THEY HAVE BEEN COMMUNI-CATING, YOU SEE, RANATECH AND THESE OTHERS, IF COMMUNICATING IS WHAT YOU CAN CALL IT. I HAVE HEARD WHISPERS, WHISPERS BEHIND THE CLOSED DOORS OF THE BOARDROOMS OF RANATECH. AND I HAVE SEEN THINGS, THINGS YOU WOULD NOT BELIEVE. SCHEMATICS. BLUEPRINTS. LANDING PATTERNS. I CANNOT RELEASE THESE YET. BUT I WILL.'

Images of papers and tablets on desks flashed onto the screen, too quickly and blurred for Jacob to see any details, and then Double M was back on screen.

'ALL YOU NEED TO KNOW FOR NOW IS ONE THING, JUST ONE THING.'

Double M leaned towards the camera, face still obscured. Their voice became deeper still. Its rumble was akin to approaching thunder.

'THE OTHERS ARE COMING. AND RANATECH KNOWS.'

The screen went black. The video ended.

Jacob continued staring at the blank screen. His own distorted, flummoxed reflection stared back at him. Still sitting against the headboard, Jacob pulled out Bomber

Jacket's watch. There was no watch face, just a circular, black disc. It was no ordinary watch, he realised, but some sort of smart device. Jacob turned it over in his hands. The strap was expensive, black leather. The RanaTech logo, an R in the middle of a golden crown, glinted up at him in the warm glow of his bedroom light. Double M's last words reverberated in his head.

THE OTHERS ARE COMING. AND RANATECH KNOWS.

Jacob was beginning to wish he had just let the boy keep it.

A few hours later and across the flat paddy fields, a black Jeep Cherokee was parked by the side of Tirinyi Road, less than a mile away from the Flynns' wood-panelled cabin. The Cherokee's black flanks and formerly pristine chrome hubcaps were streaked with red dust, having driven all the way from Jinja. The tinted window on the driver's side lowered a few inches with an electronic whine. Bomber Jacket raised a pair of binoculars. He gazed across the rippling grass at the cabin. All the lights were out. Everyone was asleep.

Bomber Jacket closed the window, placed the binoculars onto the passenger seat and drove on towards the mountain, where the glittering lights of the city of Mbale lay at its feet.

CHAPTER
THREE

Before Jacob even opened his eyes, he could sense the morning sunlight. It was an orange glare through his eyelids. The heat of it bathed him through the mesh of the mosquito net. He could hear birds chattering in the trees outside the cabin. His mother would have left for the mountain before sunrise. He had overslept.

Jacob crept out of his room and along the corridor to Kira's door, enjoying the warmth of the wooden floor on his bare feet. Jacob stood there for a moment in his boxer shorts and faded Star Wars T-shirt. He did not have to knock. All he had to do was listen.

No snoring. Kira was not there. Jacob waited until he was absolutely satisfied no one was home before trudging along the corridor towards the living room. A white straw sofa and two armchairs were gathered around a dusty television. Light streamed through the gaps in the blinds hanging in front of the square windows on either side of the front door. Jacob yawned, curling his hands into fists and twisting his arms to stretch out his body, before making his way back to his bedroom to pull on some jeans and trainers.

The paddy fields stretched into a haze of silvery mist, out of which Mount Elgon emerged with aplomb against the bright blue sky. Montane forest congregated at its base. Green crawled up the rugged slopes, their crevices an inky blue. The air was fresh, invigorating and already of a heat that was just about bearable. There was the smell of smoke from the extinguished bonfire. Jacob leaped off the porch and onto the dry grass. It crunched under his trainers as he hurried to the garage. He hauled up the door with a grating wince of metal.

The garage was almost as big as the house; it needed to be to house Eunata's old pickup truck. There was an empty space where that usually was. The Yamaha was leaning against a wall. Stacked against the other wall were piles of Jacob and Kira's old inventions. Combustion engines, go-karts, pogo sticks, catapults, remote-controlled helicopters and Barbie's Dream House were thrown in weathered cardboard boxes piled higher than Jacob himself. He walked to the Yamaha, heaved the heavy motorcycle into position and prepared to wheel it out of the garage. Kira was usually the one who drove.

'It's all good,' Jacob murmured. 'All I have to do is

point it at the great, big mountain, and not crash into it.'

There was a rustle behind him.

Jacob turned towards the heap of boxes. There was a large one, large enough for someone to fit inside, sitting away from the rest. Its lid was folded closed. Jacob placed the Yamaha back against the wall and walked over to the box. His hand wavered over the lid. No. Jacob was not an idiot. He did not need to open it. He turned away. And abruptly whipped back around, tearing the lid open. Empty. Of course it was.

'Hai!'

The cry came from behind him. Jacob wheeled round to see a fist, followed closely by his sister, hurtling towards him. He stepped aside and Kira catapulted past him and headfirst into the box, legs flailing in the air.

'S'not fair!' came her muffled cry.

'Maybe you should have read AJ's notes,' Jacob said. AJ was a Nigerian who lived in Jinja and their Dambe instructor. Eunata had booked Jacob's first session for his eighth birthday present. The Dream House had been Kira's. That had not gone down well. Their ninth birthday present had been a pair of boxing gloves each. Jacob counted himself lucky that Kira had not been following the traditional rules. If she had, her strong-side fist or 'spear' would have been dipped in sticky resin and pieces of broken glass.

The box came crashing down on Jacob's head from behind. A foot dug into the back of his knee and he collapsed to the floor. When he lifted the box off his head, Kira was already sitting on the Yamaha.

'I haven't got time for notes,' she proclaimed imperiously, 'and neither do you. We should have met Mama hours ago.'

'You overslept, too!' protested Jacob as he clambered to his feet.

'It's only oversleeping if you set an alarm.' Kira pulled the clutch and twisted the throttle to rev the Yamaha. The snarl of the engine boomed inside the garage. 'Let's go, Orangutan.'

As they thundered along the highway, the howl of the motorcycle was nearly drowned by the roar of the relentless hot air. Their clothes whipped around their bodies and Kira's French plaits fluttered maddeningly in Jacob's face. The cracked tarmac of Tirinyi Road stretched straight into the distance, where it merged in a shimmering heat haze with the city of Mbale. The mist had turned from a blanket to wispy tendrils and the slopes of Elgon were clearly visible beyond the city. It was already ferociously hot.

The Bagisu were the tribe that lived high on the mountain slopes. They called Mbale 'njia ya masaba': the gateway to the mountain. Eunata always scoffed and called it, 'Boda boda Central'. Tirinyi Road cut straight through the middle of Mbale towards where Elgon loomed. The city had been built around the point where the main road intersected with two others at a wide roundabout, around which endless motorcycles, scooters and the occasional four-wheeled vehicle seemed to circle eternally without leaving. Drivers spat, chewed gum, shouted at people walking on the pavement and blared their horns at those who cut in front of them. Telephone wires criss-crossed above the road. Palm trees lined the pavements. Locals, tourists, businesspeople, beggars and street performers milled in their shade, some of them taking the chance and darting across the street to a chorus of clamouring horns. At the centre of the roundabout stood Mbale Clock Tower. All one hundred feet of it were painted a brilliant pink. Elgon loomed overhead. There was the choking smell of hot exhaust fumes.

'I hope Mama isn't angry,' Jacob worried aloud, craning his neck to stare at the mountain's peak, shielding his eyes from the sun with his hand. The twins were caught in the middle of the sea of motorcyclists drifting towards the clock tower.

'She'll only have given Sunny some extra things to carry while she hunts elephant footprints.' Kira shrugged. 'It's not the end of the world, is it?'

'It's funny you should say that.' Jacob laughed nervously.

He grimaced as he searched for words, finding himself not able to look at Kira even though she was facing away from him, hunched over the handlebars.

'I watched one of Double M's videos last night, Kira,' Jacob said eventually. 'They say something is coming, something awful. And they say it's coming from—'

'Oi!' shouted Kira. She slammed her hand down on the horn.

'—space,' finished Jacob lamely. The word was inaudible over the wail of the horn.

'You got takataka for brains or something?' Kira hollered at a sweaty man in a stained pink shirt sidling across the road in front of them just as the traffic was herding forward. Sweat Stain stopped, inches in front of the Yamaha, and glared at them. A waft of beer and body odour washed over Jacob and he wrinkled his nostrils. Horns blared as other vehicles manoeuvred around them. Only Sweat Stain and the twins were stationary.

'Excuse us, please,' said Jacob.

Sweat Stain's eyes were glazed. There was stubble on his chin and his mouth was hanging open. He leered at the twins, looking them up and down, before fixing his gaze on their bright blue eyes. He stared at them. They stared back. Jacob felt as if his personal space was being invaded, as if it were not Sweat Stain's eyes all over him but his sweaty hands and fingers. He felt the tensing of Kira's body in front of him and knew she felt the same.

Sweat Stain spat on the road. The white globule of saliva and phlegm landed with a smack on the tarmac, inches away from the front tyre of the Yamaha.

'I know you. I have seen you before,' he hissed. 'Watoto wa mchawi.'

Watoto wa mchawi. Children of a witch.

Kira's sudden movement was utterly fluid, like the pounce of a cat. She thrust her hand first into her pocket and then at Sweat Stain. A cascade of what looked like bright orange dust exploded in Sweat Stain's face. A great deal of it went into his nose and mouth. A great deal more went into his eyes.

It was bhut jolokia. Ghost chilli powder.

Sweat Stain roared and staggered from the road and onto the pavement, screaming and clawing at his eyes. Pedestrians turned to stare at what was causing the commotion. Some shouted and gestured angrily at both Jacob and Kira.

'Move!' Jacob shouted in Kira's ear.

Kira did not hesitate. She released the throttle and kicked the Yamaha into gear. They shot onto the roundabout and joined the rest of the traffic, swooping around the clock tower. The crazed bellows of Sweat Stain followed them.

'Dirty mzungus with your strange eyes! Go back to your cabin in the fields where you belong! We do not want you here!'

'What were you thinking?' Jacob roared. 'Why did you even have that in your pocket?'

'I thought his life could do with spicing up a little,' Kira replied.

On the corner of Republic Street, on the other side of the roundabout from where a crowd was growing around the enraged sweaty man in the pink shirt, stood a palm tree. In its shade, a huge figure watched the twins leave the roundabout and join Tororo Road. The figure was clad in a black bomber jacket and sunglasses. Both sleeves were rolled up to reveal tattooed wrists, taut and rippling with muscle. In fact, Bomber Jacket seemed to be dressed in exactly the same clothes as he had been wearing in Jinja the previous day.

He was only missing his watch.

As Jacob and Kira followed Tororo Road in the direction of the slopes of the mountain, Bomber Jacket left the shade of his palm tree and crossed Republic Street.

At the same time, unbeknownst to Bomber Jacket and in an even shadowier corner of an alleyway leading off Republic Street, someone else was watching *him*. This man was leaning against the alley wall. He was skinnier and a foot shorter than Bomber Jacket but lean and wiry with muscle. The man's glinting eyes narrowed and swivelled to watch the gigantic figure of Bomber Jacket stalk across Republic Street to where his black Jeep Cherokee was parked.

The man did not follow. It was not time yet and there was no need to rush. No one could see the twenty-inch machete that was tucked into the waistband of his khaki trousers. In fact, if anyone were to notice the man, they would not cast him a second glance. He had very few distinguishing features. There was only the green boonie hat thrust downwards to hide his face.

And the blue spider tattooed on the side of his neck.

CHAPTER FOUR

Beyond the city and towards the mountain, the landscape took a gradual upward turn. Open moorlands of wiry, green and yellow tussock grass were all that could be seen on either side. The winding road became less of a road and more of a dry, red mudslide. The Yamaha spluttered but Kira forced it up and up. The higher they went, the busier the landscape became. There were groundsel plants with broad, rugged stalks sprouting a vicious bouquet of yellow-green spikes. Rocky outcrops, streaked with greys, reds and browns, began to pile as tall as buildings.

'You shouldn't have done that,' said Jacob as they climbed higher and higher.

'Switched to fourth gear for the incline?' Kira remarked innocently.

'You know what I'm talking about.'

Kira's shoulders, already hunched to grip the handlebars, jerked in a shrug.

'He deserved it. Who does he think he is, talking to us like we're scum?'

'I know exactly who he is,' said Jacob. 'I've seen him throwing his weight around town plenty of times. His plantain field is just outside the city and his crop has been failing for more than a year. He's just looking for someone to blame.'

'And he chose us because we're different?'

'We're not different, Kira.'

'He called us the children of a witch because we have blue eyes, light skin and just happen to be clever. It sure feels like we're different.'

The Yamaha burst shakily into a clearing, circled by boulders and shrubbery. Further on, the landscape became impenetrable unless travelling by foot. The mountain peak towered over feathery conifer trees. Eunata's old pickup truck was parked on the far side of the clearing, Catherine wheels of mud caking its sides. The truck had started life as a bright orange Ford Ranger twenty years ago, but parts had been replaced so many times that none of them were sure whether any of the original vehicle was left. Eunata was nowhere near the same level of engineer as the twins but still refused to buy a new truck when her old one could be repaired. Kira scooted the Yamaha over and trundled to a halt next to the truck. She kicked down the stand and wriggled backwards on the saddle.

'Off! Off! Off!' she grunted.

Jacob was forced off the back of the pillion and stumbled in the clay-like mud, hard beneath his feet.

'It comes from a place of ignorance, Kira,' Jacob said. 'He was blaming us for his own problems because he doesn't know any better.'

'It's stupidity, not ignorance.' Kira swung gracefully from the Yamaha. 'His crop isn't failing because of witchcraft. It's probably in the shadow of one of those multi-storey car parks that have been springing up around the place.'

'Even so . . .' Jacob persevered as Kira strode over to the old Ranger. 'We can't deal with people like that by—'

'I don't want to hear about it anymore, Orangutan.' Kira waved dismissively at him over her shoulder. 'I'm just glad I gave him another problem to blame on someone else.'

Jacob sighed, more to himself than his sister. He could not change how Kira felt. In a way, he knew she was right. He could never imagine blaming someone else for his own problems simply because they were different.

Kira pressed her hand against the Ranger's driver window and swiped to the side, leaving a clear arc on the grimy surface. She pushed her hands and face against the hot, dirty glass and peered inside. Jacob grimaced and looked around. A column of rocks, six feet tall, was piled next to the entrance to the clearing. Jacob wandered over. He traced his hand over the rock. It was hot on the tips of his fingers. He turned around to make sure that Kira was not watching. She was standing behind the Ranger on her tiptoes with both hands gripping the tailgate, peering into the cargo bed, piled with discarded equipment.

Jacob took a few steps back and ran at the rockpile. His foot made contact halfway up and scraped down. The rock dragged against the soles of his trainers and cut into his torso and elbows as he scrambled unceremoniously onto the peak. Crouching, he looked back at Kira. She was clambering into the cargo bed. Jacob stood up.

He stared down the tumbling moorlands. The mist had vanished now, unveiling a green patchwork of fields that stretched to the hilly skyline. Tirinyi Road was a straight line drawn by a red pencil. The sky was an intense blue above his head but lighter where it touched the horizon. Jacob spread his arms. The jump in altitude meant a slight drop in temperature. A light wind unstuck the shirt from Jacob's skin and caused it to billow across his body. Waves rippled across the grass with calming sighs. Jacob closed his eyes and breathed deeply, enjoying the grassy smell that was carried on the breeze. A black-tailed skimmer dragonfly danced through the air and low to the ground. Jacob could hear its wings whirring.

He opened his eyes again and his gaze fell on Mbale, laid at the foot of the mountain, a smouldering scorch mark of grey and black on the otherwise vast sea of green. Jacob peered through the haze of smog. His gaze was drawn to a particular building on the very edge of the city. It was a lone glass tower, conspicuous as the buildings around it were mostly low structures of brick and concrete. Its twenty storeys of black glass gleamed dully in the sunlight. The logo at the top of the building also caught Jacob's eye: an R in the middle of a golden crown. RanaTech. There was a RanaTech building in most cities. This one was brand new and had only sprung up in the last few months. It was as if it had been built out of a kit and simply dropped onto the cityscape, flattening the homes and businesses that had been there for generations.

Jacob's mind was yanked reluctantly back to Double M's video. *THE OTHERS ARE COMING. AND RANATECH KNOWS.* Could it possibly be true? Double M had never been wrong about anything before – but this, a mysterious warning about creatures from the black depths of space, was something else. Despite the heat, Jacob felt a slight, shivering chill at the very prospect that it might be real. It was enough to make his legs wobble.

A chill, and a small glimmer of excitement.

Jacob's hand closed around Bomber Jacket's watch

in the pocket of his jeans. He pulled it out and examined it in the morning sun. The RanaTech logo gleamed. Jacob turned it over and looked at the circular, black disc that was in place of a timepiece. That small feeling of giddy excitement inside Jacob grew. If he could access the information stored within the smart device, would he find out more about what, if anything, RanaTech was hiding?

There was a crash. Putting Bomber Jacket's watch into his pocket, Jacob turned and looked back up the hill. Kira was crouched in the cargo bed, hurling things over her shoulder onto the grass. An electric blender bounced in the mud with another crash.

'What are you doing?' called Jacob, jumping down.

'Mama brought it!'

'Brought what?'

Kira turned around, holding something that looked alarmingly like a ballistic missile in her hands.

'She brought my rocket!'

Jacob walked over and Kira bounded down.

'Do you think you've got that thing flightworthy?' he asked.

'There's no "think" about it.'

'How are you going to fix the hairline fractures?'

'I'm using this new propellant. It's called ammonium perchlorate. It's totally awesome. Nowhere near as fragile as the other stuff I was using. It's going to increase motor reliability and produce way more impulse per unit weight.'

'What did you use to bind it?' Jacob asked.

Kira carefully lifted the launchpad down from the truck.

'Chewing gum.'

The launchpad was a wide tripod with a single rod, pointing straight up. Kira placed it on a flat area of grass away from the truck. She kicked the rod. Satisfied, she lowered the hollow bottom of the rocket onto it so that it too was pointing straight up at the sky. Jacob saw there was a circular deflector plate between the rocket and the base of the tripod. That was to keep anything from catching fire. He took two steps back.

'Have you thought about how the trajectory's going to be affected?' Jacob asked.

'Well, I've done the driving, heavy lifting and pyrotechnics. Maybe you can do that bit?' Kira was staring down at the rocket and scratching her head. She always stuck her tongue out between her teeth when she was thinking.

'Yeah, OK,' said Jacob. He walked around the rocket. 'I guess the total thrust is going to be the sum of the three individual force readings.' He pointed at the three feet of the tripod. 'Minus twenty per cent given the unevenness of the ground.' Jacob craned his neck to look upwards, shielding his eyes from the sun. 'The trajectory will be in three phases, eh?'

'Mmm-hmm,' was the sound Kira made, meaning yes. She was crouching down and fiddling with the launchpad.

'First, the thrust phase from zero seconds to zero point eight and then the second, when the net force isn't dominated by thrust but by air drag and rocket weight.'

'Mmm-hmm.'

'And then, thirdly, the descent phase, and if I just use the drag formula without having to square the velocity, the rocket should return to the ground . . .' Jacob pointed across the other side of the clearing towards a particularly bristly groundsel plant. '. . . somewhere over there!'

'Good maths, Orangutan,' said Kira. She was wiring something that looked like a television remote control to the bottom of the rocket. The launch controller. Jacob knew she would only have to pull the switch on the controller which would supply enough voltage to spark the igniter and that would be that. Lift-off.

Kira jumped to her feet. She grabbed Jacob's elbow and pulled him backwards. She passed him the controller. It was attached to the rocket by five metres of wire. Together, they hurried to the Ranger. The wire followed them, slithering through the grass. Squatting beside it, the back tyre was as big as they were.

Jacob looked at the controller. There was something

that looked like a lock. Kira elbowed him. She was holding a key in her hand.

'Wasn't that our bathroom key?' Jacob asked.

When Kira did not respond, Jacob took the key and slipped it into the lock. He scrunched his face. Kira put her fingers in her ears.

'Bombs away,' said Jacob.

He turned the key.

A violent spurt of sparks showered from the bottom of the rocket. There was a high-pitched whooshing, like a car speeding down a rainswept highway. The rocket remained stationary for just the right number of seconds for Jacob to turn to Kira in alarm. Then, it shot up into the sky, trailing white smoke behind it. Kira jumped up and down as if she wanted to follow. Jacob stared upwards, mouth agape.

'Yes! It flies! It flies! I'm a genius!' Kira was whooping.

'Wow,' said Jacob.

'I told you! I told you! Didn't I tell you? I was like, "You can trust me!" and you were like, "Nah!" and now look! If Mama were here, she'd be like, "Kira, if there's one thing you most definitely are . . ."'

Kira stood straight and put her hands on her hips, imitating her mother.

'". . . it's trustworthy."'

BOOM. The noise was like the crack of thunder. The explosion echoed against the mountainside and rolled down the hills. Birds fluttered, screeching, from the trees.

The two of them looked up. Instead of the rocket slowly disappearing into the sky, there was a ball of flame suspended a hundred metres above them. Tongues of fire were trailing downwards. Pieces of debris, tubing and wadding landed with dull thuds around them. There was the harsh stench of burning plastic.

'Oh,' said Kira.

'Wow,' said Jacob.

'Shut up,' said Kira.

'What were you saying about not needing notes?'

'I never said that.'

'Yes, you did. You said it right there.' Jacob pointed at the white speck in the distance that was their house.

Kira kicked a piece of tubing.

'No, it's my fault.' Jacob waved the controller at her. 'I didn't realise I'd changed the setting on this to "Firework Display".'

Kira looked as if she were going to throw herself at him.

'If you two do not explain to me what is going on right now, you are going to wish you had been strapped to that rocket.'

Jacob and Kira whipped round. With her hands on her hips, exactly as Kira's had been moments before, their mother, Eunata, was standing next to the Ranger, glaring at them, having just emerged from the forest.

CHAPTER FIVE

It was easy to tell how much trouble they were in by how far Eunata had rolled up her sleeves. They were high above her elbows – strangling height. Jacob and Kira opened their mouths simultaneously to protest their case but it was in vain. Eunata silenced them with a sharp intake of breath.

'Wait! First, wait! Let us all wait just one minute!'

A man wearing a flowery shirt, dirty jeans, sandals and the biggest smile Jacob had ever known appeared from the forest behind Eunata. The man's mouth stretched from ear to ear, teeth perfectly white and utterly enormous. His name was Sunny and in the eight years he had worked for Eunata, Jacob and Kira had only ever seen him smiling. Jacob sometimes wondered whether the size of Sunny's teeth allowed for any other expression. Sunny stood between them and their mother, holding his hands up as if to shield himself from machine gun fire.

'Now, now, the children have carried out one of their little science experiments and there was a miscalculation, eh?'

Sunny turned to Kira, eyebrows raised and smiling encouragingly. Kira nodded.

'You see?' Sunny turned back to Eunata, still smiling. 'No harm done.'

Eunata turned her fiery gaze from Kira to Jacob and back again.

'You. You. Forest. Now.'

She wheeled around and, thrusting branches aside, marched into the brush. The twins followed sheepishly.

'That doesn't sound good,' Kira muttered to Jacob.

'Sunny,' Eunata snapped over her shoulder. 'Clear up this mess.'

A flaming piece of tubing floated down and settled on the mud next to Sunny. His smile faltered by a millimetre.

It always baffled Jacob that the shade of the forest was warmer than the sun-drenched mountainside. Sunlight flashed through gaps in the canopy high above as they climbed. The air smelled as hot, wet and stifling as the forest itself. Luscious, green vegetation besieged them from all sides. Eunata managed to find a corridor through the throng of brayera plants that snatched at their clothes. Jacob pushed a pronged leaf out of his way and looked at his hand. It gleamed with condensation. The wide, reddish-brown tree trunks, towering out of the bushes around them, were visibly dripping with moisture. Even the red mud steamed as it squelched and sucked at their feet. Somewhere high above them, an animal chattered. They walked for fifteen minutes, the hill getting steeper all the time, before Kira plucked up the courage to speak. When she did, she was out of breath.

'Was that a red-tailed monkey?' she asked from behind Jacob.

'Perhaps,' Eunata called back. She did not appear to have broken a sweat. 'Look before you step. Red-tailed monkeys are primarily arboreal but they can also forage on the ground.'

Jacob glanced back at Kira and she nodded meaningfully at him. Once their mother had started talking about the foraging habits of forest monkeys, it was usually safe to speak.

'Did you and Sunny find any elephants, Mama?' Jacob panted.

Eunata was lifting some bowing branches out of their path.

'Mmm-mmm,' was the noise she made, meaning no, 'but we have located some tracks leading towards Wagagai Cave. We will start there.'

It was another fifteen minutes before Jacob began

to hear Wagagai Cave and it was five minutes after that before he saw it. What he heard was the thundering cacophony of a rainstorm. What he saw was the forest opening into another clearing and, straight ahead, a sheer wall of brown and grey rock. At its base was a jagged gash like an open mouth. A waterfall cascaded in front of the cave in a vapoury haze. The dazzling sun shone through the water, creating a rainbow of colours. Eunata, Jacob and Kira crouched at the edge of the clearing, where the dense forest merged into a bank of red earth. The bank sank into a murky pool. The tops of the trees were reflected distortedly in the pool before it disappeared into the depths of the cave.

'We're going in there?' asked Jacob apprehensively. 'We've never actually gone *into* the cave before . . .'

'I want to see if there is any evidence of elephant activity,' said Eunata. 'In the old days, when elephants were a common sight on the Ugandan side of the mountain, they used to scrape the salt from the cave walls with their tusks to eat. But that was a long time ago. There has not been a sighting of a wild forest elephant in Uganda since, oh, before you were born.'

'Do you think there's one inside the cave right now, Mama?' Kira asked excitedly.

'Perhaps,' said Eunata.

'We've never seen an elephant up close,' Jacob breathed.

'Why did the Elgon elephants leave Uganda in the first place?' asked Kira.

'The city on their doorstep most likely had something to do with it,' Eunata murmured, 'as did their natural habitat being cut down to pave its way.'

She was not looking at them. Her attention was focused on the shadowy mouth of the cave. Eunata straightened and marched into the pool. She paid no attention to the brown water sloshing around her ankles. Jacob and Kira looked at each other, one with a smile of slight hesitation and the other with a manic grin of pure excitement. Kira hurried after Eunata with Jacob following closely behind.

The water was warm around their feet and shins. All three of them had dark patches stretching up to their knees as they waded closer to the cave. The waterfall washed over them like a mist. There was a moment of heavy water pounding against Jacob's head and shoulders and then he was on the other side. He looked at his mother and sister, standing in the cave mouth, which was littered with rocks and pebbles. They too were drenched. The roof of the cave was above them, a rugged, brownish-grey arch that melted into darkness after ten feet.

Jacob, Kira and Eunata stood on the rocky precipice with the roar of the waterfall behind them, staring into the gloom. It was as if they were waiting for something lurking in the blackness to reveal itself. When nothing did, Eunata unzipped a waterproof pocket in her body warmer, pulled out a bulky torch and clicked it on. The yellow circle of light swept over the interior of the cave, unveiling a rock-strewn tunnel that burrowed gradually downwards into the earth. After twenty feet, the tunnel twisted around a corner and out of sight. It was wide and tall enough for an adult to walk through.

An adult, or something bigger.

'We won't go down too far,' whispered Eunata.

'Good,' whispered Jacob.

'Come on,' whispered Kira.

As they crept into the cave, the bellow of falling water behind them became muffled and echoing. Moisture gleamed and shadows danced on the stone walls as the glare of Eunata's torchlight flashed over them. Their already sodden trainers splashed in puddles. There was the damp smell of stagnant water.

'There,' murmured Eunata.

'Wow,' breathed Jacob.

Eunata had settled her torch on a patch of wall around thirty feet into the cave. The surface was no longer black rock, glistening and wet, but a white, crystalline substance. Salt. Deep grooves had been carved into it as if it had been slashed with an axe. Eunata clambered over some strewn boulders to get closer to the salt wall and run her fingers down the grooves.

'These are recent,' Eunata whispered. 'Less than twenty-four hours ago.'

Jacob and Kira glanced at each other in the darkness. They could not see their mother's face. She was still stroking the wall reverently. But they had both heard it. Her voice had been quivering with emotion.

'Are you OK, Mama?' Kira asked.

'Yes, mtoto, I am fine.' Eunata turned to face them, smiling. 'It just always hits me, being this deep in the earth. What better place is there to marvel at the majesty of nature than here, in the very heart of the mountain? You can almost hear it beating.'

Jacob listened. She was right. He could hear water droplets trickling down the stalactites above him, quivering at the end and then dropping with a tinkle onto the cave floor. Outside was the distant thunder of the waterfall. Beyond, he could imagine the rippling of the pool, the creaking of wooden branches, the unfurling of leaves and the jabbering, squawking and growling of the infinite variety of teeming wildlife that called the forest its home.

'The natural world is beautiful,' Eunata continued. 'It must be defended. And that is exactly what we are here to do. Come. We must find out what has driven the elephants from their usual territory.'

She straightened and Jacob helped her climb back over the boulders. Having already made the journey in one direction, they returned at a quicker pace. Eunata switched off the torch. The cave mouth was a wonky circle of light just ahead of them at a slight incline, a white curtain of falling water crashing down outside it.

'It's a shame we didn't actually see an elephant.' Kira had to raise her voice over the clamouring water. 'You would have lost your mind, Jacob.'

'So would you!' Jacob protested.

'I don't think so,' retorted Kira. She turned to face them and babbled on, sauntering backwards towards the waterfall. 'We've been climbing this mountain since before we could climb onto the sofa!'

Jacob's eyes were no longer on Kira's insufferably smug face but something over her right shoulder. Was there something moving on the other side of the waterfall?

'We've seen forest monkeys, antelope, buffalo . . .'

There *was* something moving. The seething, white wall was no longer completely white. A dark shape had appeared just beyond the plunging water.

'Kira, stop!' Eunata hissed. She had seen it as well.

'There was that time Jacob tripped over that rock python and— hey, why is the ground shaking? Is that an earthquake?'

'Kira!' Jacob stammered.

Kira was right. The cave was trembling. But it was

not an earthquake. It was the footsteps of something colossal, something within arm's reach and shrouded only by the watery veil.

'What I'm saying, if you guys would just let me finish, is that there is nothing around here that could possibly surprise me.'

Kira let out her most brazen laugh before turning around to face what Jacob and Eunata were gaping at with their mouths hanging open.

'Oh,' she said.

Ten feet above the ground and towering over them, white water sprayed on top of a great, domed head. Curved, white tusks, almost as long as Jacob and Kira's whole bodies, swung from side to side. Torn, flapping ears were the size of car doors. A thick trunk dangled to the cave floor, curling and uncurling as if it had a life of its own. The skin was more brown than grey, dark rivers of water streaming down it like tears. It hung from the monolithic face in leathery drapes and folds. Jacob was reminded of the wrinkled visage of an old man. The elephant did not enter the cave. It stood there with its head on one side of the waterfall and the looming silhouette of its immense body on the other. Its orange eyes were glowing coals, with round, black pupils and fluttering eyelashes. They gazed down at Jacob, Kira and Eunata with a serene calm that Jacob found mesmerising.

Before Jacob knew what he was doing, he was reaching up and stroking the elephant's trunk. Kira was doing the same. The skin was rough and caked in hard mud. At its touch, electricity surged from Jacob's fingers all the way up his arm to touch his heart and create a sensation that was euphoric. Jacob looked at Kira and was surprised that, while she was smiling, there were tears in her blue eyes. He was even more surprised to realise that there were tears in his eyes too.

The elephant suddenly reared its trunk and Jacob and Kira leaped backwards. It blasted a trumpeting cry so deafeningly loud, Jacob felt a piercing pain between his ears. He covered them with his hands and laughed. He could not control himself. It was the most magnificent sound he had ever heard.

It was as if the elephant was announcing its intention to advance. Eunata lunged forward and hauled Jacob and Kira to the side of the cave. The head proceeded through the waterfall, followed by hunched shoulders and legs like tree trunks. Water splashed over its curved back and seeped down its sides. The cave tremored at every one of its mighty footsteps. Eunata, Jacob and Kira flattened themselves against the cave wall as the elephant passed them and into the gloom of the cave, its short tail flicking carelessly behind it.

The elephant turned the corner of the tunnel and disappeared into the depths of the mountain but it took a while longer for the spell it had cast to be fully broken. Jacob and Kira waited until the sound and shaking of the booming steps had dissipated, staring at each other and smiling. Neither of them made an effort to stop the tears, quivering in their eyelashes and streaming down their cheeks. They just let them fall.

'That,' sniffed Kira, voice shaking, 'was cool.'

'Did you see it?' Eunata asked quietly.

'See it?' Jacob nearly shrieked. 'How could we miss it?'

'I am talking about the gunshot wound under its left foreleg.'

'What are you saying?' Kira asked, finally wiping her eyes.

'I am saying,' said Eunata through gritted teeth, 'someone has shot at that elephant.'

'Are you talking about poachers, Mama?'

'I am talking about poachers,' Eunata replied and strode out of the cave without flinching under the hammering waterfall.

Before they reached the clearing where they had left Sunny, the Ranger and the wreck of Kira's rocket, Jacob knew something was wrong.

'That is why the elephants have strayed from Kenya,' Eunata was muttering. 'They have been scattered by poachers. When I find them, I will . . .'

Jacob was not listening. He already knew his mother was in a rage and not paying attention to their immediate surroundings. He also knew Kira was Kira. After the euphoria of seeing the elephant, she was skipping after Eunata with her mind even higher in the clouds than the rest of her already was.

But Jacob was Jacob and Jacob was careful. He noticed.

As the forest cleared, he could see over Eunata's shoulder. The Ranger was there, but so were the remains of Kira's rocket. Eunata had told Sunny to clear up the mess. The three of them had been gone for at least forty-five minutes. What had he been doing all that time?

'Wait!' Jacob called but by that time, it was too late.

The answer stood behind the Ranger. As all three of them rounded the truck, Jacob and Kira leaped into the offensive position they had been taught: feet apart, both fists raised, one to protect the face and the other to jab.

'I told you he'd find us,' said Kira.

'I was the one who said that,' Jacob replied.

'What on Earth is going on?' demanded Eunata.

It was the Jeep Cherokee from Jinja, still sleek, still black and still utterly menacing. The gigantic car was muddier than it had been a day previously and yet remained completely alien in Uganda. It sat there, poised on the uneven terrain. The driver's door was open and Bomber Jacket was standing next to it. His bald, muscular head and clenched jaw glistened with sweat. His mouth was nothing but a downturned slash and his sunglasses masked any other means of expression. Bomber Jacket's leather-clad shoulders loomed behind Sunny like a towering, black gravestone. Sunny's body language suggested he was indeed about to perish from sheer terror at any moment. He looked from Eunata to Jacob to Kira, smiling a hysterically nervous smile.

'Friend of yours?'

CHAPTER
SIX

Bomber Jacket scowled. It would have been easy to think he had already been scowling but Jacob definitely noticed a further narrowing of the eyes behind the sunglasses and a pursing of the lips before Bomber Jacket opened them to speak. His voice, like his face, was granite.

'I am Gustavo Yang. RanaTech Security. But you can call me Gus.'

Jacob did not alter his offensive position but stepped slowly in front of Eunata and Kira so his body was shielding theirs. Not that it would make a difference. Jacob was certain of two things. The first was he would never be calling this man Gus. The second was, if Gustavo Yang wanted to, he could snap Jacob in half like a twig under his boot.

'How did you find us?' Jacob asked.

Yang raised a hand the size of a dinner plate and clapped Sunny on the shoulder. Sunny's quivering knees almost buckled on impact and he made a sound somewhere between a nervous laugh and terrified whimper.

'My little friend told me I could wait for you here,' said Yang. 'I witnessed your altercation with that sweaty gentleman in Mbale.' His thin eyebrows rose above his sunglasses as he turned lazily from side to side to take in the wreckage of Kira's rocket. 'I also saw your flare. A nifty invention, I must say.'

'It's not a flare,' interrupted Kira. 'It's a rocket.'

'A rocket that explodes?' Yang's gaze fell on Kira.

'Yes, it's supposed to do that.'

'In any case,' Yang continued, 'I owe you both an apology. I recognised you in Jinja yesterday – those eyes of yours are difficult to miss – but my temper may have gotten the better of me. If we could start again, I'd like to—'

'Your temper may have gotten the better of you?' cried Jacob in outrage. 'You call trying to kill us your temper getting the better of you?'

Something that could have been irritation flickered across Yang's face.

'I did not try to kill you.'

'You tried to kill that boy!'

'No, I didn't,' said Yang. 'And that boy stole from me.'

'Enough!' Eunata pushed past Jacob and marched

towards Yang, who did not look perturbed by the small but furious woman hurtling towards him. He moved Sunny aside with one hand while holding up the other for Eunata to shake.

'Gus Yang.'

Like Sunny, Eunata's head only reached Yang's chest. She slapped the hand out of the way and thrust her forefinger up like a dagger to his throat. Again, Yang did not flinch. He merely gazed down at her.

'I just have one question,' Eunata said quietly.

'Go on.'

'Did you shoot that elephant?'

'Why would I shoot an elephant?'

'There is a Ruger Hawkeye .30-06 hunting rifle in the passenger seat of your car.'

Yang, Eunata and Sunny all turned their heads as one to look through the open door of the Cherokee. Sunny let out a dramatic gasp when he saw the barrel of the gun propped against the leather seat.

'I was told I'd need it in Africa,' said Yang. 'For protection.'

'You are not in Africa!' Eunata snarled. 'You are in Uganda. I suppose you would order paella in Poland since you cannot tell the difference between countries and their continents?'

Yang sighed slowly. It was as if he were calming himself. Every muscle in Jacob's body was tense. All his nerves were screaming at him to leap forward and drag his mother out of reach of those enormous hands. Jacob had seen the savagery with which Yang had treated those who crossed him in Jinja. Provoking him seemed akin to poking a black rhinoceros with a stick.

'I was told I'd need it in . . . Uganda,' said Yang. He pointed down the mountain to the black tower on the edge of the city. 'RanaTech employees have been facing aggression from local gangsters since the opening of our new building in Mbale. Threats. Muggings. A general lack of cooperation. It's been bad for business.'

Something small shifted in the ground between Yang and Eunata's feet. They both glanced down. It was a yellow forest scorpion. Eunata could identify it from the translucent yellow of its pincers, legs and tail and the brown and yellow stripes of its armoured body. The scorpion was only two inches long. Yang had seen it too. He watched it unearth itself from the red soil and scuttle out of harm's way.

'It seems RanaTech has flushed the criminal scum out of its nest,' he said.

'Mmm-hmm,' said Eunata, watching the scorpion as well. 'And I suppose the fact you built your shiny new tower on the rubble of their livelihoods has nothing to do with it?'

'In any case,' said Yang, 'the criminal uprising will be dealt with.'

He moved one of his heavy leather boots and stepped on the scurrying scorpion. There was the tiniest of crunches.

Eunata's eyes and nostrils flared. Her fists clenched. Yang stared down at her. His face could have been a glacier. It was that cold and hard.

'I haven't shot any elephant,' said Yang. 'You can check the rifle. It's never been fired.'

'Shooting a big animal. Stepping on a little one. There is no difference in my eyes.' Eunata's voice was quivering with rage. She turned from Yang to face the twins. 'We are leaving, children. Come on, Sunny.'

'Coming!' Sunny chimed.

'What did you want with us?' Kira called out to Yang as Eunata and Sunny moved towards the Ranger. Yang merely stood there. His boot was still on top of the obliterated scorpion.

'It does not matter!' Eunata snapped as she hauled open the driver's door of the Ranger.

'I am here on behalf of Amira Rana, head of RanaTech,' said Yang curtly. 'Ms Rana has a proposal to discuss with your family. You may find it quite exciting.'

'Amira Rana? Wow,' breathed Kira.

'We are going, children,' Eunata said, with one foot inside the truck.

'I will be working at the RanaTech building in Mbale for the rest of the week,' said Yang, ignoring Eunata and staring at Jacob and Kira. He pointed at the dark tower again. 'Perhaps, the three of you can visit me there?'

Jacob and Kira looked at each other. Jacob's brain was whirring. Amira Rana, head of RanaTech, had a proposal for them. What could RanaTech possibly want with two fourteen-year-olds? Double M's warning surfaced once more at the back of his mind.

THE OTHERS ARE COMING. AND RANATECH KNOWS.

Before he could make up his mind how to respond, Kira had done it for him.

'We'll think about it!' she blurted out excitedly.

'Excellent,' Yang nodded.

They could not disobey their mother any longer. Jacob and Kira shuffled towards the Yamaha, propped on its kickstand next to the Ranger. They skirted around Yang at as great a distance as possible. All the time, Yang stared at them from under his sunglasses, completely at ease with himself. He seemed to be enjoying the effect he was having.

'One more thing,' he said softly as Jacob placed a hand on the saddle of the Yamaha.

Jacob stopped. So did his heart.

'I lost something in Jinja,' Yang continued. 'The last time I saw you, you were disappearing down Wanyama Road with its thief in tow. I'd quite like it back.'

Jacob's sweating fingers reached into the pocket of his jeans. He could feel Yang's watch there, alongside his RanaPhone. Eunata, Kira and Sunny were all staring at him.

'Oh yes,' said Jacob as casually as possible.

His fingers had not settled on the watch but on his RanaPhone. He turned it on and swiped at the screen, attempting to keep the squirming of his fingers in his pocket invisible. The program he was frantically operating was a wireless hacking interface he and Kira had designed when they were nine. The app on Jacob's RanaPhone was able to duplicate the files of any device that was physically touching the RanaPhone. He was currently setting it to work by copying all the data from Yang's smart watch, nestled alongside it in Jacob's pocket. When the app had finished its job, Jacob would be able to access everything inside Yang's watch from his RanaPhone, including any secrets relating to the Others or Amira Rana's mysterious proposal. Jacob calculated it would take him four seconds to walk over to Yang and hand him the watch. The hacking process needed eight. That was four seconds more.

'Can I just ask – what kind of proposal does RanaTech have for us?' Jacob asked.

He began walking, making his steps as small and as slow as possible. There was another flicker of impatience across Yang's face.

'One that would require you to travel, let's say, out of town,' he said.

'London?' Kira gasped. 'Where RanaTech has its headquarters?'

'You would travel to London first,' nodded Yang and the downward slash of a mouth twitched into a wry smile, 'but you may end up travelling a little further than that.'

Eight seconds. Jacob was standing directly in front of Yang and staring up at him. He reached into his pocket and pulled out the watch, holding it up to Yang. It did not matter that he had separated it from his RanaPhone. Eight seconds had passed. The duplication of files was complete. Jacob now had access to all the information concealed inside the watch.

Yang gently took the watch from Jacob. The careful way he handled it was unexpected from such a brutish, muscle-bound brawler of a man. Somehow, it seemed to cause even more effortless power to emanate from him.

'Thank you,' said Yang. 'I'll expect you at the RanaTech building.'

'Do not hold your breath,' said Eunata.

Yang did not move aside as the Ranger and Yamaha rumbled close to him on their way out of the clearing. He simply stood there with his gigantic hands behind the small of his back and his boot on top of the flattened scorpion.

CHAPTER
SEVEN

'I want to talk to him,' said Kira.

'I know you do,' said Eunata, 'but I do not trust him.'

They were arguing and Jacob was doing what he always did when they argued. He was keeping his mouth shut and not getting involved.

The three of them were squeezed onto the seat swing on the porch. Kira had lit the fire in front of the house and the pungent but comforting smell of smoke wafted through the warm air. The evening sky was also alight, an explosion of vivid blues, pinks and purples. Everything from the fields to the trees to the distant mountain were bathed in orange by the red orb slowly sinking beyond the horizon. The last light bled through the translucent leaves of the banana trees. Elongated shadows spread across the grass.

'If RanaTech wants us for something and it means

we have to leave Uganda,' said Kira, 'then I want to talk to him.'

'What is it about your home that disgusts you so much that you would rather choose to trust a man like that?' Eunata asked.

'A man like what? He's not actually done anything.'

'Yang had something to do with that poor elephant. I know it. And you did not answer my question.'

Kira sighed. 'Ugandans will never treat us like Ugandans,' she said bluntly. 'This may be our home but we'll always be different here. But it's not our only home. You may have been born in Kampala, Mama, but Baba was born in London. We're just as English as we are Ugandan.'

'Your father may have been born in London, Kira, but none of his family are there now. You would be alone.'

'I'm alone here,' said Kira.

'You're not alone here,' said Jacob angrily. 'No matter how anyone else treats you, you will always have Mama and me.'

Kira looked taken aback. Even Jacob was surprised at his own outburst.

'I know that, Jacob,' said Kira firmly. 'That's not what I meant. What I meant is Baba's country is light-years more advanced than this one. You've seen it online. London's home to so many kinds of people. Surely no one could ever be treated differently there just because of who they are. Besides, do you really want to be building things out of microwaves and chewing gum all our lives? Imagine what we could accomplish at RanaTech.'

'That depends on what RanaTech actually wants with us,' said Jacob quietly.

There was a moment of silence.

'I need to speak to the office and get someone sent out to look at the wounded elephant,' said Eunata, heaving herself to her feet. 'You've heard what I've got to say on the matter.'

Neither Kira or Jacob said anything until Eunata had closed the door behind her and the wind chimes had finished tinkling.

'You don't want to go,' Kira said.

'I don't know,' said Jacob. 'It's just that . . . I think . . . I don't know,' he finished lamely.

Kira leaped from the swing to the edge of the porch with such feline fluidity that the wind chimes did not make a sound. She sat on the edge of the worn planks so her trainers were on the grass and her chin was resting in her hands.

'Did you know,' Kira remarked, 'zebras can migrate from Namibia to Botswana? That's over three hundred miles.'

'I know what you're getting at,' said Jacob, 'but don't try to sound like Mama.'

'OK. I won't try to sound like Mama. I'll try to sound like you. What's the point of reading those adventure stories if you turn down every chance of your own adventure? I bet Captain Cosmic wouldn't need any convincing to get out of his comfort zone.'

'All Baba ever did was get out of his comfort zone and look what happened to him.'

'Keep your voice down,' Kira hissed, eyes flashing to the front door. When there was no sign of their mother, she turned back to stare across the darkening fields and sighed. After a moment of silence, she decided to change tack.

'It's RanaTech, isn't it?' she asked, without turning around. 'That's what's bothering you. Does RanaTech have something to do with what you were telling me about this morning? Something about—'

'That doesn't matter,' interrupted Jacob. 'You weren't even listening.'

'You told me something was coming. From space.'

Jacob glared at Kira's hunched shoulders and plaits, touched by the flickering orange of the firelight.

'Yes,' he said slowly. 'Something is coming and I think RanaTech has something to do with it.'

Kira turned to look at him.

'What's coming?' she asked.

'I don't know. Something bad. Zachary sent me one of Double M's new videos.'

'Double M?'

'Yeah, you know, the online conspiracy theorist? He's got millions of subscribers.'

'Wow. What does Zachary's girlfriend think?'

'Zachary doesn't have a girlfriend.'

'No way.'

'Fine.' Jacob stood up. 'If you don't want me to talk to you about it . . .'

'Wait! Wait! I was just joking!' Kira's eyes were wide and pleading. 'I'm listening. I promise.'

'Give me a minute,' Jacob muttered. 'There's something I need to check before we talk about this.'

He went inside and left her there, sitting alone on the porch.

Eunata was inside her bedroom and heard her son stomping along the corridor, past her door and towards his own room. On the straw nightstand beside her bed, there was a wooden carving of an elephant, a drawing of the four of them Jacob had given to her when he was three, and a photograph of Henry. Eunata sat on the edge of the bed and smiled. Henry's blue eyes smiled back.

'It is happening,' Eunata sighed. 'I always knew it would. I have known it since they were working at university standard at the age of eight. I am just not sure why it has rattled me. Chicks of the Hartlaub's turaco leave their mother after two to three weeks. I cannot begrudge them for doing so after fourteen years. Saying that, I have clothed, fed and homeschooled them their entire lives, a little more substantial than tossing them dead caterpillars and regurgitated pulp. I even started taking them to the mountain again after . . .'

Eunata's eyes flashed to the bedroom door. When there was no sign of her children, she turned back to the photograph, leaning close but speaking quietly, almost in a whisper.

'Anyway. For a long time, it was like I was lost. I was screaming in the dark and no one could hear me. They were the light in that darkness. They were what guided me home. And it has only been the three of us, out here on our own for so long . . .'

Eunata sniffed and wiped her eye.

'Still. I suppose they will fly the nest, as all chicks must . . .'

The springs groaned as Jacob sat down heavily on his bed. Holding his RanaPhone, his finger hovered above the wireless hacking interface that had copied the files from Yang's watch. Kira would not take his suspicions about RanaTech seriously unless he had proof. Here, with any luck, was that proof. Jacob tapped open the app. A text box appeared.

> Download files?

Jacob tapped to agree and a loading bar crawled across the screen and disappeared. But, instead of a list of files, another text box popped onto the screen.

> Access denied. Classified in accordance with TRANSCENDENT.

Access denied? That had never happened before. Jacob tried again but the same message appeared.

> Access denied. Classified in accordance with TRANSCENDENT.

Jacob frowned. RanaTech must be using some incredibly powerful security measures if a hacking interface designed by him and his sister could not access its data.

Or maybe, RanaTech had something to hide.

Jacob tossed the RanaPhone onto the mattress beside him and rubbed his forehead in frustration. Could RanaTech really be attempting to cover up what Double M had leaked about the Others in their video? Why did Amira Rana, head of the company, need Jacob and Kira?

And what on Earth was Transcendent?

Jacob's eyes fell on Captain Cosmic, lying on the desk on the other side of his cluttered bedroom. Once again, memories of charging around the cabin and holding Captain Cosmic aloft swam through his head. Stories of heroes saving the world from alien hordes had played out again and again in his own imagination with the help of nothing but a scratched, plastic action figure. That same story had continued to play out in the endless adventure books he had gone on to devour in his teenage years. It was always the same. Enemies attack. Teenage hero saves the world.

Kira was right. If RanaTech did really have something to do with an alien invasion then here was his chance to play his own part in that story. Was he really going to turn that chance down?

'Fine,' said Jacob, striding back out onto the porch to find Kira still sitting in the same place. 'Talking to Yang won't hurt.'

Kira grinned, eyes wide and glittering. She leaped up to embrace him but Jacob held up his hands to stop her.

'We're just going to speak to him,' he said, 'and find out more about this proposal Amira Rana has for us. Nothing more. Got it?'

'Yeah, yeah, yeah, I got it, Orangutan.'

She hugged him tightly.

*

Eunata was not in the kitchen or living room. The twins crept down the corridor. The door to their mother's bedroom was ajar, light spilling a yellow wedge onto the floor. They looked at each other and peered cautiously inside.

'Are you all right, Mama?'

Eunata was sitting on the edge of the bed, her back to the door. She was hunched over so Jacob and Kira could not see what she was looking at but, at the sound of their voice, she whipped round to face them. If their mother had been upset, any trace of it had vanished from her face. She smiled.

'Of course I am all right! Why are you lingering at the door like a pair of hyenas? Dinner is on the table. I made matoke.'

'I love matoke!'

'I know you do,' said Eunata, 'although I have used up everything in the pantry. I will need to go to the market tomorrow. Did you two talk things over?'

Jacob and Kira glanced at each other again.

'You were right, Mama,' said Jacob. 'That Yang is a suspicious character, for sure.'

'Yeah,' said Kira. 'We'll give that one a miss.'

Eunata nodded. They were lying and she knew it.

'You'll have your chance, Kira,' said Eunata. 'You'll be chief engineer of your own tech company before you know it. And you, Jacob, you'll be CEO.'

The two of them grinned at her.

'We know, Mama,' said Jacob. 'Shall I bring you your food so you can eat on the porch?'

'No, we will eat together,' Eunata said steadily. 'We do not know how many more chances we will get, do we?'

Jacob and Kira's faces disappeared from the open door and Eunata listened to them hurrying down the corridor, whispering to each other. Eunata stood up and, brushing her fingers over the photograph of Henry, walked to the window. The first stars were starting to appear. It was as if the sky was a blue canvas with glistening specks of white paint flicked over it with a brush. Light in the darkness. Eunata Flynn smiled sadly. She switched off the bedroom light, closed the door and joined her children at the dinner table.

CHAPTER
EIGHT

The RanaTech building was a towering, black monstrosity of steel and glass that had elbowed its way onto Tororo Road among the shop fronts and cafes. It was so new that scaffolding still hugged the outside of the building, structured shakily from twisting planks of timber lashed together with rope. The tower had been designed to be modern but already looked old, its tinted windows so shiny with grease and dirt, they were more opaque than transparent.

Jacob and Kira could see it in the distance as they headed south on foot from the clock tower and towards the outskirts of Mbale. A dusty stretch of green ran down the centre of the road, separating the steady stream of motorcyclists and honking cars. Shops selling identical wood carvings to tourists wrestled for space on the red dirt footpath. The twins zig-zagged between the palm trees at the edge of the road to avoid the crowd. The smell of hot tarmac was strong and Jacob was sure that if he placed his hand on the black surface of the road, his flesh would stick. He squinted up at the blistering sun, its fierce light glaring through the palms and telephone wires that hung overhead.

'What did you tell Mama?' he panted.

Kira was one palm tree ahead.

'I told her we were going into town to pick up mangoes, which isn't actually a lie,' she said over her shoulder. 'We have to pick up half a dozen on the way back. Not from the market, though. That's where Mama said she would be today.'

'Remember what we agreed.' Jacob jogged to catch up with his sister and immediately regretted it. His T-shirt was plastered to his body and he wiped sweat from his forehead, feeling the drops spray from his fingers and spatter the red dirt. 'We're going to hear what Yang has to say and that's it.'

'Yes, yes, yes,' said Kira impatiently. She pointed up the road at the RanaTech building. 'Although, clearly RanaTech pays the big bucks. Yang may make us an offer we can't refuse.'

'We'll see,' said Jacob, looking across the road. He stopped suddenly and grabbed Kira's shoulder, dragging her back.

'Oi!' she grunted, shoving his hand away.

'Look, Kira,' Jacob murmured.

On the other side of the road was a bakery. Pancakes, waffles and mandazi were displayed in the window and customers lazed in plastic chairs in the shade outside. Beside it was an alleyway, scattered with litter and rubble. Kira could see a small heap of bricks some way down. Sitting on it was a boy, wearing a faded T-shirt that hung to his knees, a blue tattoo of a spider visible on his neck. Two of the spider's thin legs curled up onto his gaunt cheek. Spider did not seem to notice the twins watching him. His face, streaked with white dirt, was twisted in concentration, eyes fixed on a chicken pecking at the ground a few feet away. Slowly and carefully so as to not frighten it, Spider reached down, picked up a stone and threw it. The chicken squawked and flapped its wings.

'Things are different here, compared to the city centre,' said Jacob, watching Spider pick up another stone.

'Mama said RanaTech knocked down lots of housing and businesses to make space for their new tower,' said Kira glumly. 'Lots of people are living on the street now.'

She continued along Tororo Road. Jacob watched the boy a moment longer before following.

Like the exterior of the RanaTech building, the interior was also sleek, black and metal, in contrast with the burnt yellows, ochres and reds of Tororo Road outside. In fact, as Jacob and Kira entered the foyer, they saw no sign that it was situated in Uganda at all. The building would have been much more at home in the financial districts of London or New York.

'Oh dear,' said Jacob, looking down at his dirty trainers and realising he had tracked red dirt onto the immaculate marble floor.

Kira either did not notice her own dirty trainers or did not care. She bounded across the foyer and Jacob followed, walking on his toes to make as little mess as possible. The air conditioning was on full power and the sudden cold after such an intense heat felt strange on his skin. There were goosebumps on his arms and the hairs on the back of his neck were standing on end. There was a man behind a stainless-steel reception desk in a muted, black suit and with an equally muted expression.

'Kira and Jacob Flynn to see Gustavo Yang, please,' said Kira. 'He's expecting us.'

'Twelfth floor. Mr Yang's office is labelled "Head of Security",' said the man. 'He mentioned there would be an adult accompanying you. A Mrs Eunata Flynn?'

'She's not coming,' said Kira.

There were lifts but Jacob and Kira raced up a concrete stairwell in the corner of the building. The decor of the twelfth floor was identical to that of the foyer. Another receptionist led them onto a wide corridor. On either side of the black marble floor was a row of identical office doors. The far end of the corridor was dirty glass from floor to ceiling. Jacob and Kira could just about see the brilliant blue of the sky. At their current angle, there was no sign of Tororo Road twelve floors below them.

They were more than halfway up the building.

The receptionist left them at the door labelled HEAD OF SECURITY. Kira knocked. Yang opened the door. His vast, leather-clad bulk filled the frame, allowing no opportunity for them to see past him and into his office. Yang was wearing the same black bomber jacket and heavy boots as yesterday, the only difference being that he had taken off his sunglasses. His pupils were black with a peculiar glint.

'It's wonderful to see you both,' he said, with an expression that suggested otherwise. 'Do come in. Is your mother not joining us?'

'Nope,' said Kira cheerfully. 'She's busy feeding poachers to a hippopotamus.'

Yang moved aside slowly. Kira waited patiently for the gap between his colossal frame and the frame of the door to widen before striding into his office. Jacob edged after his sister, doing his best not to look at the rippling chest, shoulders like bowling balls or arms that could easily tear him in half.

They found themselves in a spacious office area, matching the black, metallic style of the foyer and corridors. The entire opposite wall was a series of glass panels, through which the criss-crossing timber planks of the scaffolding were visible. One of the panels had been slid upwards, wafting in the distant clamour of car horns and hot smells that mingled with the whirring cold of the air conditioning. The tower's location on the outskirts of Mbale meant the only view of the city through the scaffolding was one of low concrete and corrugated metal rooftops. Mount Elgon was sprawled on the horizon.

'Quite a view.' Kira whistled.

There were two leather chairs in front of a steel desk, decorated only with a peace lily in a white terracotta pot. Yang gestured towards the chairs with one gigantic hand and stalked over to his own chair behind the desk. His boots pounded and squeaked on the marble floor.

'Jacob and Kira Flynn,' said Yang. The chair creaked as he sat down and gazed at them. 'The children of a Ugandan conservationist and English mountaineer. RanaTech has been keeping a close eye on the two of you for a very long time.'

'Why?' asked Jacob.

'When a certified genius comes along, it's noteworthy, but when two appear at the same time, it's something else entirely. RanaTech has been assessing you from afar since a young age. You haven't had an IQ test yet but early estimates place you both at a level above two hundred. That makes you just about two of the most intelligent people on the planet. I believe the word being bandied about in London is "incandescent".'

'We're incandescent?' Kira grinned, the word ending in a high-pitched, childish question mark.

'You didn't realise?' asked Yang, raising his thin eyebrows.

'I always assumed everyone else was slow,' shrugged Kira.

'You said RanaTech has been keeping an eye on us,' said Jacob. 'How?'

Yang shifted his massive weight. The chair protested beneath him. He pulled out his own RanaPhone from his back pocket, tapped it a few times and held it up. Jacob was shocked to see his own face staring back at him from the screen.

'Quick! Get a good shot of it before it catches fire!' Jacob watched himself say on Yang's RanaPhone. 'In the middle of Jinja, we are surrounded by engines, guzzling fuel and coughing up carbon dioxide into the atmosphere. My twin sister and I created the atmospheric converter to recycle that carbon dioxide into fuel for this gas lantern. It works by reducing the carbon dioxide into carbon monoxide and then combining it with hydrogen to—'

Yang paused the video and slid the RanaPhone back into his pocket.

'RanaTech has been watching my videos?' Jacob murmured.

Kira rolled her eyes.

'So,' she said. 'What is this proposal RanaTech has for us?'

'I'm not the best person to answer that question,' said Yang. 'As RanaTech's Head of Security, I was sent to Uganda to deal with safety concerns surrounding our Mbale operation. Making contact with your family was an additional assignment tasked to me by Ms Rana. As you may have guessed, public relations are not my strong suit.'

'I've always thought of you as a people person, actually,' said Kira.

Yang raised his wrist so the sleeve of his jacket fell down his brawny, tattooed arm, revealing the watch he had taken back from Jacob the previous day. Yang reached for the circular, black screen with his other hand and removed it from the leather strap with a click.

Jacob inhaled sharply. He had examined Yang's watch so many times and not once realised! It was far more than a smart device. Yang placed the small, round disc on the steel desk in front of them with a dull clang.

'Is that an Oracle Mark I?' Kira breathed. 'I've only ever seen them online.'

Yang still did not answer. Instead, he pressed a tiny button on a section of the strap. When he did, the disc emitted a whine, which began as the low drone of a mosquito but rapidly rose in pitch until it was so high, it was impossible to hear. At the same time, the disc glowed brighter and brighter until it was blinding. But Jacob and Kira were no longer looking at the disc. They were both goggling at the woman who had flickered to life on top of the desk.

The hologram was only two feet tall but the image of Amira Rana was crystal clear and completely lifelike. Jacob thought she was beautiful. Long, black hair with streaks of brown flowed down the white sari which swathed her elegant form. The white of the fabric seemed to glow as if it were an angel that had appeared to them, and not a sophisticated holographic projection. Jacob gaped at her, ensnared by Amira's hazel eyes.

'If she says, "Help me, Obi-Wan Kenobi," don't pass out,' Kira muttered in Jacob's ear.

'Hello, Jacob and Kira,' Amira said. Her voice was deep, with the slightest edge, like the purring of a cat. 'I'm terribly sorry not to have been able to meet you in person. It's with the greatest of pleasures that I deliver this message to you.'

Amira's red lips broke into a perfect smile, revealing perfectly straight, white teeth.

'I'm here to talk to you about Transcendent.'

'What's Transcendent?' Jacob asked the hologram.

Kira elbowed him.

'She's a hologram, doofus. She can't hear you! Don't embarrass us after they've just called us incandescent.'

'Transcendent began as an idea,' Amira continued, 'to bring together a group of remarkable young people, people who are most equipped to save the planet from the greatest threat it has faced in its four-and-a-half-billion-year history.'

Jacob's stomach clenched. Was Double M's theory about to be confirmed?

'The trials for Transcendent will take place in London next week.'

'London!' Kira gasped.

'If successful, you will travel to RanaTech Spaceflight's facility in Cornwall.'

'Cornwall!' Kira exclaimed.

'The next day, you will fly via rocket to RanaTech's private orbital space station, the Garden.'

Kira made a noise somewhere between a whimper and a scream.

'On the Garden, in low Earth orbit, you will be equipped with the best tools and scientific equipment RanaTech can provide. You and the other members of Transcendent will begin work safeguarding the planet from the deadliest danger it has ever faced.'

'What danger?' Jacob almost shouted at the hologram. 'What threat are we fighting?'

'I'm sure you have many, many questions,' said Amira

as if she did not hear Jacob, which, of course, she could not. 'That's all the information I can give you for now, I'm afraid. I'm very much looking forward to meeting you face to face in London and telling you more, should you be successful in the trials. Goodbye, Jacob and Kira.'

Amira faded out of sight like breath on a mirror. Yang picked up the Oracle and clicked it back on the strap on his wrist.

'So,' he said, 'while Ms Rana was the most qualified person to make the introduction, I have been fully briefed on Transcendent and am capable of answering your questions, although certain pieces of information will be classified until after the trials, of course.'

Jacob's mouth opened but no words came out. The only sound he could make was a faint gurgling. Kira too appeared unable to speak. She was gaping at Yang with a slack-jawed expression. In fact, if her jaw had dropped any lower, Jacob thought it would have landed on the black marble floor of the foyer.

'I understand,' said Yang, the slash of his mouth twitching slightly. 'I'm sure you weren't expecting this afternoon to be so surprising but, I promise you, that is where the surprises . . . stop.'

Yang broke off. His thin eyebrows were raised and his hands, which had been laid flat on the steel desk, curled into gigantic fists. Yang's black eyes were fixed on a point just over Jacob and Kira's shoulders. Jacob and Kira twisted round.

There was a man standing on the scaffold outside and bending to step through the open window. He was wearing khaki. His eyes were wide with fury and lips pulled back over his gums and teeth in a vicious snarl. There was a blue spider tattooed on the man's neck.

And a machete in his hand.

CHAPTER
NINE

Machete took his second step into Yang's office, teeth bared. He was well built, his back and knees were bent and he was ready for a fight. He crept towards them, twirling his weapon. The length of the blade was the distance between his hand and elbow, around twelve inches. There was six feet between Machete and the twins. Jacob's feet seemed to be frozen to the floor. The only movement he was capable of making was to tear his eyes from Machete's blade and turn desperately to Yang, who was already making his way around his desk, fists raised and tendons straining like industrial cables in his neck. His black eyes were bulging. There was almost no white in them at all. Yang broke into a charge and Machete raised his weapon above his head, preparing to slash downwards. The sun glinted hideously on its vicious curve.

Before either man had made contact with the other,

there was a loud, fleshy smack. Yang skidded to a halt. Machete dropped the blade. It landed with an evil clatter on the marble floor. Machete clasped both hands to his face and staggered back. He had time to issue a pathetic groan before he was careering out of the open window. There was a crash as he landed on the timber scaffolding. Kira tucked her slingshot back into her pocket.

'Nice shot,' said Yang. He prowled over to examine Machete's limp form through the window. 'You knocked him out cold. Do either of you recognise him?'

'No,' said Jacob, hurrying over to look at the unconscious Machete. Jacob was not frozen any longer. Seeing his sister leap into action had brought him to his senses. 'But I do recognise *that*.'

'What?' Yang asked.

'Spider tattoo on his neck,' said Jacob, pointing.

'What is the significance of that?'

'Your little friend in Jinja had the same tattoo,' said Kira. 'We saw him outside.'

'So, they're part of the same gang?' Yang asked. 'Why are they coming after us? And will there be more of them?'

As if on cue, they heard running, squeaking footsteps in the corridor.

'Does that door lock?' Jacob asked sharply. So much adrenaline was pumping around his body that he was almost shaking.

Kira darted to the door and jammed the lock closed. Less than a second later, the locked door jolted on its hinges as someone barged against it from the other side. They heard shouting. The door jolted again but held steady.

'We need to escape through the window,' said Yang.

Pretending they had been waiting for Yang's instruction and not come to the same conclusion thirty seconds earlier, Jacob and Kira turned their backs on the trembling door and ran to the open window. Yang stood aside and gestured impatiently for Jacob to go through first.

Jacob placed a hand on the glass panel on either side of the open gap. He poked his head out of the air-conditioned office and into the scorching heat. Yang's window was twelve floors above Tororo Road. That was more than one hundred and thirty feet. Through the levels of timber walk boards and ladders leading down to the street, Jacob could just about see the tiny people sitting on their tiny, plastic chairs outside the tiny bakery. Tiny cars and motorcycles trundled up and down the road. Jacob leaned back into the office.

'I can see a route down the scaffolding,' he said breathlessly.

'Let's hurry this up,' said Yang, dragging Machete's unconscious body into the office while glancing back at the door. 'Come on. It's just platforms – like Donkey Kong.'

'It's great how you're able to relate to the modern generation,' said Kira.

There was a louder bang against the door. Kira's eyes narrowed. It would not hold for much longer.

The sweltering wall of heat engulfed Jacob as he stepped out of the window. The peeling sheet of timber sank a little under his weight and his stomach lurched. There was no barrier apart from a series of upright, timber beams. Jacob gripped one of them tightly, feeling splinters bite into his hand. There was no downward ladder on their level but the overlapping succession of walk boards stretched along the full width of the building and turned a corner on each side. They would have to work their way around the building to find a way down. The scaffold gave another alarming shudder as Yang stepped out of the window.

'Your turn,' he said to Kira.

Kira held the sides of the window and placed one foot onto the low, glass ledge between the office and the scaffold. The other foot remained inside the room. The fierce sunlight that was dashing off the darkened glass glinted in her eyes so they were as blue as the sky. She was staring at Jacob.

Kira did not need to say anything. Her eyes said it all.

'No,' said Jacob simply.

'I'm going to buy you guys time,' Kira replied.

'Absolutely not!' roared Yang.

Jacob let go of the timber beam and lunged for his sister, who slipped back through the glass panel, shutting it behind her. It landed with a *thunk* between them and locked with a *click*.

'Kira!' Jacob bellowed. He slammed his fist against the window but it barely shook. Through the grimy surface, he saw Kira running towards the door.

'That sister of yours is incredibly stupid,' said Yang.

'No,' Jacob said miserably. 'She's incredibly clever. That's the problem.'

Kira smiled grimly as she stood next to Yang's office door, back against the wall. She had always suspected but Yang had confirmed it: she and Jacob were different from other children. Kira had suspected it from the moment people had given the two of them strange looks when their mother had first taken them into Mbale. Their blue eyes. Their light skin. Their cleverness. Jacob at least had some friends, but Kira had no one. Of course, she had always had Jacob and their mother. She never felt alone when she was with them, but would she always have them? What would happen when Kira and Jacob left home? What would happen when they inevitably parted ways?

Kira was different from anyone else she had ever met except her brother, and her brother would not always be there. She had thought their father would always be there and then, one day, he was gone. Kira was like her model rocket, blasting into the sky, brighter, cleverer, higher than anyone else, except she did not know how to make it back to Earth. How long until *she* was the one to spectacularly combust?

As Kira raised Yang's potted peace lily above her head, she decided the trials for Transcendent in London would be the perfect place to find people not so different from herself.

With a thundering crash and flurry of dust, the lock finally broke and the door flew open. Jutting through was a boot dusted with red dirt. It lowered to the marble floor with a thud and was followed into the room by its hunched, hulking owner. Khaki. Machete. Spider tattoo. The man was grinning, showing off a cracked, front tooth.

Kira swung the potted peace lily as hard as she could. The pot collided with Broken Tooth's forehead and disintegrated. He dropped like a sack of bricks in the doorway amid a mess of white terracotta shards and lumps of brown soil. The limp, green remains of the peace lily were strewn across Broken Tooth's unconscious face.

Kira sighed gleefully. It was a wonder she struggled to make friends.

She was jogging along the corridor towards the

stairwell when she heard a small scream behind her. Kira spun like a weathervane in a gale. Down the corridor was a cleaner not much older than she was, pushing a trolley laden with a mop and a yellow, plastic bucket. Between the cleaner and Kira was the open door to Yang's office. Protruding from it at odd angles were Broken Tooth's khaki-covered legs and a scattering of terracotta and soil. The cleaner trundled to a halt.

'What is going on here?' the cleaner gasped. A badge on her apron announced her name as Amy. Amy's shaking hands were gripping the trolley so tightly that the plastic bucket rattled. Soapy water sloshed around inside it. Kira edged closer with her palms held in front of her.

'I didn't kill that man!' she cried before realising that was the most suspicious thing she could have said.

There was a harsh whine from Broken Tooth's unconscious body. Kira had not noticed it but there was a bulky walkie-talkie attached to his belt. A raspy, crackling voice emitted from it, loud enough for both Kira and Amy to hear.

'Did you get the big man? What is taking so long? Shall I come up?'

Yang. They were after Yang. And there were more of them.

'Amy.' Kira flashed a grin. 'Can I borrow your bucket?'

*

Twelve storeys above the ground, there was no breeze. There was just the dry smell of hot wood. Jacob and Yang edged around the corner of the building so they had their backs to the busy street. Rooftops of concrete and brickwork stretched away around them. A white snake eagle sailed past like a kite, cawing as if surprised to see them. The flimsy walk boards sank under each step and the entire scaffold swayed with a straining creak. Jacob was breathing heavily, cheeks bulging in and out like a paper bag. If either he or Yang were to fall, they would break every bone in their body. They came to a makeshift gap in the walkway and a ladder leading down to the next level. Yang went first.

'Water pipes!' Jacob heard Yang remark from below as he descended after him.

'I thought you'd let that one go,' Jacob muttered, focusing his attention on his quivering hands as they gripped each rung. 'It wasn't me who dropped them on you anyway. It was Kira.'

'No. Water pipes. Look.'

Jacob's trainers landed shakily on the walk board of the eleventh level. There was indeed a pallet, stacked with blue water pipes, dangling in the air six feet from the scaffold. The stack of corrugated tubes was hanging from a frayed rope winch somewhere above. Below, a small construction site was squeezed into the alleyway between the RanaTech building and the opposite building, which was an ugly concrete structure. Its rooftop was flat and eleven storeys tall, the same height as their level of the scaffold. It was nearly fifteen feet away. Too far to jump. The stack of water pipes was directly between them and it.

'Let's find the next ladder,' said Yang and started edging past the windows of the eleventh floor.

'Kira better be staying out of trouble,' said Jacob.

'Don't worry. I'm sure Kira is smart enough not to draw too much attention to herself.'

There was the splintering of glass and something large burst out of the window panel a few feet ahead of them. It crashed onto the walk board, which dipped under its weight, causing the one underneath Yang and Jacob to spring upwards. The scaffold rocked horrifyingly. Jacob yelled and scrambled for one of the upright timber planks. Yang's feet remained planted where they were. He held up his arms like tree branches to balance himself.

A man in khaki was lying on his back on the scaffold in a litter of broken glass. On the man's head was a yellow, plastic bucket. He was drenched in soapy water.

Yang glanced at Jacob and they edged along the scaffold to peer into the window. There, standing with her hands still outstretched, was Kira.

'Kira Flynn, step out of this window right now,' commanded Jacob.

Kira was about to respond when there was a sudden

whine of static at Jacob's feet. Kira saw that, just like Broken Tooth, there was a walkie-talkie fixed to Bucket Head's belt.

'Do you have the big man?' a scratchy voice whispered from the device. 'Boss will be there soon. He is stuck dealing with the Flynn witch at the market.'

Despite the suffocating heat, Jacob felt the blood turn to ice in his veins.

He is stuck dealing with the Flynn witch at the market.

They had his mama.

Jacob and Kira's eyes met. No words needed to pass between them. Before Jacob could stop her, Kira turned and sprinted back down the corridor. He heard the squeak of her trainers on the marble floor and the slam of the door to the stairwell.

'No!' Jacob started to follow her, but Yang grabbed his shoulder and hauled him back.

'It's not safe.' Yang's voice was steady but strained.

'We need to go and help my mama!' Jacob shouted.

'We will,' said Yang through gritted teeth, 'but first I need to get you down from here. Are you good? Can you remain calm?'

Jacob took a deep, furious breath and nodded. Yang let Jacob go and jogged to the end of the scaffold.

'There's no ladder on this side!' Yang called back to him.

But Jacob was not facing Yang. He was facing Bucket Head, who was clambering to his feet between Jacob and the smashed window. Bucket Head lifted the bucket from his head and tossed it from the scaffold. Jacob raised his fists and spread his feet apart to assume the offensive position he had been taught. The news about his mother had nearly spun his mind out of control but he forced himself to think. To fight Bucket Head would be a mistake. This was a big man who would be capable of inflicting a lot of damage. Jacob knew what to do.

Turning his back on Bucket Head, he sprinted after Yang. The scaffold shuddered under his footsteps but Jacob ignored both this and the dumbfounded expression on Yang's face. Jacob passed Yang and took a running leap through the air. The construction site loomed below. Just as it was about to rush up to meet him, the hanging stack of water pipes rammed into Jacob's stomach. Breath was punched out through his mouth. His hands and fingernails scrabbled at the curved plastic ridges until he grasped a knot of rope. The muscles in his arms burned as he hauled his legs up. Finally, he was crouching on top of the stack, keeping his centre of gravity low. The ropes from which it was suspended, already taut, screamed under the extra weight. The pallet was revolving. The RanaTech building passed by in a blur again and again as the stack of pipes spun round and round. The pull of gravity was intense. Jacob could feel it inside his head as he stood up, every muscle in his body straining against the g-force. He took three running steps along the tops of the pipes and hurled himself once again through the air.

Jacob's feet were running through nothing, and then nothing was replaced by a grey sea of gravel and he landed flat on his face on the rooftop opposite the RanaTech building. Small stones tore at his knees, chest and hands. There was a horrible scraping as he skidded on his front. A cloud of dust drifted in his wake. Jacob came to a stop and lay there for a few seconds, panting. He dragged himself to his feet. His hands were bleeding. From the way his trousers and T-shirt were plastered sorely to his body, so were other places.

Jacob looked back. Fifteen feet away, Yang was still perched on the scaffold, facing Bucket Head, who was barrelling towards him.

'Watch out!' Jacob shouted.

Yang stayed where he was, letting Bucket Head come. When they were about to collide, Yang turned casually to the side. His hands moved in a blur and, in a matter of seconds, Bucket Head had been thrown over his shoulder and flung onto the walk board like a rag doll. Still moving quickly, Yang bent down. There was a brittle snap. When Yang straightened, Bucket Head was clutching his wrist and screaming.

Yang took a few steps so his back was against the

window and rubbed his hands together. He burst into a run, hurling himself from the scaffold.

'Wait!' Jacob screamed. 'You're too heavy!'

Yang's hands came down on a pipe in the lower corner of the stack. One of the ropes holding the pallet in place snapped, making it lopsided. It swung back and forth between the scaffold and the opposite building in huge arcs, all the time spinning like a nightmarish fairground ride. With a surge of strength, Yang threw himself up and grabbed the pipe at the top of the stack. The one he had been clinging to slid between his legs and dropped out of sight. Yang twisted his neck to look around. As the pallet swung towards the concrete building again, he flung himself towards the roof. Yang slammed into the side of the building, huge legs thrashing and one hand gripping the concrete ledge. Jacob dived towards him.

'Come on! Come on! Come on!'

Grunting, Jacob managed to help Yang haul himself onto the roof. Yang lay on his back, black clothes battered with dust and sweat pouring from his face. Jacob stumbled back onto the gravel. The two of them remained that way for a few moments, panting like dogs.

'Right,' said Jacob, staggering to his feet. 'Let's go get my mama.'

CHAPTER
TEN

Gravel crunched underfoot. Some rooftops were so close, Jacob and Yang could hop between them as they would a bus to the pavement. With others, they had to pick up speed and hurl themselves over a plunging drop, swinging their legs forward and landing ungracefully on the other side. Narrow streets flashed past underneath them. They soared over a garden and a clutch of chickens squawked and scattered. A woman screamed.

'Samahani!' Jacob yelled over his shoulder as he sprinted on.

They were getting closer to the cluster of high-rises in the city centre. The towers looked aflame, sunlight gleaming on glass. Slumped at their feet in a dull heap was Mbale Central Market. The market building itself was a square with a courtyard and three levels. It had once been a bright red but the paint had baked over time until it was more like the colour of the soil that lay beneath it.

At last, they came to a slope of rusting metal slanting down onto the market roof. Jacob slid down and crawled clumsily to the edge. Yang slithered along like a python.

Jacob spotted his mother immediately. She was in the middle of the crowd that was crammed into twisting lanes between stalls. Most of the stalls were covered by tattered canopies. Eunata was standing unnaturally straight and still in the midst of the heaving throng. Sunny was next to her. He looked petrified. There were three men in khaki huddled around them. One was wearing a green boonie hat. He looked like the man in charge.

Staring down into the courtyard in disbelief, Jacob desperately tried to think about how this could have happened.

It had happened because of fish eyes.

Eunata's mother used to say *it was always in the eyes*. She would say it when Eunata was a child and they were perusing the markets of Kampala, one of the few happy memories Eunata had of their time together. If a fish's eyes were clear, it was fresh and had been caught that very day. If a fish's eyes were foggy and unclear, that fish was not fresh. You may as well throw a fish with foggy eyes back in the Nile, Eunata's mother used to say. Some sellers even went as far as gluing googly eyes onto their fish to create the illusion that they were fresh.

It was always in the eyes.

At the same moment as Jacob and Yang were clinging to the scaffold and Kira was preparing to clobber Broken Tooth with a peace lily, Eunata had arrived with Sunny and stood in the pathway between the fish stalls at the entrance of the market. She was struck by the watery reek every time. The stalls were piled with tilapia, perch, catfish and more, their mouths filled with tiny, sharp teeth and hanging open in morbid surprise at their predicament. Beyond the fish stalls were masses of stalls laden with everything else that could be imagined. Everyone was shouting. Bootleg DVDs were thrust into peoples' faces. Fruit and vegetables tantalised with their fresh and fragrant scents. Above, garish tapestries assaulted their eyes, hanging from the balconies of the upper levels beneath the brilliant, blue square of the sky.

'We will see the twins, eh? If they are looking for mangoes?' Sunny had asked cheerily. He was wearing a different but equally loud and flowery shirt as the day before.

'Mmm-mmm, Sunny,' Eunata had said thoughtfully. 'I did not believe for one second that the children went into town to pick up mangoes. No, they have gone to speak to that man from RanaTech. What can I do? I have given them my opinions but they are old and wise enough to choose their own path.'

That was when Eunata had spotted the man in the green boonie hat, slinking along with the mass of people meandering through the maze of stalls towards the exit on the other side of the courtyard. She had decided straight away that he was somebody who needed to be followed.

Elbows and the corners of bags dug into their sides as they travelled deeper into the market. They were within ten feet of Boonie Hat, standing by a jewellery stall that did not sell any real jewels, when he suddenly turned around. Eunata had pretended to examine a bead necklace. In the corner of her eye, she could see under the shadow of the hat and the dark pits for eyes that glowered there. They never fell on Eunata or Sunny but swept over where they were standing. There was no sign of suspicion on Boonie Hat's face. It was neutral, yet there was something in his gaze. His eyes were the cold, unfeeling eyes of a crocodile watching a herd of wildebeest approach a riverbank. Tiny beads of sweat dotted his skin. He was gripping the strap of the sports bag on his shoulder. When Boonie Hat had finally turned away from them, Eunata had glimpsed a tattoo on his neck. A blue spider.

At that moment, there had been a particularly sharp jab in Eunata's side. She had recoiled and turned to confront what she assumed was an aggressive shopper. Instead, she was confronted by another man in khaki. On his head was a tangle of dreadlocks rather than a boonie hat but the cold, unfeeling look in his eyes was the same. The curved edge of a machete was being held against her stomach. All Dreadlocks had to do was apply a little more pressure and there would be no difference between Eunata and the gutted fish she had been looking at on the table. A quick glance had told her there was a third man in khaki holding his own machete inconspicuously to Sunny's side. Sunny was not smiling anymore.

Boonie Hat was suddenly between them. He was relaxed and smiling with crooked, yellow teeth. His gums were like raw meat.

'You tell me why you follow.' Boonie Hat's voice was a hoarse whisper. He gestured at the other two men in khaki. 'Or they cut you up like jackfruit.'

'First,' Eunata whispered back, 'you tell me why you have an elephant tusk in that bag of yours.'

Boonie Hat's smile vanished and Dreadlocks lunged so close that Eunata could see the hairs in his flared nostrils. She felt the tip of the blade poke into her jacket, almost cutting through the material and piercing flesh.

'They are the poachers! But how did you know?' Sunny whimpered.

'I knew as soon as I saw him,' said Eunata grimly.

'No one grips a bag that tightly unless they have something to hide. Also . . .'

She spat into the red dirt and looked squarely at the two black pits glowering at her from underneath Boonie Hat's boonie hat.

'. . . it is always in the eyes.'

'Stay here,' murmured Yang, starting to crawl away.

'I don't think so,' said Jacob. 'We don't need any more broken wrists, thank you.'

'OK,' growled Yang, stopping and turning back. 'What do you suggest?'

Jacob spoke quickly and clearly.

'Let's take a walk. Somewhere more private, eh?' Boonie Hat whispered to Eunata, jerking his head in the direction of the exit by the fish stalls. 'So we can talk.'

Eunata felt a sharp stab of pain in the small of her back from Dreadlocks and started to walk. The third man shoved Sunny forward, who looked as if he were going to burst into tears. Boonie Hat sauntered ahead, still gripping his sports bag. He was barging anyone who might have gotten too close and realised there was a hostage situation taking place in the middle of the crowded market. Eunata was walking with her shoulders back and chest forward to keep her back as far from the tip of the machete as possible.

As they neared the entrance, Eunata thought she saw something large and dark drop from the higher levels and bounce from one of the canopies. There were shouts from that direction but she dared not turn her neck.

They came to the fish stalls. That familiar stench seemed to emanate from the ground itself, slick with water and dark patches of blood. It was like standing in a swamp. The crowd swelled as it funnelled in and out of the archway, only adding to the pungent odour. Eunata felt something stir at the back of her throat. She needed to retch. She swallowed the cough but it scratched its way back up her throat like some awful insect trying to burst out of her mouth. Her eyes watered. Her midsection contorted. If she were to cough, Dreadlocks might mistake it for a cry for help and slip the machete between the vertebrae of her spine, much like the tooth of a lion puncturing the trachea of a zebra. To make a sound was to die.

Eunata could hold it in no longer. She was going to explode.

Then a lot of things happened quickly. One of the tables was overturned and a silver mountain of fish spilled onto the floor. The crowd erupted. People threw themselves onto their hands and knees to snatch up the fish. Eunata no longer felt Dreadlocks' presence behind her and a quick glance to the side told her Sunny had also been separated from his captor. Boonie Hat swung round. He brandished his machete, no longer caring about witnesses. He took two strides towards Eunata and was broadsided by a gigantic woman clutching a tilapia triumphantly in each hand. The gang leader was knocked off his feet and engulfed by the riotous crowd. At the same time, Eunata felt a hand curl around her own. She turned and was greeted by the filthy, bleeding face of her son.

'Run!' Jacob cried.

'Sunny!' Eunata barked.

'Coming!' Sunny chimed.

Eunata allowed herself to be led towards the exit on the other side of the courtyard. The three of them broke away from the edge of the crowd and wound their way through the emptying passageways between the stalls. The archway that would bring them into an alley and to safety was just in front of them when, out of nowhere, Boonie Hat pounced from behind an underwear stall. The shadowy crevices under the brim of his hat were livid. Boonie Hat spat some foul insult but his voice was lost over the roar of the crowd. Eunata and Sunny lurched to a halt.

Jacob did not stop running. He flung his right arm forward and opened his fist. A small bundle sailed through the air and exploded in Boonie Hat's face in a cascade of orange dust. Boonie Hat roared and staggered back.

'What was that?' Eunata cried.

'Bhut jolokia,' Jacob said grimly. 'Sometimes, Kira's methods are the best.'

He attempted to tug his mother towards the archway.

'Wait!' Eunata shouted. She snatched the sports bag, containing the broken elephant tusk, from Boonie Hat's shoulder. The gang leader was no longer paying attention to them, crashing around in agony and clawing at his eyes. Jacob, Eunata and Sunny ran and did not look back.

They burst through the archway and into a deserted alley. Only a plastic bag tumbled noiselessly over strewn rubble. The wall behind them was the crumbling, red brick of the market building. The wall in front was the black glass of the office of a financial services company. One of the glass panels had been shattered and left that way, cracked into a spider's web. In the other glass panels, they could see their hazy reflections.

Jacob looked at himself. His clothes were torn. His face was bleeding. The adrenaline that had surged through him in Yang's office was beginning to wear off. Jacob realised for the first time that he was exhausted.

There was the sudden crunch of running feet on gravel. Jacob tore his hand free from Eunata's and raised his fists wearily. He did not think he could survive another fight.

Kira skidded around the corner. Jacob lowered his hands.

'Oh, you got to her first,' she grinned, clattering to a stop in front of them. She was barely out of breath. 'Nice one, Orangutan. Everything all right, Mama?'

'I am fine, Kira,' said Eunata, 'thanks to your brother.'

'And no thanks to you,' said Jacob.

Kira threw her arms around Eunata, spinning her round and round.

'Were you followed?' asked Jacob.

'Of course I wasn't followed,' said Kira. 'You know me. I'm basically a ninja.'

There was a high screech like the yowl of a mountain cat and the sound of running feet – much smaller feet than Kira's. The boy they had named Spider hurtled into the alley. Spider did not heed the sharp stones cutting into his bare feet. His shrill cry ricocheted off the walls. His long T-shirt flapped around his spindly frame. There was a rock the size of a passion fruit in his hand. Spider threw it. The rock clipped the left side of Eunata's head. She grunted and staggered back, dropping the sports bag and clasping her hand to her face. Kira screamed and grabbed hold of her, shielding her mother with her own body.

A haze fell over Jacob.

He stepped in front of Eunata and Kira. Spider was still running even though he had used his only weapon.

His lips were drawn back in his high, continuous screech. Jacob lunged and grabbed hold of the front of Spider's T-shirt. The frenzied boy's sticklike limbs flailed, trying uselessly to scrabble at Jacob's body. They were not strong enough. Jacob hauled Spider up so the boy was dangling in front of him, face to face. Flecks of spit struck Jacob's face.

'Watoto wa mchawi!' Spider rasped in a cracked voice, the small, black dots of his pupils darting between Jacob and Kira.

For the briefest moment of pure instinct, all Jacob wanted to do was strike Spider as hard as he could for what he had done to his mama. His gaze fell on his reflection in the darkened window of the office building, standing there with Spider dangling in front of him. Yang had almost struck Spider a few days ago in Jinja. Jacob and Kira had been outraged at the time – but now, here Jacob was, on the verge of doing the same.

Jacob shook his head roughly. He loosened his grip and lowered Spider gently to the ground. He stood over the boy, breathing heavily. Spider was gasping for breath and glaring up at him in hatred.

'Are you all right, Mama?' Jacob asked Eunata.

'I am fine, mtoto,' smiled Eunata. She touched the side of her forehead and winced, smearing a small smudge of blood. 'It is just a scratch. I will clean it at home.'

'We need to take the boy to Maluku Police Station first,' said Jacob. 'They'll be able to find help for him there.'

'He doesn't deserve our help!' Kira protested. 'He's the reason all of this happened! See how he hurt Mama!'

'He's a desperate child who doesn't know what he's doing,' said Jacob firmly. 'He needs our help.'

Before Kira could argue further, there was the squeal of tyres and a black Jeep Cherokee skidded to a halt at the entrance of the alley. The driver's door swung open and they were greeted by a sweating, scowling face they all knew.

'Get in,' said Gustavo Yang.

CHAPTER
ELEVEN

Eunata's sleeves were rolled all the way up to her elbows. She threw a tea towel over her shoulder and leaned against the kitchen worktop. There was a plaster on the left side of her forehead. A pot of matoke was bubbling on the stove. The sweetness of steamed bananas wafted from underneath the lid. It was late evening and pleasantly warm. The blinds were closed and the living room was basked in dim lamplight. Yang was sitting on the straw sofa. After refusing multiple times, he had finally allowed Eunata to wash his bomber jacket. He was hunched in his black T-shirt, huge, tattooed arms resting on his knees, which were squeezed into the tight space between the sofa and the coffee table. It was as if Eunata had invited the elephant from Wagagai Cave into her living room.

'Samosa?' offered Eunata, carrying the plate of

triangular, vegetable-filled pastries over to the coffee table and sitting in the straw armchair opposite him.

'Thank you,' said Yang. He picked a samosa off the plate with his forefinger and thumb. 'Is everything resolved with the police? I couldn't understand what you and the officer were saying at the station.'

'We were speaking in Luganda,' said Eunata. 'We speak lots of languages in Uganda but mostly Luganda and Swahili.'

'Those men were after me today, weren't they?' Yang asked. 'Because I work for RanaTech.'

'Yes,' said Eunata. 'According to the police, they call themselves the Blue Spider Gang. They are a fairly new criminal organisation in Mbale and have taken to poaching elephants in the Elgon National Park. According to the police, that boy is their youngest member. He discovered you worked for RanaTech when he tried to rob you in Jinja. The gang's plan was to kidnap you and demand RanaTech pay a ransom for your release.'

Yang did not seem bothered by this news. He finished the samosa and picked up a napkin from the coffee table to clean his fingers. When he was done, he folded the napkin neatly and placed it on the plate.

'I could tell they were inexperienced,' he said. 'Too many mistakes. The man who came through my window attacked me with his machete. I would have been difficult to kidnap if I had been cut up into little pieces.

He panicked. That was his mistake. Plus, he made his move too early. If the men in the building had attacked at the same time, they would have had slightly more of a chance of taking me alive.'

'Slightly?' Eunata raised her eyebrows.

'Slightly,' nodded Yang. 'As criminal vermin go, I've handled worse in my time.'

'Do not call them vermin,' Eunata said sharply. 'They did not start life as criminals. They are working people who turned to poaching and kidnapping out of desperation because RanaTech knocked down their homes and businesses to build that ridiculous tower. The gang's actions are despicable, yes, and poachers fill me with a rage unlike any other. However, RanaTech cannot possibly blame others for a problem it itself created.'

Yang considered this.

'Why were they after you?' he asked. 'You don't work for RanaTech.'

'No,' said Eunata, 'but they know who I am – an environmental conservationist who has been the thorn in the side of many a poacher in her time. I ran into their gang leader at the market by coincidence. I think I startled him by telling him I knew about the elephant tusk in his bag. He was going to interrogate me to find out what else I knew. Interrogate me, or worse.'

'You handled yourself well,' said Yang.

'He needed more than three men,' Eunata shrugged. 'Then he would have had slightly more of a chance.'

'Slightly?'

'Slightly.'

Yang's slash of a mouth curled into something resembling a smile.

'I apologise for accusing you of shooting that elephant,' said Eunata.

'Apology accepted.'

'So, what is it RanaTech wants with my children, Mr Yang?'

Yang took a deep breath and leaned back on the sofa. It creaked under his weight.

'Jacob and Kira have been chosen as candidates to try out for Transcendent, an initiative that will equip the best and brightest minds with the most advanced scientific tools on the planet. If you all agree to take part and the twins are successful in the trials in London next week, they will be launched to RanaTech's private space station, the Garden, in low Earth orbit. Onboard the Garden is the most sophisticated laboratory this planet has ever seen. With minds like theirs, the breakthroughs and discoveries Jacob and Kira could make would be beyond anything we can imagine.'

'You want to shoot my children into space?' Eunata said slowly.

'They would be launched from RanaTech Spaceflight's

facility in Cornwall, yes,' said Yang. 'If they are successful in the trials.'

'Into space,' Eunata said again. She could not believe she was even saying the words.

'Like a lot of large companies, RanaTech is beginning to abandon the planet's surface and do business in orbit,' said Yang. 'With all the recent environmental changes, a lot of the planet that was hospitable even a few years ago is now inhospitable. There are, I think, around a hundred space stations in low Earth orbit right now. There's a launch facility close to most major cities. Even the process of preparing for launch has been radically streamlined and can happen in a matter of days. It's just like popping to the shops, really.'

Yang's black, glinting eyes examined the conflicted expression on Eunata's face. He leaned forward again. When he spoke, there was a kinder note to his voice.

'What I mean to say is, it's not as scary as it sounds. Amira Rana oversees Transcendent and she is one of the wealthiest, most famous and successful women in the world. Jacob and Kira have nothing to fear.'

Eunata sighed heavily. She was about to say something when there was a theatrical, protracted yawn from behind her. Kira had emerged from her bedroom, barefoot in pink pyjamas with teddy bears on the front.

'How was your nap, mtoto?' Eunata asked, turning around in her chair.

'It was OK, Mama.' Kira jumped into the other armchair. 'How's Orangutan?'

'Jacob is fine. He is outside. I patched him up but I think he is still feeling a little tired.'

'He's milking it,' Kira sniffed. Her nostrils wrinkled and she clasped hold of the armrests. 'Is that matoke I smell?'

'It is.'

'I love matoke!'

'I know you do.'

Kira settled back into the chair. Her fingers and toes wiggled.

'Kira,' Eunata began, glancing at Yang. 'What are you thinking about London and—'

'I want to go.' Kira's reply came before Eunata finished speaking.

'Yes,' Eunata sighed. 'I thought you would say that.'

'Mr Yang?' Kira asked.

'Yes?' Yang's thin eyebrows raised. He had not expected to be included.

'You said there are going to be trials in London. Does that mean there will be other people like me and Jacob there?'

'RanaTech has been gathering a handful of the greatest young minds from all over the world,' said Yang. 'The other candidates will join you in London for the trials, yes.'

Kira nodded. She seemed pleased with the answer.

'It is a hard decision, Kira,' said Eunata. 'Are you sure?'

'Actually, it might not be,' said Yang. 'You may be right that RanaTech is the cause of the conflict in Mbale but that doesn't change the fact that this Blue Spider Gang have shown themselves to be capable of acts of extreme violence. As far as I understand it, their leader is still on the loose. I may have been the Blue Spider Gang's original target but, after today, I wouldn't be surprised if the Flynn family has also been added to their list. All of which is to say . . .'

'Leaving Uganda for a while may not be such a bad idea,' Kira grinned. Her blue eyes sparkled.

Eunata dragged a hand down her face and groaned.

'Do you really not want us to go, Mama?' Kira asked, her face falling.

'No, it is not that,' Eunata smiled weakly. 'I have just realised I will have to leave Sunny in charge of the house.'

Kira squealed and clapped her hands.

'I'll go and tell Jacob!'

'Put on some shoes!' Eunata shouted but Kira had already bounded out of her chair and charged out of the front door, slamming it shut behind her.

Jacob was lying in the cargo bed of the Ranger, parked in front of the garage next to Yang's Cherokee, gazing up at the infinity of stars. The air was tinged with the scent of distant bonfires. For a long time, the only sound had been the pulsing chirr of crickets. Now, he heard approaching footsteps on the grass.

'You know, sooner or later, we might get a closer look at those stars,' came Kira's voice.

'We have to go to London, don't we?' said Jacob, sitting up and looking down at her.

'Yeah,' said Kira.

Jacob sighed. His cut and bruised face was illuminated by the white glow of the RanaPhone in his hand.

'You know, it wasn't just the stars I was looking at up here,' he said.

'Well, hang those ridiculously long arms down here so I can climb up and you can tell me all about it,' said Kira.

Jacob leaned over and grunted as he heaved Kira into the cargo bed. His body still ached. They cleared some of the clutter, pulled out a rough, chequered rug and laid it out. They lay on top of it, side by side. The glistening stars spread into the blackness at the very edges of the night sky, spiralling from the kaleidoscopic glow of the Milky Way.

The two of them stared up in silence for a while. Then Jacob spoke.

'There's been a new post from Double M,' he said.

'What did they say?' Kira asked.

'They didn't say anything. They just posted a photograph.'

'Let's have a look, then.'

Jacob hesitated, then passed Kira his RanaPhone.

The picture at first seemed to be nothing more than a black square with two dots of luminous green close together at its centre. Kira squinted and realised with mounting repulsion that the green dots were eyes, with vivid, black pupils that burned off the screen with pure, inhuman hatred. Around the eyes was a shapeless mass of bristling, black hair and underneath the hair was a body, segmented like a spider's but shaped like man's, with two arms and two legs. The creature was a tarantula in human form. Its hands were a glistening grey and, aside from the fact that there were six fingers on each, could actually have been human. Kira could even see chipped, black fingernails.

She managed to tear her eyes from the RanaPhone and look at Jacob. She chuckled. Despite her best effort, the laugh sounded hollow. Her mouth was dry.

'I hope it's not a self-portrait,' she said in a hoarse voice.

'I've been staring at it for ages,' Jacob said quietly.

'Why? It's horrible.'

'It's a picture of one of them.'

'One of what?'

'They're called the Others. Or, at least, that's the name they've been designated by RanaTech.'

'How can Double M possibly know that?'

'Double M's a spy inside RanaTech,' murmured Jacob. 'He managed to download this image from their private server. He must be the best hacker in the world. Not even our hacking app was able to break into Yang's Oracle.'

'So, has RanaTech been in contact with these Others? Is that how they have a picture of one of them?' Kira shifted uncomfortably. 'I don't know, Orangutan. This sounds like one of your Captain Cosmic adventures to me.'

Jacob had lowered his RanaPhone and was staring up at the sky, into the intense blackness between the pinpricks of the stars.

'Why else would RanaTech want to send us to space to fight the greatest threat this planet has ever faced?' Jacob asked, shivering a little in the slight breeze. 'What other threat could it be?'

'If that really is what's happening here,' said Kira, 'why has Amira Rana chosen us? What can two fourteen-year-olds from Uganda do against an alien invasion?'

'Maybe RanaTech needs our intelligence.' Jacob sighed again. 'You were right, Kira. Believe me, I don't want to leave Uganda. But it's the right thing to do.

I've been reading stories about heroes fighting bad guys and saving the world my entire life. Now, here's my own chance. Captain Cosmic wouldn't turn his back on a fight like this. We need to go to London. But there's only one way I can do it. And that's if you're with me.'

Jacob heaved himself onto his side and winced. There was a nasty bruise above his waist. His blue eyes were staring at Kira while she continued looking up at the sky.

'Today,' said Jacob, 'you ran off and Spider followed you. Because of that, Mama was hurt. If we had stuck together, everything would have been OK.'

'I know,' said Kira. 'I'm sorry.'

'If we go to London, I want you to promise me something,' said Jacob. 'Promise me you won't do anything like that again. That we'll stick together.'

Kira turned onto her own side and looked at her brother.

'I promise,' she said.

'Good,' said Jacob.

They both rolled onto their backs and said no more, gazing up at the stars. After a while, Jacob's hand reached out across the rug to his sister's. Kira squeezed it and did not let go. That was how they remained until they heard their mother's voice from the porch, telling them that the matoke was getting cold.

CHAPTER
TWELVE

Jacob and Kira had their faces glued to a window of the Gulfstream electric business jet, flying low on its approach to London City Airport. At first, they could see nothing at all. The city was submerged in a colourless smog. Gradually, towering skyscrapers emerged like ships from a sea mist. Rain was falling. As the jet fell further beneath the clouds, drops pattered against the windows and distorted the already murky view. Jacob and Kira looked at each other, shrugged, and sat back down.

It was the first time they had shown any interest in the view since boarding at Entebbe Airport. There were no rows of seats as on normal planes but two long white sofas on either side. Jacob and Kira had spent most of the eight-hour flight asking Yang questions about the automated piloting system. The cockpit looked like any other, apart from the lack of pilots. It was unnerving to watch the flight instruments operate themselves, the needles on the altimeter and airspeed indicator spinning and the Gulfstream tilting of its own accord to adjust its course.

Eunata had simply watched in silence as the sparse, glittering lights of Africa disappeared from underneath them, to be replaced by nothing but a black void, which meant they were speeding over the Mediterranean Sea.

The journey from Mbale had been a blur. Entebbe was five hours west and that meant following Tororo Road through both Jinja and Kampala and skirting along the northern shore of Lake Victoria. Tororo Road cut ramrod straight across the green countryside and the Ranger and Cherokee had careered along it, weaving around each other with clouds of red dust billowing behind them. The sun had glanced off their orange and black chassis as they tipped from side to side like bucking bulls, the roar of their engines rumbling over the plains. Kira had stood on the cargo bed of the Ranger and gripped the chrome bar on the roof of the cabin, frizzy hair fluttering behind her and cheeks rippling. Jacob sat in the passenger seat, his arm resting on the lowered window as he offered the occasional disapproving glance at his sister.

Yang had rushed them through Entebbe Airport. Jacob remembered his mother breaking down in tears as they walked onto the tarmac as she realised she and her children would be leaving Uganda for the first time. Jacob and Kira had hugged her while Yang had seemed taken aback by this display of emotion. He had cleared his throat and pointed to the Gulfstream, with its sleek, white body, pointed wings and two cylindrical, electric engines.

'I understand this may be difficult for you but, if it's any consolation, you will be leaving in style.'

'That's awesome,' Jacob said.

'Where's the pilot? Is it you?' asked Kira. 'Because I really think you should take those sunglasses off for that.'

Yang's mouth twitched.

'What pilot?' he asked.

Both twins' mouths dropped open.

'No . . .' began one.

'. . . way,' finished the other.

Now, as they descended on London, they finally saw something other than the dark shapes of skyscrapers looming out of the smog. The silvery curve of the River Thames was like a wide strip of glass winding through the city. The runway was floating on the water, a thin stretch of land surrounded by the Royal Docks. Jacob could see an industrial wilderness of towering cranes and mountainous stacks of shipping containers on both sides of the river.

The landing gear collided with the ground and the

cabin and everything inside bounced roughly. When the frantic whirr of the electric motors had died and the Gulfstream slowed to a stop, the airstair, unassisted, opened and extended down to the runway.

The cold sank its claws into Jacob as soon as he stepped off the jet. It was a biting cold that gnawed at his insides like rats. His fingers were numb. What hit him next was the smell. London stank. There was a stench of sewage and smoke so powerful, it was choking and a hundred times worse than the fish stalls at Mbale Central Market. Both Jacob and Kira coughed as they shuffled down the airstair and onto the tarmac. They could hear the clanging and hammering of dockland machinery and the hiss of drizzling rain, which fell in misty, billowing clouds. They were soaked in seconds. Still coughing, they hurried off the runway and into the terminal, suitcases trundling noisily on the wet tarmac.

There was a Jeep Cherokee waiting for them outside the airport, identical to the one Yang had driven in Uganda. The huge, black car seemed far more at home in London than it did in Uganda and yet still dwarfed the vehicles around it. Cars whooshed past, headlights casting dirty beams of yellow into the grey fumes that hung over everything. A driver wearing a dark suit and wireless earpiece got out of the Cherokee. While Yang helped the driver fling their suitcases into the back of the car, Kira turned to Jacob and grinned with some difficulty. She needed to blink through the rain.

'What do you think?' she asked.

Jacob did not answer at first. He was looking around in wonder, lost in the onslaught of traffic and pedestrians. He had never seen so many white faces. Jacob considered Kira's question before turning back to her and replying honestly.

'I'm not sure,' he said and shivered.

'Where exactly in London is this RanaTech facility?' asked Eunata, covering her mouth with her hand and staring, aghast, at everything around her.

'You'll see,' said Yang.

The driver navigated expertly through East London and in the direction of the city centre. The streets were far wider than those of Mbale. As they joined the slow-moving traffic, the buildings began to get taller and the crumbling, graffiti-covered brickwork of the docklands was replaced by towering structures of steel and glass. Digital billboards on every surface hurled their reflections onto the tinted windows of the car. They tinged the grey smog with fluorescent greens, pinks, blues and all manner of neon colours. Fizzy drinks, fast food, the latest RanaPhone, underwear worn by athletic models – all these and more leered in front of garish backgrounds. The flashing colours were reflected in rippling puddles on the pavement.

Jacob noticed the people hurrying through the streets mostly had their heads down to shield themselves from the rain. No one was paying real attention to the lurid advertisements. Looking closer, Jacob noticed the faces of the people were not just white. They were pale, gaunt, and almost as colourless as the ever-present smog. Everyone seemed to be avoiding everyone else's gaze, determined to walk to their destination as fast as they could. They appeared and disappeared in the gloom like haggard ghosts.

The Cherokee crossed Tower Bridge. The smog was clearer over the slate-coloured, lapping water of the Thames and Jacob could see all the way across the river to a cluster of skyscrapers, jutting from the north bank. One of them caught his eye straight away. One side of the building was straight and vertical but the other was tilted so the building was the shape of a gigantic, glass wedge. Amira Rana's smiling face was emblazoned on the tilted side of the building, on a billboard the size of a runway. It was a video, the same three-second clip repeating one time after the other. The luscious, black and brown hair that flowed down the two-hundred-metre height of the building was flicked over Amira's shoulder and she smiled the same, dazzling smile again and again, all hazel eyes, red lips and white teeth. At the bottom of the billboard was the R in the middle of the golden crown that was the RanaTech logo.

'That's cool,' Kira noted, 'and only a tiny bit narcissistic.'

'That's the Leadenhall Building,' said Yang, turning around in the passenger seat, 'otherwise known as the Cheesegrater for obvious reasons. I'm sure you recognise Ms Rana.'

'Just look at her,' Jacob breathed. 'Her life must be perfect.'

'She certainly is the envy of millions,' said Yang.

The Cherokee left Tower Bridge and continued south of the river. Jacob pulled out his RanaPhone and lowered the car window. The icy, fetid stench of the streets flooded the car. Drops of rain splashed against the leather seats.

'Mama! Look what he's doing!' Kira protested.

'Just quickly,' he mumbled.

Jacob stood up and leaned through the window so his head and shoulders were outside the moving Cherokee. He squirmed with one arm to lift his RanaPhone and started filming.

'Hey, guys, it's Captain Cosmic here,' Jacob grinned at the screen. 'I've arrived in London Town and, I've got to say, at first glance, it's a little—'

The Cherokee jolted to a stop. The car had pulled up outside a marble entrance hall behind gigantic, glass doors and a row of steel columns. With his RanaPhone camera still filming, Jacob goggled up at the building above the entrance hall and the slanting, glass panels slicing towards a jagged peak three hundred metres high. He recognised it from all the postcards and online photos he had ever seen of London.

'Amira Rana works at the Shard?' Jacob blustered.

'Son,' said Yang. 'Amira Rana *owns* the Shard.'

Their footsteps and trundling suitcases echoed as they wandered through the entrance hall. As soon as they stepped into the lift, it shot upwards at such a speed that Jacob's feet glued themselves to the floor. He felt not just his feet but his bones and guts pulling themselves down, as if the lift wanted to leave his body behind. The doors opened onto the thirtieth floor and he staggered out.

'Welcome to the Lounge,' said Yang.

The sloping windows were thirty feet tall and should have offered a sweeping view of the London skyline. But Jacob could see nothing at all. There was just grey cloud, pressing relentlessly against the glass. The view from every window was nothing but grey. The effect was suffocating. Jacob did his best to ignore the murky vapour and appreciate the lavish interior of the Lounge. Kira's mouth was hanging open.

'We're staying here?' she asked, dumbfounded.

There was a bar in one corner with a black, marble counter and glasses hanging from the racks above. In another corner was a pool table. There were leather sofas and displays of succulents and ferns. The one wall that was not glass was vertical concrete and painted white. The other side of that wall housed both the lift shafts and, according to Yang, the Transcendent candidates' living quarters. Everything was brand new. There was still the smell of fresh paint.

'I'm told the other candidates arrived earlier today,' said Yang. 'You will meet them this evening at a charity event Ms Rana is hosting at the National Gallery in Trafalgar Square.' He eyed Jacob and Kira's damp T-shirts, jeans and dirty trainers. 'Someone will fetch you more suitable clothes. Now, I think you should get some rest. The trials will take place tomorrow.'

With that and no goodbye whatsoever, Yang left them. When they heard the *ding* that indicated he had stepped back into the lift, Kira took a running jump and hurled herself onto one of the sofas.

'I could get used to this,' she said cheerfully, bouncing up and down.

Eunata sighed and said nothing.

CHAPTER THIRTEEN

The dinner jacket fitted Jacob perfectly. He walked to the window, polished Oxford shoes tapping the glass floor. When he raised his hand to smooth his lapels, a white sliver of his crisp dress shirt was visible at his wrist.

Night had fallen but the rain clouds were as oppressive as ever. The view out of the windows was entirely black. It was disconcerting to be so high in the sky and yet not see anything outside. Jacob attempted to focus on his reflection in the window and straighten his bowtie. His electric blue eyes stared back, betraying the anxiety and excitement battling each other in his head. Jacob had made it to London, so ridiculously far from home, he may as well have travelled to another planet. But he had Kira by his side and, together, they were going to find out what Transcendent was all about.

Jacob, Kira and Eunata had each been given a private

room. Jacob's was much bigger than his bedroom in Mbale but almost empty, with just a bed and bedside table. One wall was entirely glass and slanted at an angle like the windows of the Lounge but, as Jacob could not see anything through it, he had not paid much notice. What he had noticed straight away was a dark suit carrier laid across his bed. Jacob had never worn a dinner jacket or even a dress shirt and had spent the last hour fiddling with each new piece of clothing. Gazing at his own reflection now, Jacob was pleased with the result. He thought he looked like a spy.

There was a clatter behind him. Jacob turned and burst out laughing. Kira was stumbling towards him in an elegant, green evening gown that hung to her ankles and left her arms bare. There was a pair of matching, green high heels on her feet. Kira had never worn anything remotely similar before and it was obvious from the thunderous expression on her face. She was walking like a new-born giraffe.

'Keep laughing and you can meet us on the pavement,' Kira growled, 'without taking the lift.'

'You look lovely,' said Jacob in a choked voice, struggling to keep his face straight.

'Forget this,' she said, taking a few more steps before turning shakily around. 'You look like a spy by the way.'

'Really?' said Jacob, looking himself up and down.

'No,' said Kira over her shoulder as she stumbled back to her room. 'You look like a penguin with a stick up its—'

'Kira!' Eunata had emerged from her own room, wearing an orange gomesi, a floor-length dress with a square neckline and short, puffed sleeves. There was a blue sash around her waist. She had brought the traditional Ugandan dress with her from Mbale.

'You look really nice, Mama,' said Jacob.

'Thank you, mtoto,' Eunata said without smiling. 'Hurry up, Kira. Our driver is waiting downstairs.'

Nelson's Column stood in the middle of Trafalgar Square. Four bronze lions crouched at its base. On either side was a fountain, decorated with elaborate statues of mermaids, mermen, tritons and dolphins. The water erupting from each fountain was illuminated in blue from beneath. The buildings surrounding Trafalgar Square on three of the four sides were adorned in the same digital advertisements Jacob had seen all over London. Their neon colours lit up the puddles on the paving stones, gleamed on the bronze of the statues and irradiated the mist of constantly falling rain.

The north side of the square was occupied by the pillared entrance of the National Gallery. A red carpet spilled down stone steps, covered by a canopy. Photographers crowded on the steps on either side of the red carpet, wearing anoraks, drenched and glistening in the rain. The aggressive flashes of their cameras forced Jacob to squint, even from inside the tinted windows of the Cherokee. He and Kira were sitting at the back. Eunata was in the passenger's seat. The same driver who had picked them up from the airport was driving. As the Cherokee neared the entrance, the photographers became more animated and started running down the steps.

'Is that for us?' Jacob asked in amazement.

'No, boss,' the driver chuckled. 'It's not for you.'

A startlingly pink Aston Martin Rapide E had slipped silently into Trafalgar Square in front of the Cherokee and was pulling up at the bottom of the stone steps. The photographers bustled around it. Cameras snapped excitedly. Jacob pressed his face against the window and had an excellent view of what happened next.

The driver's door of the Aston Martin swung open. First to exit was a stiletto heel, straps glittering with diamonds and laced around an ankle, swiftly covered by a flowing, pink lehenga. A dupatta of the same colour was draped around the waist and elegantly thrown over the shoulder. A turquoise choli was worn underneath, leaving the stomach bare. If Amira Rana could feel the freezing cold or see the clamouring photographers around her, she gave no indication. She strode along the red carpet, up the steps and into the

National Gallery, black hair and pink lehenga billowing behind her.

'So,' said Eunata, 'that's Amira Rana.'

'Our turn!' said Kira, preparing to stand up.

'No, it's not,' said the driver, chuckling again. 'We're using the back entrance, boss.'

The walls of the central hall in the National Gallery were a blood red underneath an elevated glass rooftop. The floor was polished oak. Oil paintings of lavish landscapes lined the walls. The hall itself was crowded with guests, each wearing an outfit more extravagant than the last. Waiters in black tailcoats wandered through the hall, carrying silver platters of canapés. All eyes were on Amira Rana, who was standing on a raised stage at one end of the room. Next to the stage, a string quartet had lowered their instruments and were listening intently.

As Jacob, Kira and Eunata entered quietly at the other end, Amira's speech was coming to a close. Jacob was mesmerised. Her voice was like butter melting in a pan.

'With wildfires still raging in the Amazon rainforest, twelve million hectares have already been burned to ashes. That equates to an area roughly the size of Greece. The flames are threatening millions of people and over a thousand animal species and every one of them is desperately in need of aid. I hope you find it in your hearts to give generously. Thank you.'

There was a polite smattering of applause and Amira smiled and left the stage. Conversations recommenced. The string quartet began playing Bach.

'What do we do now?' Kira asked. She and Jacob were looking around awkwardly.

'It's a party,' said Eunata. 'Enjoy yourself. Try the canapés. Make polite conversation.'

Jacob and Kira looked at each other. They had no idea what they were supposed to make polite conversation about.

'Perhaps you can try and find the other Transcendent candidates,' said Eunata. 'Mr Yang said they would be here this evening.'

'OK,' said Kira. 'What are you going to do, Mama?'

Kira turned to look at her mother but Eunata was already marching purposefully into the revelling crowd.

'I will be back,' said Eunata darkly.

Kira looked at Jacob and shrugged.

'I guess she'll be back.'

Jacob was not looking at Kira. He was looking at an elderly woman, wearing a black, feathery dress, who was standing amongst a close group of people, all holding champagne flutes and engaged in lively discussion. The woman was not joining the conversation. She was staring across the hall at Jacob and Kira. As soon as Jacob met her gaze, the woman turned abruptly back to her companions and began speaking in hushed tones.

'What are you looking at?' Kira asked, who had not noticed what had happened.

'Nothing,' said Jacob, grabbing Kira's bare shoulders and steering her towards the other end of the hall. 'Let's go and find these Transcendent candidates.'

The oil painting was of a night sky, so vibrant and pulsing with energy that it could have been alive. The moon was an orange sickle, radiating with fierce yellow. Swirling through the sky was the wind and, bursting through the blues and blacks of the sky and the swirl of the wind were the stars. Their light roared in the face of Amira Rana, who was gazing at the canvas with an expression that was entirely unimpressed.

'It is beautiful,' said Eunata. She had quietly appeared next to Amira and the two women were staring at the painting, side by side. Amira was a foot taller than Eunata but she did not turn to look down at her. Instead, her hazel eyes danced over the painting like those of a cat.

'You think so?' asked Amira. 'Apparently, Vincent Van Gogh painted *The Starry Night* from the window of his asylum room at Saint-Rémy-de-Provence. I had it shipped here from the Museum of Modern Art in

New York especially for tonight. On seeing it, I'm not entirely sure what all the fuss is about.'

'I think it is the stars,' Eunata said. 'They remind me of my home in Uganda. Whenever I am feeling low and in need of hope, I look up at the night sky.'

'That must be nice,' said Amira absently. Her demeanour was different from the warm and vivacious woman who had been speaking on stage. Now, her voice was bored and drawling.

'That was a powerful speech, by the way,' said Eunata. 'Congratulations.'

'I'll tell that to the people who wrote it,' said Amira. 'Excuse me.'

At the swish of Amira's dupatta and lehenga, Eunata caught an aroma of expensive perfume. There was a golden pendant hanging from a chain around Amira's neck, the snarling face of a tiger with tiny emeralds for eyes.

'You seem a little less passionate than you did on stage a moment ago,' said Eunata. Amira stopped and turned back to *The Starry Night*, changing direction as gracefully as a swan on water.

'Once you reach a position like mine,' Amira said, 'you find yourself saying a lot of things other people have written down first. You get bored of it after a while.'

'You are the head of RanaTech,' said Eunata,

astonished. 'How could having the power and resources to change the world ever be boring? Some people would call that a privilege.'

'Some people would call it a world not worth saving,' replied Amira icily. Her eyes narrowed and looked Eunata up and down, as if she were properly noticing her for the first time. 'What are you doing here, may I ask? You don't strike me as one of the usual social climbers I meet at these things.'

'My children are Jacob and Kira Flynn,' said Eunata. 'You have chosen them as candidates for Transcendent.'

Amira laughed. It was a cold sound.

'Ah, yes, Transcendent. It sounds like your children are the ones who will be saving the world. And we'll all be so grateful.'

'I would like your guarantee that they will be safe,' said Eunata.

'Don't worry,' said Amira. 'That's one thing you'll learn about RanaTech. Nothing will happen that has not already been planned down to the last detail. Every. Last. One.'

Eunata was about to reply when another woman, wearing a grey trouser suit and tightly curled hairstyle, appeared at Amira's side in such a hurry that the two almost collided.

'What is it, Kelly?' Amira asked with obviously false sweetness.

'Ms Rana, the Bolivian ambassador wishes to speak with you,' said Kelly breathlessly.

'Oh, has that bumbling old goat not croaked it yet?'

'Pardon me, Ms Rana?'

'I said, "Lead on, please."'

And, with that, Amira walked away, heels rapping the wooden floor. She seemed to have forgotten about Eunata already.

Eunata stayed where she was, gazing at the night sky above Saint-Rémy-de-Provence. She was completely taken aback. Amira Rana had not been what she had expected and Eunata had no idea what to make of their brief conversation. But there was one thing of which she was very certain.

Eunata did not trust her one little bit.

Jacob and Kira wormed their way through the crowd in search of the other Transcendent candidates, catching snippets of conversation from the other guests as they passed.

'. . . it's worse than ever . . . all the fumes . . . can hardly breathe outside nowadays . . .'

'. . . it's their fault . . . coming from these other places . . . insisting on taking those kinds of jobs . . . driving RanaCabs . . . driving trucks to and from the docks . . .'

'. . . it's an infestation . . .'

'. . . the Prime Minister said as much herself this morning . . .'

Kira nudged Jacob and pointed at a teenage girl hovering in the corner of the central hall. Lulu Laei was also fourteen and looked so overjoyed to be there that she did not know how to contain it. She was wearing a flowery dress and seemed to immediately recognise Jacob and Kira as other Transcendent candidates. Beneath black, curly hair, her sun-kissed face broke into a wide, warm smile. Her eyes, brown but just as sunny, were magnified and made even sunnier by the thick lenses of gold-framed spectacles.

'I'm a marine biologist,' said Lulu excitedly after introducing herself. 'RanaTech recruited me for the Transcendent trials after they saw my work reversing coral bleaching around the Solomon Islands in the southwest Pacific.'

'That's incredible!' Kira grinned.

'How are you guys feeling?' Lulu asked. 'This is all pretty crazy! You must be nervous, right?'

'No,' Jacob lied.

'I suppose you guys are all here for Transcendent as well, then.'

Jacob, Kira and Lulu turned to see another boy and girl. The girl looked to be their age but the boy seemed older, around sixteen. The girl was wearing a lace dress. Her straight hair was jet black, her face pale, slight and serious. She was very pretty. Her eyes were also black and glittered like gemstones.

'Sakari Ekho.' She smiled a slight smile, hesitantly offering her hand to shake.

'Nice to meet you, Sakari!' Kira and Lulu shook her hand vigorously, one after the other. When Jacob took Sakari's hand, he felt the strange flutter of something inside himself that he had not experienced before. Sakari was the same height as he was, which made avoiding her sparkling eyes difficult. After Lulu explained her work in the Solomon Islands, Sakari turned to Jacob and Kira.

'What about you two?' she asked. 'Are you biologists as well? Would I have heard of some of your projects?'

'No,' said Kira, a little sheepishly. 'We just build things.'

Sakari smiled again at that and appeared to relax a little. Her black eyes flicked between the two of them, eventually settling on Jacob. His cheeks burned.

'That's how I started out,' she said. 'I've been developing a device that will refreeze melted ice caps and restore the habitats of displaced bowhead whales. I'm based on the Alaska North Slope, north of the Arctic Circle, so the temperature in London is actually warmer than what I'm used to.'

'That's amazing!' Kira beamed.

'Seriously impressive,' Jacob said shyly.

Sakari nodded appreciatively, then lowered her voice. 'I guess you've all been given the brief on Transcendent like I was, but has anyone been told anything about what our work on the Garden will actually be about?'

When Jacob, Kira and Lulu all shook their heads, Sakari nodded and bit her lip.

'I wonder if we'll be told more after the trials tomorrow,' she said anxiously. 'It all feels very mysterious, doesn't it? Makes you wonder what RanaTech might be hiding.'

Jacob was about to ask Sakari what she thought RanaTech might be hiding when the older boy next to her chose that moment to introduce himself. He was short, around the same height as the rest of them, with straw-coloured hair, reddish skin and watery eyes. He was wearing a waistcoat and open-necked shirt.

'Peter Presland,' he announced. 'I'm a physicist based in New York. I've already done some work for RanaTech Defence, developing a new model of their surface-to-space missile.'

'That's brilliant!' enthused Kira.

'It will be when it works,' said Peter pompously.

'So,' Kira clapped her hands together. 'We're the five Transcendent candidates. It will be all of us up there on the Garden! I can already tell we're going to be best friends.'

'Sure we are,' said Lulu brightly. 'That is, if we all get through the trials tomorrow. I'm sure we will!'

'What exactly will happen during these trials?' Jacob asked.

'Sakari and I were just talking about that.' Peter shrugged. 'We have no idea, but I suppose it won't be long until we find out.'

The five of them stood in thoughtful silence.

'So, where are the two of you from?' Peter asked after a while.

Jacob and Kira looked at the others before realising he was speaking to both of them.

'Uganda,' said Jacob.

'That's interesting,' said Peter. 'I mean, you do look kind of African but, really? With eyes like those?'

'Yes,' said Kira.

Jacob heard the hardness in his sister's voice. 'We should probably go and find our mama,' he said quickly. 'We'll see you guys at the Lounge later?' Jacob manoeuvred Kira back towards the middle of the central hall, away from a potential argument.

'I wonder if it'll really be the five of us up there on the Garden,' said Jacob. 'Do you think that will be the first time we'll be the least interesting people in a room? And what could Amira Rana have chosen us all for?'

Kira did not respond. She was frowning.

'Jacob, why are people staring at us?' she asked.

Jacob glanced around. Kira was right. As soon as his eyes met those of at least three people in the hall, they quickly looked at the people next to them or down at their drinks to avoid eye contact. He had the abrupt and unpleasant sensation of crawling skin, as if there were worms all over his body. He was used to being treated differently in Uganda because of the way he and Kira looked. He was used to children calling them names from far away and even to men hurling abuse at them on the street. Somehow, staring was worse than all of that. Kira was breathing heavily. Her fists were clenched and shaking.

'How much debt will I be in if I tear one of those paintings off the wall and put a rich person's head through it?' she muttered.

'Kira, please calm down,' breathed Jacob.

'Excuse me.'

Jacob froze. The voice had come from behind him. He had recognised it instantly. He felt his body seize up. It was as if it wanted to fold itself into a ball and throw itself away.

'I would say, "Excuse me," again but the last person who made me repeat myself took an unfortunate tumble out of a window. I'm trying to get past.'

Jacob and Kira glanced at each other. They turned slowly with forced smiles as they came face to face with

Amira Rana at last. Amira did not smile back. She simply stared, blinking expectantly at them. If looking at Amira from a distance was mesmerising, being in her close vicinity put Jacob into a state of stunned delirium. He opened his mouth to speak but could only conjure a hoarse croak. Amira took hold of her dupatta and retreated a few steps.

'Don't you dare be sick on me,' she said.

'Excuse my brother,' said Kira quickly. 'Kira and Jacob Flynn. We were just leaving. We're getting a bit bored of the crowd around here.'

'Likewise,' said Amira. Her gaze fell on Kira. Something flickered in her hazel eyes. 'Nice trainers.'

Kira looked down at the dirty trainers under her green evening gown. She had switched the high heels before leaving the Shard. When she looked up again, Amira had already swept past. Jacob managed to catch the scent of expensive perfume and the jangle of jewellery before the crowd parted before her like the Red Sea and she was gone.

CHAPTER
FOURTEEN

Raindrops rippled across the surface of St Thomas Street. Neon advertisements crackled and sparked. There was a splash and the Aston Martin Rapide E drew up to the pavement outside the Shard. The eight-hundred-volt electrical battery purred under the bonnet. Glowering headlights hurled dirty yellow beams into the smoky gloom.

'Drop shields.'

At Amira's command, the tinted windows turned from opaque to transparent in an instant. Light fell across hazel eyes. Inside the marble entrance hall, Amira Rana could see the suited receptionist leaning back in his chair and staring up at the cavernous ceiling.

'Call reception,' she said.

She watched the man scramble forward to pick up the phone.

'Ms Rana.'

'Raymond.'

'It's, erm, Ramone, Ms Rana.'

'It's raining.'

'I see.'

Thirty seconds later, the doors slid open and Ramone hurried onto the pavement, brandishing an umbrella. He held it above Amira's head as soon as she stepped out of the car.

'Welcome back to the Shard, Ms Rana,' said Ramone.

'Thank you, Raymond,' she replied.

Amira took her private lift to her private office which occupied the entire seventieth floor of the building, forty floors above the Lounge. The office was entirely bare, with just a desk and chair sitting in the middle of a frosted glass floor. Outside the windows, rain fell in great, billowing sheets. There was a brief, vapoury gap in the colossal, black clouds and Amira's eyes were drawn to something on the other side of the Thames. At the sight of it, her lip curled in disgust. Intense hatred bubbled up within her, like venom to the fangs of a snake.

For a few seconds, Amira's own face stared back at her from the side of the Leadenhall Building, adorned on a billboard the size of a runway. The gigantic image, visible only due to thousands upon thousands of red, blue and green light-emitting diodes, flicked its dark, flowing hair over its shoulder and smiled a stunning smile. The real woman of flesh and blood, standing on the seventieth floor of the Shard, glowered across the river at her grotesque caricature with an expression that could only be described as purest loathing.

What was it that Ugandan woman had said at the National Gallery? Something about stars?

Amira looked up. Falling rain cast rippling shadows over her face. They could almost have been tears. As always, not a single star could be seen in the night sky. At no point in her thirty-eight years, either in Delhi or London, could Amira remember looking up and seeing anything other than smoky murk. She could only imagine the stars, twinkling ominously above the rolling, gargantuan storm clouds.

There had been something about those twins of that Ugandan woman. Jake and Kristen. Were those their names? No. Jacob and Kira. Candidates for Transcendent. It was a shame. There had been a spark of something in their blue eyes.

Amira had almost liked them.

CHAPTER
FIFTEEN

The next morning, Eunata sat on one of the black leather sofas, away from the others, gazing out of the slanted window of the Lounge. The rain clouds had cleared. Only the tops of skyscrapers were visible above the haze of dirty smog. Jacob, Kira, Sakari, Lulu and Peter were sitting together in a cluster of sofas some distance away. They had all changed into hoodies, jeans and trainers. Eunata could hear them laughing. Kira was sitting between Sakari and Lulu and had her arms around the shoulders of the other girls, looking more happy and comfortable with anyone apart from her family than Eunata had ever seen her before. Jacob and Peter were sitting together on a sofa across from them.

'The first thing we're going to build on the Garden is a zero gravity jacuzzi!' Kira was saying loudly. 'Only girls allowed!'

'Absolutely!' Lulu clapped.

'I don't think that will be allowed at all, actually,' muttered Sakari.

'What are *you* going to build first, then?' asked Kira, rolling her eyes.

'I'm going to wait till we find out what we've actually been called together to do,' said Sakari. 'Until then, I'm not sure I want any part in Transcendent. I don't like the fact that RanaTech is keeping secrets from us.'

'I always expected that to be the case,' said Peter bullishly. 'The RanaTech lab in New York is the same. We're just cogs in a machine. We're never going to know all the secrets. We'll be told what we need to know, when we need to know it.'

'You're not the only one who's worked at a big company before,' said Sakari, cheeks flushing. 'I was eleven when I finished my master's degree and, since then, I've been contracting with various think tanks and tech companies, all while working on my own conservation projects in Alaska.'

'I've only got two bachelor's degrees,' said Lulu, fiddling bashfully with her hair. 'I graduated at twelve. It took longer because I was studying biology and marine sciences at the same time.'

'It's not a competition,' declared Peter, 'but I finished my doctorate a few months ago.'

'So, you guys are all used to working away from

home already?' Kira asked. 'Is that why none of your parents have come to London with you?'

Peter, Sakari and Lulu shrugged and nodded.

'We've never been to university,' Kira said, dejected. 'Our mama's still homeschooling us.'

'I just assumed universities in Africa were hard to come by,' said Peter. 'Anyways, as I was saying, this is all to be expected. We'll find out more at the trials today.'

'There are around fifty universities in Uganda alone, actually,' said Kira, eyes narrowed, before turning to Jacob, who was not really listening. 'Do you think they sell bhut jolokia in London?'

'One person who is not what I expected,' said Eunata loudly from the other side of the Lounge, 'is Amira Rana. That woman has a sliver of ice in her heart.'

Jacob's ears perked up. He had been deep in thought. Amira Rana had not been what he had expected either. He swung himself off the sofa and walked over to Eunata. Sakari and Peter both watched him as he crossed the Lounge.

'Do you think Amira's hiding something, Mama?' Jacob asked.

Eunata sighed and looked out of the window at the colossal billboard on the other side of the Thames. Jacob followed her gaze. It was the only part of the dreary cityscape that could have been called warm or colourful and yet, despite Amira's brilliant smile, there was a coldness in those eyes. Could it really be that Double M was right and Amira, head of RanaTech, knew all about the Others? Was that really the threat Transcendent would face up there on the Garden?

'I do not know, mtoto,' Eunata said, standing and hugging him tightly. 'Keep your wits about you. As long as you and your sister stick together, no harm will come to either of you.'

Jacob closed his eyes and sighed, nestling into her embrace.

'That's what I'm counting on, Mama. I couldn't do this without her.'

Eunata pulled back and held up her RanaPhone. It displayed a map of London.

'I think I will go for a walk. Mr Yang said I will not be able to accompany you for the trials.' She pointed at a wonky rectangle of green labelled as HYDE PARK. 'I want to visit here. Good luck! I think Kira is excited.'

Jacob smiled as Eunata walked towards the lifts that would take her down to the ground level. He turned and found himself suddenly face to face with his sister.

'What are you thinking about, Orangutan?' Kira asked, curious eyes and furrowed brow filling his vision.

'I . . . I just . . . erm . . . I'm not sure if . . .' Jacob was disconcerted. 'I'd just like to know a bit more about what Amira Rana is up to . . . and what we're all doing here.'

'Amira said we'd find out after the trials.'

'Do you think . . . there might be a way to find out sooner?' Jacob asked. His eyes searched the glass ceiling.

'Oh, Orangutan!' Kira elbowed him, smiling conspiratorially. 'It's usually me who suggests that sort of thing!'

'You don't want to find out more?' Jacob's eyes lowered hesitantly to meet Kira's.

'Oh, I've been thinking about it all morning. I just can't believe *you* said it first.'

'What are you guys talking about?' Sakari called over.

'We were wondering whether . . .' Jacob began as they rejoined the others.

'. . . Amira Rana has something to hide?' Sakari finished for him.

'Yeah,' said Kira gleefully, 'and we're going to find out what!'

'I don't think we're supposed to leave the Lounge until we're called,' said Sakari.

'Don't you want to find out sooner?' Lulu asked.

'Of course I do,' Sakari flicked her black hair over

her shoulder and Jacob once again felt the strange flutter of something inside his stomach, 'but I'm not sure I want to break the rules to do it.'

'Don't worry,' Kira grinned. 'My brother and I have been breaking rules for as long as we've been breaking wind.'

'I'm game,' said Peter, 'and that's disgusting.'

'Me too!' squeaked Lulu, raising her hand.

They all looked at Sakari, who thought for a moment and then shook her head.

'Sorry, guys,' she said, 'but I don't feel comfortable doing that. I'll stay here and cover for you. I'll say you've all gone for a walk along the Embankment or something.'

'Thanks, Sakari.' Jacob smiled, managing to look unflinchingly into her black eyes for the first time. That strange flutter seemed to swell.

'So, how are we going to do this?' Peter asked.

'Amira's private office is forty floors up,' Lulu said.

'And what?' Peter scoffed. 'We're going to stroll in there and demand she tell us the purpose behind Transcendent?'

'Not exactly.' Kira reached into her back pocket and pulled out her RanaPhone with a flourish. 'You guys clearly haven't needed to eavesdrop on anyone before. That's why you haven't developed a spyware app to listen in on conversations.'

Kira waved the RanaPhone at Sakari, Lulu and Peter, who stared at her in astonishment.

'Oh, yeah,' Jacob heard Kira mutter to herself, quietly enough that the others would not hear. 'That's right. We're just as good as you. Yeah, baby.'

Dressed in round glasses and a white laboratory coat, Professor Jermaine Kowalski's hair was as thin and wispy as he was. Ramone the receptionist looked up from behind his marble desk as Kowalski approached.

'Ms Rana's expecting you. Go straight up, Professor,' said Ramone.

The Shard was a working office building during the day and people were walking in and out in a steady stream. Kowalski made his way to the lifts, sidestepping men and women in business attire with mumbled apologies. He did not notice the two teenagers, a boy with straw-like hair and a girl with gold-framed glasses, lingering by a potted plant and out of sight of the reception desk. The boy was holding a RanaPhone to his ear.

'Man in the white coat,' Peter whispered into the RanaPhone as Kowalski passed.

Kowalski managed to fight his way into a lift as the doors were closing. There was a smothering, sweaty smell inside. The metal box, with its marble finish, was packed with more people in business dress, all of them looking anywhere other than at anyone else. Kowalski was crammed into a corner, where there was a glass panel with more than seventy glowing, circular buttons.

'Excuse me!' said a cheerful voice beside him.

Kowalski was not able to turn his body as elbows, briefcases and handbags pinned him into his corner of the lift. He turned his head awkwardly to see the startling blue eyes of a mixed-race girl who could not have been older than fourteen. The girl beamed up at him.

'Would you mind pressing the button for the thirtieth floor?' the girl asked brightly. 'I can't reach from here and my brother can't reach either, even though he's got these ridiculously long arms and—'

'That's not true!' said a muffled voice from the other side of the crowded lift.

'OK, OK, no problem,' wheezed Kowalski, hauling his hand up to reach for the panel.

'Thank you!' said the muffled voice.

'No . . .' Kowalski began. As he stretched out to press the glass button with his left hand, the sleeve of his coat moved a few inches, revealing the simple, brown leather strap of an Oracle Mark I on his right wrist. Kira whipped out her own RanaPhone and brushed it lightly against the circular screen of Kowalski's Oracle. There was the quietest of beeps and the RanaPhone was shoved back into Kira's pocket.

'. . . problem,' finished Kowalski.

A few minutes later, the lift reached the seventieth floor and only Kowalski was left inside. He pulled a damp handkerchief from inside his white coat and wiped his face roughly.

There was a *ding*. The lift door opened.

Amira Rana's fists and insides clenched at the sound. Dressed in a green sari, she turned slowly from the window of her office. There were two people standing by her desk. One of them was her personal assistant. Kelly was always letting herself in. One day, Amira would have to do something about that.

'I'm sure you didn't forget your meeting with Professor Kowalski, Ms Rana,' Kelly chimed.

'Of course I hadn't forgotten,' said Amira in a honeyed tone. 'How could I forget? Take a seat, Professor.'

Amira had, of course, completely forgotten. She gave no intimation of this and strode past Kelly, sitting down on the other side of the desk. Kowalski smiled and wiped his balding head with his damp handkerchief. He pulled out a seat. Amira winced at the scraping sound.

'There was something else, Ms Rana,' said Kelly. 'Another message from your solicitor.'

'Very good. Thank you, Kelly,' said Amira.

Kelly handed her a tablet computer, paper-thin and with RANATAB emblazoned on the back, before turning and marching out of the room. Amira imagined blasting her in the back with a double-barrelled shotgun every time her high heels struck the glass floor.

'Thank you for seeing me at such short notice, ma'am,' said Kowalski.

Amira leaned back in her chair. She raised her hands.

'Think nothing of it. I'm happy to have such a familial relationship with every branch of RanaTech, especially one as exciting as our Spaceflight division. To be honest with you, I'm all about the domestic approach.'

She flashed an artificial smile, the same one magnified a hundred times on the other side of the river. Kowalski glanced at the RanaTab. Kelly had left it unlocked. DIVORCE SETTLEMENTS shone at the top of a digital document in bright red capitals. Amira saw him looking. She thought about how messy it would be if she shot him in the head there and then. All she needed was that shotgun. And a mop.

'Well, yes,' said Kowalski. 'The advancements made at our little facility in Cornwall have been nothing short of stratospheric. It's quite extraordinary, the breakthroughs we've been making. But, I'm rambling, ma'am. I'm actually here to give you some bad news.'

'I'd appreciate it if you wouldn't.'

'Give you bad news?'

'No. Ramble.'

'Ah. Of course. Well, the way I see it, you are one of the few on the planet in a position to actually do something about this.'

'Do something about what?'

Kowalski frowned. It took him a moment to find the right words.

'One of our satellites has made quite a . . . distressing reading,' he said cautiously.

Amira leaned forward.

'What kind of reading?' she asked softly.

'It'll be easier if I show you.' Kowalski detached the circular screen of his Oracle from the brown, leather strap on his wrist. He placed the device onto the middle of the desk. The Oracle started to glow and a hologram burst into being. Its white light illuminated Amira's face, expressing something between polite curiosity and cold calculation.

Hovering between them was a perfect representation of the solar system. The moons revolved around the planets and the planets revolved around the Sun, which blazed with a white, eerie light. Stars shimmered. The asteroid belt was a ring of sprinkled pepper between Mars and Jupiter. The Earth was a blue and green marble.

'Let me zoom in,' said Kowalski. He tapped the Oracle.

'How close is that?' Amira breathed when she saw it.

'Too close for comfort,' he replied. 'It's coming, and a lot quicker than we first thought.'

'Who else knows about this?' she asked.

'Only the higher-ups at RanaTech Spaceflight. I won't lie to you, ma'am, everyone's freaking the hell out. That's why I'm here. I know Transcendent is nearly ready but it needs to be accelerated. We need it. Now more than ever.'

Jacob, Sakari, Lulu and Peter were crowded around Kira as she held her RanaPhone aloft, allowing them to listen to the entirety of Amira and Kowalski's conversation. A robotic, emotionless voice suddenly rang out of hidden loudspeakers all around the Lounge and everyone jumped up. Lulu let out a small scream.

'All Transcendent candidates are to make their way to the lifts at once. The trials will now take place in the lower levels.'

'Do you think they know we were listening?' Sakari asked urgently.

'No way,' said Kira, tapping her RanaPhone hurriedly with both thumbs. 'The program's untraceable. I'm deleting it from Kowalski's Oracle now. He'll never know we were there.'

'So, something is coming,' murmured Peter, 'and RanaTech needs Transcendent to stop it. What do you think it could be?'

Jacob thought he knew the answer to that question. He still could not fully bring himself to believe that Double M's warning about the Others could possibly be true, but what else could Amira and Kowalski have been speaking about?

'All Transcendent candidates are to make their way to the lifts at once,' the invisible speakers barked again. 'The trials will now take place in the lower levels.'

'That doesn't sound ominous at all, does it?' Kira remarked.

CHAPTER
SIXTEEN

Jacob's face smacked against a smooth, flat surface. He lay on his front, eyes squeezed shut and arms and legs spread as if he had been splatted like a fly on a windscreen. He groaned. Even though everything was still, Jacob's stomach was clenched and his head was spinning. He had once felt something similar after riding a rollercoaster in Uganda. It was as if his brain had thought his body was still flying through the air and not standing on solid ground. This felt a lot worse than that.

'Hello, I am the system interface,' said a voice that emanated all around him. 'Apologies for the delay. We needed to synchronise your sensory nervous system with our application server. You are now ready to begin your trials for Transcendent. Please be aware that you may experience an initial period of amnesia. This will soon pass. Shall we begin, Jacob Flynn?'

Jacob groaned again. He recognised the voice. It was the one he had heard from the loudspeakers in the Lounge, artificial and without emotion. It had ordered them to take the lift down to the lower levels. But what had happened after that?

'I am sorry,' said the interface, not sounding sorry at all. 'I do not recognise that response. Please try again.'

Jacob rolled onto his back and opened his eyes.

At first, he thought someone was shining a torch into his face because all he could see was blinding white. Jacob lashed out to grab the torch but grasped at nothing but air. He decided to wait for his eyes to adjust, but they did not. He sat up and looked around. All he could see was white. Jacob scrambled to his feet and looked down. Beneath him was white, too, and not the dirty white of a T-shirt. It was a white so pristine, it made Jacob's eyes hurt. He jumped up and down. Not a sound. He did not even cast a shadow. Jacob was definitely standing on something but from what it looked like, he was floating in an utterly blank nothingness.

'Hello?' Jacob shouted, hurling the word into the whiteness. 'Where am I?'

'I am sorry. I do not recognise that response,' answered the interface in the same monotonous tone.

'Where am I? Where's Kira?'

'I am sorry. I do not recognise that response. I will repeat the question. Shall we begin, Jacob Flynn?'

Jacob paused. While it had begun as robotic and unemotional, something that could have been impatience was beginning to creep into the voice of the system interface.

'OK, then,' said Jacob.

'There will be three trials,' said the interface. 'The first trial will be a test of intelligence. The second trial will be a test of resolve. The third trial will be a test of comradeship. The first trial, a test of intelligence, begins now. There will be ten questions. Good luck, Jacob Flynn.'

Jacob said, 'Tha,' but before he could say, 'nks,' there was the glimmer of something in front of him. Gold letters materialised. They floated, shimmering in the air, as if someone had written them with a sparkler. Together, they formed something Jacob recognised:

$x^3+y^3+z^3=k.$

It was an equation, the Diophantine equation to be exact. It was one of the most difficult mathematical problems ever devised. Jacob swiped his hand at the apparition, feeling nothing. The golden letters merely flickered as his hand passed through them.

'What am I supposed to do?' he asked.

'Simply use the index finger of your right hand to show your working,' said the interface.

Jacob held up his finger to the empty space just below the equation. To his surprise, a line of gold trailed after his fingertip like paint from a brush. Jacob drew a zig-zagging pattern in the air. When he was done, he closed his fist and the line was cut from his finger. The crude drawing hung in front of him. Jacob laughed in delight.

'There will be ten questions,' said the interface. 'Good luck, Jacob Flynn.'

Jacob screwed his face and examined the sequence of letters. $x^3+y^3+z^3=k$. The aim of the Diophantine equation was to find the sum of three cubes, or the value of x, y and z for every value of k, from one to a hundred. It was thought to be nearly impossible for a human brain and it had once taken a supercomputer to complete it. All Jacob had was a finger.

'Good luck, Jacob Flynn,' the interface repeated. Was there a hint of mockery in its voice?

Jacob smiled and got to work.

It took him over an hour to conquer the Diophantine equation or, at least, he thought it did. Without Jacob's watch on his wrist, there was no way of telling the time in this netherworld in which he had found himself. After that, the questions came thick and fast. The Poincaré conjecture. Fermat's Last Theorem. The classification of finite simple groups. Each was more complex than the last. By the time ten questions were done, the space around him was more gold than white due to his madly scribbled calculations. Jacob sat down on what looked like nothing but at least felt solid. He was exhausted and his finger ached. His brain was pounding. It had never been put through its paces quite like that before and he was actually sweating from the exertion.

The interface did not give him a moment to rest.

'Well done, Jacob Flynn,' it said, a little sulkily perhaps. 'Your first trial, a test of intelligence, is now complete. Your second trial, a test of resolve, will begin momentarily. You will be taken to your second trial in three . . . two . . . one . . .'

'No! Wait!' Jacob mumbled wearily. 'Just give me a minute!'

It was too late. A swirling, multicoloured vortex was opening beneath him and Jacob felt an immense force tugging at his body as if he were being sucked down a gigantic plughole. Lights and colours as bright and vivid as the neon streets of London crackled like lightning around him. Down he tumbled, leaving the white nothingness behind.

Jacob was thrown into a chair and was alarmed to immediately smell something burning. He opened his eyes and realised he was held tight by something bound across his chest. The seat of his chair was shaking violently and so hot that it almost seared Jacob's back.

Sparks cascaded around him. There was the rumbling of engines and the wail of an alarm.

'The second trial, a test of resolve, begins now,' came the voice of the system interface over the cacophony. 'Good luck, Jacob Flynn.'

Jacob was sitting in what appeared to be a cramped, two-man cockpit. Lights flashed on and off and, through the horrible strobe effect, Jacob could see an empty seat next to him. In front of the seats was a control console, from which a torrent of orange sparks and black smoke gushed. All that could be seen from the window that stretched around the front and sides was raging storm clouds. Lightning forked across the sky. Rain lashed against the glass like bullets.

'Interface!' Jacob shrieked. 'What am I supposed to do?'

'A scenario has been devised based on readings from the amygdala in your brain. Your current predicament has been calculated as the one to cause you the most possible distress.'

'You're making me live out my worst fear?' Jacob moaned.

'Yes,' said the interface in a rather petulant tone. 'The second trial, a test of resolve, is based on your handling of this scenario. Good luck, Jacob Flynn.'

Even though the system interface was clearly an artificial intelligence and to resent it would be like begrudging a toaster, Jacob was determined that it would not see him panic. He scrabbled at his chest, found a red, circular button and slammed his fist against it. The straps flew off him. Jacob leaped to his feet and immediately banged his head on the low ceiling and fell against the console. He gasped in pain as the hot metal scorched his fingers and collapsed back into the chair. The cockpit lurched to the left and he almost flew over the armrest.

Jacob thought it fairly obvious that he was in some kind of virtual simulation, although that did not explain the burns on his hands. Could he be killed during the simulation too? Jacob did not want to find out. He tried to focus on the shaking, sparking console. It looked as if it belonged to some kind of suborbital spaceplane. He would have been overjoyed at the prospect of sitting in the cockpit of a suborbital spaceplane, if it was not also a crashing one.

Taking a deep breath, Jacob stared down at the console's flashing lights and sliding levers. Should he try to stabilise the orbit? No. It was too late for that. The clouds meant the spaceplane was already hurtling down through the lower atmosphere. He had to keep it level.

'Level with what? The clouds?' Jacob cried to himself. He clasped his hands to his temples. 'Oh, I can't do this on my own!'

There was a hissing behind him and the door at the rear of the cockpit slid open. In tumbled Kira, holding her arm over her mouth, coughing dramatically and followed by a cloud of smoke. She elbowed a switch on the wall and the door slammed shut. She was wearing a military flight suit. Jacob realised for the first time that so was he. It was as if they were dressed to fight a war. What kind of wars were fought in space?

'Computer! Status report!' Kira bellowed. She leaped into the chair next to Jacob's.

ENGINE ONE HAS FAILED.

The sentence sprang onto a cracked, black screen on the console, one green letter at a time.

Jacob stared in dismay, first at the screen and then at his sister. Was she part of the simulation too?

'Erm, what are you doing here?' Jacob had to ask loudly.

'I'm trying to get this bird facing upwards,' grunted Kira. 'Are you going to help or not?'

Jacob considered. If Kira was part of the simulation then she was nothing more than an impressive computer graphic, like the seats and the spaceplane and the sky through which they were tumbling, all of which had been designed to test him. On that front, Jacob had to admit, he was not doing a very good job so far.

'Of course I'm going to help,' Jacob said, trying to sound more assured than he felt. He thought about all the video games he had played in his life. Surely, this simulation was simply a more sophisticated version of those, although one that had proven it could hurt and, perhaps, even kill him. 'Computer!' Jacob shouted. 'Can you set us a flight path?'

> *AUTOMATIC PILOTING HAS FAILED.*

'Nothing's working!' Jacob groaned.
'Computer,' said Kira. 'What is working?'

> *NOTHING IS WORKING.*

'OK. What's the least "not working"?'

> *ENGINE TWO AND MANUAL PILOTING ARE FAILING. ALL OTHER SYSTEMS HAVE FAILED.*

'We can't lose Engine Two!' Kira cried.
She threw herself out of her seat and staggered to the door, slamming her fist against the switch. The door slid aside with another hiss but stopped jerkily after opening only a few inches. Jacob and Kira had just enough time to squeeze through before it slammed shut again.

The corridor on the other side stretched away until the smoke became too thick to see any further. Pipes ran along the walls and ceiling and underneath the grated floor. Red warning lights flickered overhead.

'Where are you going?' Jacob yelled.

'We need to patch that engine!'

'The computer said that manual piloting is *failing*, not failed! Kira, we can land this thing!'

'If that engine explodes, there'll be nothing left to land!'

The corridor shook as if from an earthquake and Jacob fell painfully onto the grating. When he looked, there was a red grid cut into his palm.

'Kira,' Jacob panted as she heaved him to his feet. 'This thing is in free fall. If we don't at least try and land it, we are probably going to die.'

'If that engine explodes, we are *definitely* going to die.'

Jacob was about to shout something back when there was the muffled boom of an explosion outside the plane, followed by the scream of tearing metal. The wall on the right side of the corridor tore itself away as easily as a foil wrapper from a chocolate bar, flooding in light and unveiling rolling storm clouds and flashing lightning. Wind and rain howled through the gutted plane. Jacob had been standing by the wall so was able to sling his arm around a pipe and cling to it. The g-force lifted his feet in the air and dragged at his body, the flight suit rippling as if it was going to tear from him. Kira had been standing in the middle of the corridor and was not so fortunate. She looked at Jacob. Her eyes glinted with as much spark as the lightning bolts in the sky behind her.

'Told you,' she said.

Then Kira was plucked into the air and whisked out of the plane and out of sight.

Jacob's mouth opened to scream but there was no sound, or at least none that could be heard. His body was numb and he would have lost his grip if not for what he saw next through the gaping tear in the hull. There was something moving in the clouds. It was a dark, fleeting shape, like a shark under the surface of the water. Jacob did not need the system interface to tell him what he was looking at. The plane to which he was clinging desperately was obviously not crashing of its own accord. It had been shot down by something else.

The noise reached a thunderous crescendo. Jacob squeezed his eyes shut, the sheer force of gravity causing tears to run sideways across his face. The impact came with an ear-shattering boom like the eruption of a volcano. Jacob finally lost his grip and felt himself falling. His last thought was not, as he would have thought, of his impending, inevitable doom, crushed under tonnes and tonnes of crumpling metal. It was . . .

'Kira,' he managed to gasp before consciousness slipped from him and everything turned dark.

CHAPTER
SEVENTEEN

Jacob opened his eyes but the darkness remained. He was lying on his back on a metal surface. It was hot to the touch. The air was close and sour with an oily tang. Apart from the heavy patter of rain outside and the crack of distant thunder, everything was silent and still.

Jacob was wondering what could have woken him when it happened again. A drop of something splashed against his cheek, and again a few seconds later. Whatever it was felt warm on his skin, mingling with the sweat that plastered the sodden flight suit to his body.

It must be water, Jacob thought.

Slowly feeling around with his hands, he realised that he was lying on the cockpit door. Jacob was staring back up the corridor which was now an upright shaft, still drenched in the red of the warning lights. Through the crooked teeth of the tear in the wall, he could see the gleam of falling raindrops in the darkness. The spaceplane must have crash-landed and was lying vertically against the side of a crater somewhere.

There was only the occasional sound of a warm drop of water falling down the full length of the upright corridor and landing with a smack on Jacob's cheek.

He had no idea how he could have survived a plane crash from outer space. Either, Jacob thought, the spaceplane had some considerable inertial dampeners installed, or whatever was controlling this nightmare, simulation or otherwise, had allowed him to survive.

'Hello?' Jacob called out. His voice was small in the shadowy ruin. 'System interface? Are you there?'

There was silence from the interface but, as if in response to the sound of his voice, something stirred in the gloom. Jacob's eyes darted to the very top of the shaft. He peered at a point thirty feet above where the red glow of the warning lights faded into nothing but shadow. Jacob squinted, waiting for his eyes to grow accustomed to the intense blackness and coiling smoke, and saw something that caused the cold hand of fear to tighten slowly around his warm and beating heart.

He was not alone.

Thirty feet above Jacob was a hunched figure. Its arms, legs and head were pulled close to its body. The figure was suspended there by what looked like the black threads of a spider's web. Every piece of its segmented body was prickling with long, coarse hairs. The mere sight of the figure caused goosebumps to erupt across Jacob's shoulders and ripple down the middle of his back. It had the body of a tarantula in human form and much like a tarantula, the very idea of the figure bursting into sudden movement and scuttling towards him made Jacob want to scream. But it did not move. It dangled above him, poised, utterly still, utterly silent and utterly horrifying.

It was an Other.

It looked exactly like Double M's photograph, except the creature above him was no image. Did it know Jacob was there? Was it watching him? Eyes as wide as golf balls and fixed on the Other, he crept his left hand towards the door control. His heart was beating like an embuutu drum in his chest. He could feel it in his ears. Jacob spread his trembling fingers but could only feel the smooth surface of the wall. It was like stumbling around finding a light switch in the dark. His eyes welled with tears of terror and frustration.

Finally, Jacob's fingertips settled on the hand-sized panel. All he had to do was press down and the door underneath him would slide open. If he could get himself inside the cockpit, that would at least place a sheet of solid metal between him and it. Jacob permitted himself a small sigh of relief. It was like slightly releasing a pressure valve.

And then another drop of something warm landed on his cheek.

There was no water leaking from the crashed plane. There was something dripping from the Other, saliva or some other foul excrement. And it had touched Jacob's skin.

Jacob lost control. He screamed and scrabbled noisily for the switch and slapped it with his palm. There was a hiss beneath him and Jacob felt the door move aside, moving him aside too, before stopping after opening only a few inches. He was about to squeeze through the gap when the door slammed shut again with the slicing sound of a guillotine blade. The same thing had happened when he and Kira had first left the cockpit. The door was jammed and, if he had been caught between it and the metal door frame when it closed, he would have been cut in half.

Tears were streaming down Jacob's cheeks. He hammered the switch again and rolled through as soon as the door opened. Jacob fell a few feet and pain flared in his lower back as he landed on the hot control console. He looked up and saw a pair of luminous, green eyes in the gloom at the end of the corridor. Then the door sliced shut and they were gone.

Jacob lay uncomfortably against the console, aching

hands and feet resting against the twisted walls of the cockpit. He could feel the wet tracks his tears were leaving down his grimy face. He strained with his ears but all he could hear were his own rapid, rasping breaths. No noise came from the other side of the door. Jacob slowly turned his head to examine the smoking cockpit around him. If any equipment could have been used to ease his escape, it made no difference now. The place was a wreck. Jacob shifted his arm and his elbow knocked a broken, glass dial. It made the slightest scraping sound.

The plane suddenly shook and Jacob yelled in shock. There was the savage thrashing of something heavy on metal. It was the sound of something large rushing down the corridor towards the cockpit. And then everything was silent and once again still.

Jacob glared at the cockpit door as if he were able to see through it. He imagined the Other hovering there, poised inches from the metal, alien slobber drooling from whatever foul crevice it had in place of a mouth. There was silence for such a long time, it was unbearable. Jacob almost screamed and sobbed just to break it.

Then there was a violent pound against the door and a dent appeared in the metal. Jacob really did scream. There was another bang and a larger dent appeared next to it. It was going to tear its way into the cockpit. And then it was going to tear its way into him.

It was all a test. Jacob knew that and he was not going to survive by fighting his way out of it. He needed to think. Jacob looked around the ruined cockpit frantically before his eyes finally settled on the door switch.

Another dent appeared and Jacob could not wait a second longer. He kicked the switch once. Nothing happened. With crazed, panting breaths, he summoned all his strength and kicked the switch so hard that pain rattled up his leg. The door slid open with a hiss and stopped. A thin beam of red light bled in from the corridor. Jacob's heart felt as if it was pummelling against his ribcage as hard as the Other had against the door. Now with the door opened, however, it had stopped and was, once again, hideously silent.

A hand slithered through the crack. It was grey and glistening. Apart from the wiry bristles on its spider-like arm, the hand was upsettingly human. There was a black fingernail on each of the six fingers, which gripped at the door for a few agonising seconds as if they were going to wrench it open.

The door flung itself shut again and sliced through the Other's hand like a cleaver through meat. There was a splatter of bright, green gore. Flecks of the stuff flicked onto the walls of the cockpit and six grey fingers toppled onto Jacob's chest. He cast them aside in disgust. The Other's shriek of pain emanated through the door and Jacob clenched his teeth. Its inhuman cry was the most horrifying sound he had ever heard. It was the screech of fingernails being dragged down a blackboard.

There was an echoey clanging and the cries grew quieter. Jacob remained sprawled on the console, panting and listening. He waited for what could have been hours but the noise did not return. There was only the sporadic drumming of raindrops on the fuselage. The Other had retreated.

Eventually, Jacob attempted to speak but all he managed was a weak croak.

'System interface? Are you here? I've completed the second trial. You can take me out of here now!'

Again, there was no reply.

Jacob rolled painfully onto his side and tried to look out of the window. It had been smashed to such an extent that the thick glass was white and opaque. He had to get out of the cockpit. Jacob struck the glass with his palm and felt it budge. Grinning with exertion, he punched it a few more times and the front section fell away completely. Rain billowed into the cockpit, lashing Jacob's face. He scrambled through the gap, gasping in pain as a jagged shard of glass snagged his side. Blinking through the watery onslaught, he could just see the boiling night sky. By the time he was all the way out, he was soaking wet. Jacob perched himself on the collapsed nose of the spaceplane.

As he did so, a streak of lightning tore the darkness aside like a curtain, revealing a brief, uninterrupted view of where he was standing.

Mount Elgon.

The spaceplane had crash-landed on the mountainside and was lying vertically against its rugged slope. The nose was entrenched in a deep, muddy gash and had been twisted upwards so Jacob was able to stand on it and look down, past the tumbling moorlands to the city below.

The ruins of Mbale were laid out like a burning rug. The buildings were charred skeletons and the clock tower, once a bright pink monument, was nothing but a pile of rubble. Flames as high as the buildings themselves leaped upwards, ghoulish, orange light flickering across the blackened fields. Jacob could hear their crackle and feel their fierce heat searing his skin even at a distance. Worst of all, faint but very much there alongside the sound of a city on fire, was the sound of screaming. The strength slipped from his legs and he fell to his knees with a thump onto the nose of the fallen spaceplane.

'No,' Jacob said simply. He was not able to hear his own voice because, as he spoke, there was a roar overhead. He looked up and saw a dark shape gliding through the rain. It was huge, almost as wide as the mountain itself. The main structure was a shapeless, hairy mass, poked through by jagged spikes instead of wings and lashed together by black strings of web. It was a gigantic spider nest. Bursts of green fire blasted from its rear as the flying nest swept over Jacob's head in a rumble of thunder and descended upon Mbale. Jacob knew he was looking at what had shot down the spaceplane. It was the Others' vessel, their spaceship which had carried them from whichever dark and dripping corner of the universe they had originated from. Jacob had survived one Other by the skin of his teeth but here was an entire nest full of them. If it came down to a straight fight, the human race would not stand a chance.

As if in confirmation, a blinding, green beam of light streaked over Jacob's head from the base of the nest, throwing long shadows across the landscape. A distant column of flame leaped into the air as the beam struck somewhere within the city. In the brief moments the mountain was illuminated by laser, Jacob glimpsed movement on the slopes around him. He heard a faint but painfully familiar screech and, looking frantically around, realised there were countless pairs of luminous, green eyes darting through the darkness. Jacob could see hordes of hairy figures scrambling over themselves and clawing at the grass. Thousands of Others were stampeding down the slopes towards Mbale, rushing past on either side of the spaceplane. Jacob stood on the mountainside, watching the Others sweep down the moorlands and into Mbale like a dark flood, their hovering nest razing everything that lay before them, and came to one last, awful realisation.

The interface must be showing him a vision of the future. Jacob knew it. Double M had been telling the truth. The Others were coming and they had to be stopped.

Otherwise the world was going to burn and everybody with it.

CHAPTER
EIGHTEEN

'This is the system interface. You are now being ejected from this Oracle Mark II holographic simulation. Have a nice day.'

'Jacob! Can you hear me? Snap out of it, Orangutan!'

For a few seconds, all Jacob could see was a spinning rainbow of colour before it melted away and he was looking into the worried face of his sister. Kira's piercing blue eyes were close to his and Jacob could feel her fingers pulling at some kind of equipment that was clamped to his head. When he was free, Jacob dropped to his knees onto a smooth, metal floor. It was hard and cold on the palms of his hands. The dizziness was overwhelming. Jacob stayed as he was, heaving and coughing. His eyes were watering and he could feel his stomach wrenching itself in knots. For a moment, he was worried he was going to vomit but managed to get himself under control. Jacob looked up at the startling sight of two Kiras standing in front of him.

'Are you feeling OK?' both Kiras asked at the same time.

No. There was only one Kira. Jacob's vision was blurry and his eyes hurt. Kira looked like she was wearing the same clothes as that morning in the Shard. Was it still that same morning? It felt like days or even weeks ago.

'Kira,' Jacob panted. 'You're really there?'

'S'up?' Kira said.

Kira really was really there. There was a look of amused concern on her face. Her blue eyes were shining. All of her freckles were exactly where they were supposed to be. Jacob thought she looked magnificent. The sight of her stirred a wave of emotion that washed over him and rushed him onto his feet. Jacob staggered to Kira and hugged her tighter than he ever had in his life.

'Can't breathe!' she gasped as Jacob squeezed her tighter still.

'I thought I'd lost you,' he breathed.

Kira finally tore herself free and put her hands on his shoulders.

'You know Transcendent is only for geniuses, right?' Kira grinned. 'I was in the next room, Einstein.'

'What happened to us?' Jacob asked faintly.

Kira's grin widened.

'Turn around,' she said.

Jacob did and, as he turned, was finally able to absorb his new surroundings. Jacob and Kira were standing on a raised gangway, suspended in the middle of a room the shape of a perfect sphere. It was as if they were inside a gigantic hamster ball. Grey walls curved all the way around them and were dotted with small, metal discs, spaced apart at equal distances from each other. The spherical shape of the room meant there was a disc pointing at Jacob and Kira from every angle. Jacob thought the discs looked familiar. He walked unsteadily to the edge of the gangway to get a closer look at one of them. There was nothing to hold on to so he was careful not to fall and topple the few feet onto the curved floor below.

What was it the system interface had said? *You are now being ejected from this Oracle Mark II holographic simulation.* Of course! Jacob had seen both Gustavo Yang and Professor Kowalski wearing identical discs on their wrists. Yang had called the device an Oracle Mark I and he had used it to project a holographic image of Amira Rana back at the RanaTech building in Mbale. All the Mark I had been able to offer was a relatively small image from a single projector. Jacob, however, was standing in a room filled with over a hundred projectors pointing at him from every possible angle. If the Mark II was the upgraded version of the Mark I, the leap between the two was extraordinary.

'Was I just inside a hologram?' Jacob asked.

Kira nodded excitedly.

'Look at this!'

The gangway ended in the middle of the room where, hanging from the ceiling, there was a robotic arm like the ones used to build cars in factories. The arm was the same colour as the room itself, a dull grey, and hung from the ceiling to Jacob's chest height. There were multiple joints along the arm which, Jacob assumed, meant it was completely manoeuvrable. At the end of the arm was a harness which, Jacob realised, he had just been attached to.

'You were strapped in here,' Kira explained, bounding around the bottom of the arm. 'And this was strapped to your head.' She showed Jacob a circular piece of wire that was joined to the harness by a bundle of cables. 'Not only does this device connect to the cerebral cortex in your brain, it also pairs with your sensory nervous system.'

'But, that would mean . . .' Jacob looked at his hand. When he had been running, or thought he had been running, down the corridor of a crashing spaceplane, he had fallen and cut his hand. Jacob remembered the pain and the red scratch on his palm. When he looked at his hand now, though, it was unscathed. In fact there was no mark anywhere on his body. He had not actually fallen from space or been hunted by a bloodthirsty alien. He had been right here in this room, playing what was essentially a technologically advanced video game.

'Wow,' Jacob murmured. 'That's both amazing and terrifying.'

'Yep,' Kira agreed. 'The Oracle Mark II must be the most sophisticated virtual simulation ever invented. Not only does it create a scenario from your own imagination, your worst fear or whatever, and show it to you as a perfectly realistic hologram, it—'

'It makes you feel it,' said Jacob, looking wearily at his hand.

'I think Sakari's nearly finished her simulation,' said Kira eagerly. 'Let's take a look.'

At the point where the gangway met the edge of the room was a door with a large, circular window. Jacob and Kira jogged to it, the thumps of their trainers on the smooth metal echoing around the room. Kira pushed the door open onto an empty, concrete corridor, painted a stark white and lined with identical doors on either side.

'Where are the others?' Jacob asked, looking up and down the corridor.

'There's a simulation happening behind each of these doors,' said Kira. 'I was in the room next to you and completed my simulation first, obviously. That's why I was able to come and get you.'

'What did you see during yours?' Jacob asked.

Kira ignored the question and hauled him over to another one of the doors.

'Check it out.'

Jacob gawked through the glass. On the other side of the round window was not another room, but an icy tundra.

The landscape and sky above it were flat and white. Sakari Ekho was standing a few metres away but looked tiny and insignificant in the vastness of snow, stretching for hundreds of miles in every direction. Sakari was wearing a parka made from tattered caribou fur, along with gloves and long boots. She was carrying nothing but a driftwood harpoon with a bone tip. Something moved in the snow some distance away and Sakari wheeled round to face it, raising her harpoon. At first, Jacob thought it was a gigantic snowball rolling towards her at frightening speed. But it was not a snowball. It was a polar bear.

'NANOOK!' Sakari screamed.

The bear was galloping at Sakari, white fur tinged with yellow and black eyes and snout wide with fury. Its teeth were bared. Paws pounded the snow as the animal, weighing more than one and a half thousand pounds and the size of a car, hurtled closer with every second. Sakari stood her ground and prepared to lunge herself, and her harpoon, at the snarling predator. She was snarling too.

'We need to get her out of there!' Jacob cried.

'She's in no real danger,' said Kira. 'If she's seriously hurt or even dies, the simulation will just end. Look.'

Sure enough, just as the bear was about to collide with Sakari, Jacob saw the snowy scene fade away in a shimmer of colour. Soon, Sakari was in exactly the same place, except she was not wearing caribou fur or holding a harpoon. She was wearing the T-shirt and jeans she had been wearing earlier, and was strapped by a harness to a moving robotic arm hanging from the ceiling of an identical spherical room. The projectors on the walls glowed with a bright light which eventually faded. The moving arm, which had allowed Sakari her full range of movement while strapped into the harness, lowered her back onto the platform and was still.

'Because the arm is wired to her cerebral cortex, it moves with her thoughts. She thinks she's been moving freely when it's actually the arm doing all the work, while she's safe and sound in her harness. Cool, huh?' Kira remarked.

Sakari's hair hung dishevelled in front of her face, which was flushed and dripping with sweat. She jerked suddenly, pulling the wire band from her head and began to struggle in the harness. Jacob had his hand on the door handle when he heard harsh footsteps.

'Welcome to the Oracle Mark II, developed right here at RanaTech. May I ask what you are doing out of your harnesses?' said a cold voice.

A woman approached. She was small, thin and wearing a white suit that matched her white hair, which sat in a tight, white bob on top of an even tighter, whiter face. There were pointed, white high heels on her feet. Jacob thought the shoes must have been uncomfortable because of the awkward manner in which she was hobbling towards them. The woman's face appeared to be drawn back in a permanent grimace. Her mouth was so thin, it could have been a short line drawn with a pencil. Jacob was not sure whether that was because of the shoes or the sight of the two teenagers in front of her.

'I am Doctor Arianna Shaw,' said the woman, squinting down her thin nose at the RanaTab in her hand. Her scratchy voice sounded like a boot scraping broken glass into the ground. 'I was planning to safely disengage you from your harnesses myself. Your names are?'

'Kira and Jacob Flynn,' said Kira.

'What are you doing out of your harnesses?' Shaw repeated, not looking up from the RanaTab.

'I completed my simulation first,' said Kira, 'and went to help Jacob.'

Shaw looked up and peered at Kira. Meanwhile, her claw-like fingers scuttered over the screen like a crab.

'You woke up inside your simulation chamber, disorientated, likely exhausted and with no memory of how you got there,' Shaw said, eyes narrowing, 'and your first thought was to help this young man?'

'Well,' Kira shrugged, 'he is my brother.'

'I see,' said Shaw.

'What are we even doing here?' Jacob stammered, looking between Kira and Shaw. 'How did we get into those things? Did you drug us?'

'As you have already been told by the interface,' said Shaw patiently, 'mild amnesia can be a side effect of your first simulation. You have met me already and I explained all of this to you then. You entered the Oracle of your own free will. No one forced you.'

There were two bangs and Lulu and Peter burst from the doors next to Jacob and Kira. Peter staggered to a wall and leaned against it, muttering something darkly. Lulu tottered over.

'I think I'm going to be sick!' she gasped.

Jacob and Kira jumped back in shock.

Lulu took some deep breaths. 'Actually, I think I'm fine.'

She smiled reassuringly. Jacob and Kira relaxed and stepped back towards her.

She was not fine. No sooner had Jacob taken a step

forward then Lulu was violently sick. Vomit splashed noisily over his trainers and up his trousers.

'I'm so sorry,' Lulu whimpered, wiping her mouth.

'It's fine,' Jacob said. 'Don't worry about it.'

Shaw had observed all this with scrupulous interest. Her fingers were still rapidly tapping the RanaTab screen, as if she were recording some fascinating observation.

'It would appear,' she mused, 'that the remaining candidate is having some difficulty.'

Jacob had been grimly inspecting his ruined trainers but looked up sharply at that. Sakari had still not emerged from her Oracle. He leaped to her door, feet squelching, and pulled it open.

Sakari was still ensnared in her harness but the robotic arm was throwing her wildly around the room. Now that the door to her Oracle was open and Jacob, Kira and Lulu were running down the gangway towards her, they could hear Sakari screaming. There was the high-pitched whirr of a machine working overtime as the arm hurled her up, down, left and right. While the middle of her body was held tightly by the harness, her arms and legs were being thrown around like those of a toy. Her black hair whipped around her head.

'Turn it off!' Jacob bellowed as he jumped up and down, trying to grab Sakari's feet.

'There seems to have been some malfunction,' said

Shaw from the door, not sounding particularly concerned.

'I can see the controls!' Kira cried. There was a small, glass screen on the wall next to the door on the inside of the room. She and Lulu ran to it and started prodding, looking for a way to shut the Oracle down. There was not an obvious one. All they could see were lines of scrolling code.

'I've never seen an interface like it,' muttered Lulu. 'This system is more than cutting edge. It's like something from another planet.'

'Jacob!' Kira shouted over her shoulder. 'Come and help us with this. What are you standing around for?'

As Kira and Lulu had their backs to the rogue, mechanical arm, they did not see Jacob bend down low and wait for Sakari to swing over his head again. When she did, he hurled himself as high as he could, grabbed onto the harness and then he too was being flung around the room like a kite in a hurricane.

'Never mind then, Jacob,' said Kira, oblivious to the chaotic scene behind her. 'I'll take care of everything, like always.'

Sakari was screaming into Jacob's right ear. Her hair lashed at his face. Everything else was a blur. With one hand, he scrambled for the buckle across Sakari's stomach that held the harness in place. Jacob could feel the fingers of his other hand slipping. If he were to let go, he would be thrown against the curved wall of the Oracle, likely snapping his spine.

'Hold on!' he managed to hiss through gritted teeth.

'System shutdown!' Lulu said delightedly. 'There it is!'

She pressed hard against the screen. All the lights turned off and the whirr of the machine lowered dramatically until it was silent. Just as the mad thrashing of the arm slowed to a complete stop, Jacob pried the buckle loose and he and Sakari tumbled with a crash onto the gangway. Jacob broke Sakari's fall and the metal surface slammed into his shoulder. He grunted as pain, very real this time, jolted through him.

Kira and Lulu finally turned to see Jacob and Sakari sprawled on top of each other.

'Oh, goodness,' said Lulu, covering her eyes.

'If the two of you are going to get on with that nonsense,' said Kira, 'you should get your own holographic simulation chamber.'

Jacob helped Sakari to her feet, severely hoping she would think his face was red from exertion and not because he was blushing. Kira and Lulu hurried over. The three of them huddled around Sakari and made their way along the gangway together and out into the corridor where Shaw and Peter were waiting.

'I'm OK,' Sakari panted, sounding better than she looked. She was bleary-eyed. Tears gleamed on her cheeks. 'Thank you so much, guys. How are all of you? Can you believe how crazy this is?'

Shaw nodded approvingly at Sakari. 'Showing concern for your fellow candidates despite your own distressing situation. Good. Very good.' She looked pointedly at Peter Presland. 'Perhaps, you would care to explain what just happened?'

Peter was leaning against the wall of the corridor, arms crossed.

'What do you mean?' he asked, looking surprised. His watery eyes bulged.

'Your fellow candidate was in peril,' Doctor Shaw raised her eyebrows, 'and you chose not to offer assistance. A poor show of comradeship, wouldn't you say?'

'I prefer to take care of myself before I take care of anyone else.' Peter shrugged but Jacob heard a shake in his usually pompous voice.

'I see,' said Shaw. She turned back to Jacob, Kira, Sakari and Lulu. 'Congratulations to the four of you,' she said matter-of-factly. With that, she turned and shuffled away down the corridor. All five of them watched her go.

'Thanks, I guess?' Kira called after her. She turned to Jacob. 'Why did she just congratulate us?'

Jacob had been staring at Shaw hobbling away when realisation hit him like a train. He smacked his forehead so loudly that everybody jumped.

'Remember what the system interface said? There were meant to be *three* trials – a test of intelligence, a test of resolve and a test of comradeship. I only went through *two* trials in the Oracle, intelligence and resolve!'

'Me too,' said Kira.

'And me,' said Lulu.

'And me,' murmured Sakari, still dazed.

'So, that means . . .' said Kira.

'What just happened was the third trial? The test of comradeship?' Sakari asked.

'Yes,' said Peter solemnly, 'and I failed.'

Jacob, Kira, Sakari and Lulu stared at him, no one knowing quite what to say. Then a second realisation came to Jacob, slower than the first. It crept over him like a shadow at sunset.

'If that was the third trial,' he said slowly, 'did any of it really happen?'

Everyone's eyes widened as they looked at each other. Instinctively, Kira reached out and held on to Jacob's hand. Right on cue and in answer to Jacob's question, an unnaturally loud and definitely smug voice echoed around them.

'This is the system interface. Well done, candidates. Your third trial, a test of comradeship, is now complete. You are now being ejected from this Oracle Mark II holographic simulation. Have a nice day.'

'We're still inside the simulation,' said Jacob.

'We can't be!' Lulu stammered. 'This is real. It must be real. I know it's real!'

'Jacob . . .' Kira whispered. For the first time in his life, Jacob could see the slightest hint of panic in her eyes. He squeezed her hand tighter.

'We'll be all right, Kira,' he said, trying his best to sound brave. 'We'll be back together in no time.'

Already, though, Jacob could see his surroundings beginning to fade, only to be replaced by a swirling vortex of iridescent colour. The colours grew brighter and more lurid until soon, they were all he could see.

'Jacob?' Kira's voice sounded very far away.

'We'll be all right, Kira!' Jacob repeated but even his own voice seemed to be calling from a distance.

Kira's hand dissolved like sand through his fingers and, once again, Jacob was falling into nothingness.

CHAPTER
NINETEEN

This time around, Jacob really did vomit.

He managed to tear himself loose from the harness and drop on his knees onto the gangway before spilling his breakfast onto the curved floor. The dizziness was far worse than the last time. Jacob leaned back on his heels, swaying slightly, and wiped sweat from his brow.

The Oracle Mark II looked exactly the same as it had done in the simulation. Jacob was kneeling on a metal gangway underneath a robotic arm hanging from the ceiling of a perfectly spherical chamber. He glanced around. Sure enough, there were the tiny holographic projectors placed at equidistant intervals across the curved walls. It looked and felt real – but then, it had done the last time.

'Jacob!'

The door at the end of the gangway was thrown

open and Kira clattered into the room. She ran forward as if to hug him.

'Wait!' Jacob shouted and held up his hand. Kira stopped a few feet away.

'What is it?' she asked.

'If this is real,' Jacob panted, still holding his hand up to her, 'if you are real, tell me something only you would know.'

Kira rolled her eyes in exasperation.

'Remember when we were eight and Mama bought me Barbie's Dream House and you asked to borrow it because you said you were interested in vernacular architecture but really—'

'OK, I believe you! You're real! You're real!' Jacob staggered to his feet and hugged his sister.

'That was a really sly move by Amira,' said Jacob as the two of them walked along the gangway together.

'You can say that again,' nodded Kira. 'Dropping us into a hologram without us realising. Twice!'

'At least we made it through the three trials,' said Jacob. He opened the door onto the white corridor. 'I wonder what happens next?'

'What happens next,' said a familiar voice, 'is you will be debriefed by Ms Rana herself tomorrow evening. For now, I suppose you have all earned the afternoon off.'

Doctor Arianna Shaw looked just as unfriendly as

the holographic version of herself, lurching along the corridor towards them as Peter, Lulu and Sakari emerged from their own chambers.

'Will there be any side effects from what we've just been through?' Sakari asked. She was still agitated. Lulu put her arm around her.

'You may experience some peculiar dreams,' remarked Shaw, 'but nothing too distressing. You may now make your way upstairs.'

They started to walk hastily towards the end of the corridor where the lifts were. Everyone was eager to get themselves as far from an Oracle, and from Doctor Arianna Shaw, as possible.

'Peter Presland!' came Shaw's cold voice and they all turned to look back at her. She raised one thin finger and beckoned to him. 'I should like to speak with you for a moment.'

Peter's shoulders sank. He hung his head. Without a word to Jacob or the others, he followed Doctor Shaw. It was absurd to watch the frail, crooked woman leading him away like a naughty schoolboy. But no one felt like laughing. In glum silence, Jacob, Kira, Sakari and Lulu walked to the lift that would take them back up to the Lounge.

CHAPTER
TWENTY

Hyde Park was smothered in smog. On the map, the park had been a wonky, green rectangle but there was no green here. Eunata's walking boots crunched on the wide, gravel path as if she were walking on dry bones. She could not see further than a few metres. Dead trees clawed out of dead grass like gnarled hands, silver, petrified forms leering out of the pale haze. Eunata came to a cast iron bench at the edge of the path and sat down. She had zipped her body warmer all the way up to shield her mouth and nose from the unbearable smell of London. Her arms were wrapped tightly around herself to stave off the cold. Her teeth clacked like billiard balls.

'This is the end, Henry,' Eunata whispered. 'This is the end of the path started in Mbale. This is where it leads.'

At the thought of Mbale, Eunata felt an ache of longing deep in her heart for Uganda. At this time in the early evening, she would be sitting on the porch, rocking on the swing seat. Eunata closed her eyes. She could feel the warmth of the setting sun, smell the burning logs, hear the creaking banana trees and see the lush, rippling grass of the paddy fields. She opened her eyes and looked up. The rain clouds had cleared but there was no sky. There were no stars. There was only writhing, grey smoke.

Eunata pulled out her RanaPhone and began scrolling through it. She did not know why. Perhaps it was the thought of home and the fact that she was further away from it than she ever had been in her life, but Eunata was about to do something she had not done in twenty years, since she had eloped with Henry from Kampala. She found the contact named MAMA and tapped it before holding the RanaPhone to her ear.

Eunata listened to the mundane beeping of the outgoing telephone call. It lasted for a minute before suddenly stopping. The person on the other end had cut the call without answering.

Eunata remained as she was for a few minutes, sitting on the bench with her RanaPhone to her ear. She gazed into the nothingness of the colourless fog. Tears began to swim in her eyes.

'Mama! What's wrong?'

There were scraping footsteps on the gravel. Jacob and Kira emerged from the smog a few feet away.

'Nothing, children,' Eunata sniffed, wiping her eyes and smiling. She shoved her RanaPhone back into her pocket. The twins sat down on either side of her.

'Are you sure?' asked Jacob.

'Of course I am sure!' Eunata said, putting her arms around the pair of them. 'How could anything be wrong when I have everything I need right here? Shall we walk?'

Jacob and Kira sat on another bench while Eunata paid for dinner from a battered burger van on the other side of the path. The twins pulled the cords of their hoods tight to stave off the cold. It was evening and the park was empty but the stink of exhaust fumes was as suffocatingly present as ever. All that could be seen around them were the crooked shapes of the dead trees, lurking in the darkening smoke like terrible scarecrows. Jacob looked at Kira as she stared into the smoke. Her face was pale from the chill and there were pink blotches on her cheeks.

'What did you see inside the Oracle?' he asked.

'What's that now?' Kira answered absently.

'Don't pretend you didn't hear,' said Jacob. 'I asked you before and you ignored me then too. We all had to take the intelligence test so I guess your first trial was exactly the same as mine. We were all placed into the third trial together so I know what you saw for that. But the second trial should have been different for all of us. The interface said it was based on our worst fear. So what did you see?'

Kira mumbled something.

'What was that?'

'I said, "I don't want to talk about it!"' she blustered.

'Fine,' said Jacob.

He stared into the semi-darkness. The face of the Other, dripping and bristling with coarse hairs, took shape at the back of his mind like a reflection in a murky puddle. Jacob was not sure if it was due to the cold but he felt a prickle on the back of his scalp.

'I saw them, Kira,' he said.

'Saw who?'

'The Others. I had visions of what they are and what will happen when they get here. They'll turn this planet into a scorched wasteland. Humanity won't stand a chance.'

'How can we be sure they're real?' There was disbelief in Kira's voice.

'Amira knows about them,' Jacob said. 'She said as much to Kowalski.' He gave a slow nod. 'We'll confront her tomorrow when she briefs us about Transcendent. We'll confront her about the Others.'

There was silence for a while. Then Kira cleared her throat. When she spoke, her voice was no more than a whisper.

'I saw my rocket.'

'What did you say?' Jacob turned to her.

'I saw the model rocket I tested on Mount Elgon. But it wasn't a model. It was the real thing. I was inside a real rocket and I was blasting into space. There was a malfunction, a hairline fracture that was going to cause the rocket to explode. I managed to fix it. I thought that was the test but . . .'

'But, what?'

'But, when I fixed the problem, there was nothing to stop the rocket. It reached the edge of the atmosphere and kept going into space. It kept blasting higher and higher and the planet behind me got smaller and smaller until it was just a dot and then it was nothing. I was all on my own, flying higher than every other person in the world and I didn't know how to make it back to Earth.'

'Your worst fear is being blown up in a rocket,' Jacob said slowly.

Kira sniffed.

'No,' she said. 'My worst fear is what came afterwards. I was . . . I was all on my own.'

'Kira, you've always had Mama and me and you always will,' said Jacob.

'That's just it!' she cried. 'What if I don't? What happens if you and I choose different paths?'

'That's never going to happen, Kira,' said Jacob.

'How do you know?'

'Before we left Uganda, you promised we'd stick together. Whatever Amira reveals to us tomorrow about Transcendent, we'll be together. That's the only reason I know I can do this. I can handle anything Amira Rana, or even an army from outer space, can throw at me. Only because you'll be by my side.'

Kira breathed a long, rattling sigh of relief. She shivered a little in the cold. Jacob moved closer to her on the bench and put his arm around her shoulders.

'OK, Orangutan,' she said.

'You two better not tell me you're hungry again before we get back to the Shard,' said Eunata, footsteps trudging on the gravel path. She handed each of them a vegan cheeseburger.

'Thank you, Mama,' said Jacob.

'Not quite matoke, is it?' said Kira, sniffing the burger.

'What is?' Eunata sighed as she sat down.

When they finished eating, they took the 452 bus to Sloane Square and the tube to London Bridge, changing at Westminster. Back at the Shard and stepping out of the lift into the Lounge, they discovered that one of the candidates for Transcendent had already left.

There was no sign of Peter Presland or any of his things.

CHAPTER
TWENTY-ONE

Jacob woke but he did not open his eyes.

Sleep slipped from him like a thin veil that had been tugged away. He was wide awake and lying on his back with his arms and legs spread slightly apart – exactly how he had been lying on the cockpit door of the crashed spaceplane inside the Oracle. He was completely still. His eyes were closed and his mouth was shut but Jacob felt as if electricity was coursing through him, all the way to the tips of his nerve endings. His ears twitched. Something had woken him. Jacob strained with his remaining senses to work out what it had been.

He did not usually have nightmares. There had been one evening when he, Kira and Eunata had watched a horror film in which aliens descended upon a rural town similar to Mbale. That night, Jacob had demanded to sleep in his mother's bed, adamant he could hear a monster breathing under his own. Of course, when Jacob had repeated this story to Ian and Zachary, that had been the moment Kira had chosen to explain that it had really been her lying on the floorboards and breathing through a toilet paper roll. There had been no monster.

But that was then and this was now.

Just as he managed to convince himself he had been dreaming and the dark veil of sleep was beginning to envelop him once more, the breath of the monster returned. Jacob did not hear it – he felt it instead. It began at the tip of his nose, as if someone were waving a feather. Jacob squeezed his eyes shut so hard that they ached. All he could see was black. He stared at the insides of his eyelids, wishing desperately that he could see through them yet also convinced that to open them would be a bad idea. Jacob wrinkled his nostrils, trying his best to ignore the tickling at the end of his nose that was now spreading to his cheeks. It could easily have been a breeze from an open window.

Except Jacob was on the thirtieth floor of the Shard and there were no open windows.

There was a loud snort and a burst of hot, putrid air pummelled Jacob's face with such force that his eyes flew open. When they did, he screamed. But not for long.

The face of an Other was inches from his, hairy body

tangled in black webs and dangling from the ceiling. Poisonous green eyes and intensely black pupils burned down at him with bestial hatred. Coarse, bristling, black hairs stood on end like wires. Small, sharp teeth champed and sprayed with saliva. A few warm drops pattered Jacob's face with every one of the monster's rasping, haggard breaths. A grey hand with six fingers lunged down and smothered Jacob's mouth. Its skin was cold and wet, like that of a dead body rotting underwater.

And then Jacob woke up again.

This time, he opened his eyes straight away and sat bolt upright. It was still night-time. Jacob's eyes darted over the slanted window and three white walls of his bedroom, paying particular attention to the ceiling and its shadowy corners. There was no sign of the Other. Jacob touched his cheeks with shaking fingers. Had he really been dreaming? Shaw had mentioned strange dreams might be a side effect. He shuddered and wiped his mouth roughly. Since his experience in the Oracle, Jacob did not think it was wise to make hasty assumptions about what was real and what was not. In any case, he was in no hurry to close his eyes again.

Jacob swung his legs out of bed and shivered as his bare feet touched the cold floor. His Captain Cosmic action figure was on its back on the bedside table. Jacob padded in his Star Wars T-shirt and boxer shorts towards the window. Oddly, the smog had disappeared.

The London on the other side of the glass looked like an electrified circuit board. He could see into the bowels of the city, the glistening maze of streets and the headlights of the cars and buses streaming up and down them. The lights of the South Bank glittered across the black surface of the Thames. Jacob stared at the Leadenhall Building. Amira stared back.

'What are you hiding?' Jacob murmured. Amira winked and flicked her hair over her shoulder in response.

There was a deafening blare outside the window and the room was flooded with a hideous, green light. Jacob pressed his hands and face against the window and the glass hammered against him. The whole building was shaking. Something colossal was moving through the air above the Shard. With mounting horror, Jacob realised what it was.

Another nest. It was one of the Others' vessels, like the one Jacob had watched destroy Mbale inside the Oracle, except this was far, far bigger. It looked like a gigantic, furry spider's nest with jagged, black spikes protruding from it instead of wings. It roared overhead. It kept coming and coming and Jacob thought it was never going to end. It seemed enormous enough to cover the city. Jacob craned his neck. He thought he could see tiny figures crawling over each other within the vast, shapeless mass of black hair.

Others. Thousands of them.

The nest stopped moving and hovered overhead, blotting out the sky. Its centre began to glow with the same poisonous green. Jacob pounded his fists against the glass but they could not be heard over the thunder of alien engines. He knew what was coming. There was nothing he could do to stop it. A green beam of light plunged from the base of the nest and landed in the middle of the Thames, just in front of Tower Bridge. Jacob watched the water froth and boil and cascade over the banks.

'No! No! You can't!' he screamed but even that he could not hear.

There was just enough time for one last cheeky wink from Amira Rana on the side of the Leadenhall Building before a whirlpool of fire exploded from the river at the point of the light's impact and spread outwards with ferocious speed. Tower Bridge was the first to vanish, its two turrets vaporising into ash. It was as if a volcano had erupted in the centre of the city and was engulfing everything in every direction. Jacob watched the wall of flame tear towards the Shard, its light blinding and heat burning and then . . .

Jacob woke up again.

He knew he was awake this time. The bedsheets were drenched and his sodden T-shirt was plastered to his body. Jacob could actually smell his own sweat. He heaved himself upright and ran his hand through his moist hair. He looked out of the window. The smog was there as it always had been. Its dark haze blurred the night sky.

There was no way Jacob was going to sleep again tonight. He leaned out of bed and scooped his RanaPhone from the floor. The screen cast its cold, white light over his clammy face. He wanted to find out everything that Double M, whoever they were, knew about the Others.

Because, tomorrow, he was going to find out everything Amira Rana knew about them too.

CHAPTER
TWENTY-TWO

It was late in the afternoon and the four remaining candidates had dragged two of the Lounge's leather sofas to form a semi-circle by the window. Kira was again sitting between Sakari and Lulu on one of them. Jacob had taken the other entirely for himself. His head was resting on one end and his legs were flung carelessly over the other. That was until Eunata marched over and slapped him hard on the knees. Jacob scowled and shifted himself to an upright position, giving his mother enough space to sit next to him. He was exhausted. He had hardly slept the previous night and his mind was as foggy as the view from the window. The cogs of his brain turned slowly and jerkily.

It was not raining but everything about the view suggested it would be soon. The clouds had returned and were rallying against the window. They were immense, rolling and black, like great waves on a storm-ridden sea.

'I wonder what Amira will tell us this evening,' said Lulu.

'Hopefully, she'll start by explaining exactly what we'll be doing up there on the Garden and exactly what threat we'll be fighting,' said Sakari. 'Although, given how needlessly mysterious everything about Transcendent has been so far, Amira will probably wait until we're all sitting in the rocket before holding up a sign outside the window.'

'Well, I'm excited whatever happens,' said Lulu.

'Yes, we must hope tonight brings answers,' nodded Eunata, 'but if you are true to yourselves, all your steps will be in the right direction. Are you listening, Jacob?'

'Yeah, yeah,' Jacob said vaguely. He was leaning back on the sofa and gazing up through the slanted, glass window, beyond which the mighty clouds rolled.

Eunata was about to prod further when they heard the thud and squeak of heavy leather boots behind them, followed by a familiar, stony voice.

'Candidates, if you're ready, Ms Rana will meet you downstairs,' said Gustavo Yang. 'Mrs Flynn, you're welcome too.'

Yang was standing to attention with his hands behind his back and feet shoulder-width apart. As always, his face could have been carved out of granite. The slash of a mouth was downturned in its usual scowl. Jacob would have thought the face unreadable if not for the slight glint in the black eyes that betrayed that Yang was at least a little pleased to see them. Jacob recognised the same bomber jacket from Uganda.

'Do you just own seven of those outfits and nothing else?' Kira asked.

'No,' Yang replied. 'On Sundays, I wear plaid.'

Before they could decide whether or not he was joking, Yang was leading them towards the open lift. He pressed the button that would take them to the lower levels. The lift travelled silently at a sudden speed. Jacob still had not grown accustomed to the dizziness it brought on every time. He leaned against the wall and avoided the others' gaze. Kira and Sakari were glancing at each other nervously. Lulu was doing her best to look cheerful.

There was a *ding* and the lift doors opened. As they stepped out, it took Jacob a moment to recognise where they were. They were standing at the end of a white, concrete corridor with a row of doors on either side. On every door was a round porthole.

'We're not . . .' he began.

'No Oracle today,' said Yang crisply. 'This way, please.'

Yang gestured down another corridor with a door at the very end. There was no round window or even a handle – it was simply a sheet of solid steel with a small, glass panel on the wall beside it. The six of them proceeded down the corridor. Despite his weariness, Jacob felt excitement growing with every step. He looked at Kira. A silly grin was spreading across her face. Yang brandished a security card and swiped it against the glass panel. There was a *beep* and the door clicked open. Yang pushed against it with a gigantic hand and they all shuffled underneath his tree branch of an arm.

Jacob could not see anything. The room was in darkness. He was not sure it even was a room. From the echo of their footsteps, where they were standing could have been as cavernous as an aircraft hangar, directly underneath the Thames.

'Hey, who turned out the lights?' Sakari asked.

'She likes it in the dark,' Yang murmured.

'Who does?' asked Lulu.

'The Queen of Sheba,' said Kira cautiously, squinting into the black. 'Who do you think?'

A voice, warm like poured caramel and yet with the slightest, grating growl, drifted from the darkness.

'At last. I thought you'd have me standing here all day.'

There was the booming thrum of high bay lights and a sudden fierce, white glare made them all cry out and cover their eyes. When Jacob was finally able to lower his fingers, he saw they were standing in a gigantic concrete bunker. The bunker was so long, two jumbo jets could easily have been parked inside it from nose to tail. The ceiling was tall enough that three could have been piled on top of each other.

A few feet away from them was an arrangement that looked bizarre in such a large, empty space. Amira Rana was standing there, wearing a yellow sari. There were five folding chairs in a row in front of her. For a few moments, the four candidates did nothing but gape. Eunata, on the other hand, was determined Amira would not see her looking impressed.

'Really?' Amira said, eyebrows raised. 'You're just going to stand there after I went to all that effort of asking someone to carry these chairs down here?'

Snapping out of his trance, Jacob was the first to approach and sit in the chair directly in front of Amira. The sound of the chair scraping on the concrete echoed in the enormous space. Kira, Sakari and Lulu looked at each other and followed suit. Eunata took the chair at the end of the row, dragging it a few feet away from the candidates, who were all staring up at Amira. Yang stood a few feet behind Amira, feet spread and hands clasped behind his back.

Everyone waited for Amira to speak. She flashed a gorgeous smile and clapped her hands together. Eunata was the only one to notice that her smile did not reach her eyes.

'Firstly, I would like to congratulate you for your success in yesterday's trials and for making it through to Transcendent,' beamed Amira. 'You will travel to Cornwall tomorrow morning and spend an intense twenty-four hours in training at RanaTech Spaceflight's state-of-the-art facility. At noon the very next day, you will be launched via rocket to the Garden, where you will start work safeguarding the future of humankind. Before that, however, I'm here to explain exactly what Transcendent means and what your part in it will be.'

'You're not really here, though, are you?' Kira interrupted. 'You're just another hologram being beamed from Tokyo or wherever you really are right now. See?'

Kira pulled a pen from her pocket and, before Eunata could stop her, hurled it at Amira. Rather than passing through her as Kira expected, it bounced off Amira's shoulder and landed with a clatter on the floor. Amira's eyes flickered down to the pen and back up to Kira. She raised her eyebrows.

'Oh,' said Kira. 'Sorry.'

'As I was saying,' Amira continued, 'given the gravity of such a venture, the board thought it best I deliver this information to you in person. Before I begin, my associate, Mister . . . erm . . .' Amira gestured vaguely towards Yang, 'will distribute your identification passes.'

Yang did not seem offended by Amira not knowing his name. He strode forward and handed each candidate a sleek, metallic card. Jacob took his and looked down at it. There was a photograph of him looking shell-shocked, his name and TRANSCENDENT printed underneath.

Amira raised a hand, as slender and elegant as the neck of a swan. Jacob noticed that around her wrist, underneath glittering, golden bangles, was the diamond encrusted strap of an Oracle Mark I. Amira unfastened the circular projector and bent gracefully to place it on the concrete floor.

'I would appreciate it,' she said, 'if the crowd could refrain from any further interruptions whilst I'm making my presentation.'

There was a whine and the Oracle shone brightly for a few seconds before a hologram of the Earth sprang out of it. The perfect sphere of sparkling, blue ocean, green land mass and white clouds was the size of a beach ball, suspended and revolving slowly over the projector. Amira paced in front of the hologram. The cold light of the Earth shone around her.

'Around every hundred million years,' Amira began, 'our world experiences a mass extinction event, a moment when life is destroyed on a global scale. It has happened five times in the history of our planet. The last mass extinction event wiped out the dinosaurs when a meteorite collided with the Earth and obliterated three quarters of living species. Just yesterday, I was visited by a professor from RanaTech Spaceflight who confirmed our suspicions that, according to their readings, the next mass extinction event is very much . . . on its way.'

Jacob and Kira shared a quick, worried glance with the other candidates.

Amira stood back and gestured at the hologram of the shimmering, revolving planet.

'After the meteorite annihilated the dinosaurs, the Earth recovered as it always has. Every form of life, baboons and bacteria and people and plants, plays a part in allowing the planet to prosper. Mighty herds fertilise the soil, allowing plants to grow, which are then pollinated by the tiniest insects. Great shoals of fish recycle nutrients in the ocean which, in turn, produces over half of the world's oxygen – the very air we breathe. Our world is one that, for the last ten thousand years, has existed in perfect harmony with itself. Until now. A menace has arisen that threatens to overturn our world and leave it nothing more than a smouldering ruin.'

Jacob felt as if he had swallowed a chunk of ice. This was it. He recollected frightening images of the Others, of black, hairy spider nests descending from space, glowing, green eyes and freakishly human hands with six fingers.

Amira was silent for an agonisingly long time. She seemed to be enjoying herself.

'That menace,' she purred, 'is the human race.'

Jacob had the sudden and violent sensation of being

dunked into freezing water. *The human race?* What was Amira talking about? Her voice floated to him from further and further away. It was as if he were sinking deeper and deeper beneath an ice sheet.

'The utopian nature of our planet has given humanity a unique opportunity. Usually, animals adapt by developing a physical gift to survive: wings, flippers, claws, long necks to reach high places or gills to breathe underwater. Humans were given something else. We were given the gift of intelligence. We discovered fire, invented the wheel and farmed our own food. Our pace of progress has been like nothing else on the fossil record.'

The hologram flickered from the image of the Earth to grainy black and white footage of smoking factory chimneys, tanks rolling across cratered fields, troops of soldiers marching with bayonets held aloft and, finally, hideously, the mushroom cloud of a nuclear explosion enveloping the horizon at the distant edge of an ocean.

'Since the Industrial Revolution and fuelled by colonisation and segregation, our pace of change has become faster and faster. There are no longer any threats to our survival. Any potential diseases or predators have been overcome and eradicated. As a result, the human population has skyrocketed. There were a billion humans on the planet two hundred years ago. Now, there are eight billion.'

The image displayed by the Oracle changed again and there was a flurry of horrified gasps. At first the image appeared to be of a crumpled tent on burnt, yellow grass. Then, broken tusks and limp, torn ears could be seen. It was a dead elephant. The elephant's insides had wasted away so its loose skin, which was turning white and mouldy, was thrown over a protruding mess of a gigantic skeleton. Its four legs were splayed, eyes nothing but sunken, lifeless pits. Jacob turned around in his chair to look at his mother. Eunata was staring at the image with an expression of abject horror.

'Our success has come at a price. The African elephant is sensitive to high temperatures, disease and disappearing vegetation. If we continue to destroy its habitat to build our cities and farm our cattle, this is the inevitable result. We have cut down three trillion trees across the world – over half of the planet's rainforests. There are now half the number of wild animals in the world that there were seventy years ago. We are burning more and more fossil fuels, trapping carbon dioxide and other greenhouse gases in the atmosphere, causing our planet to get hotter and hotter. The weather is more volatile. Flooding and wildfires are rife across the planet. Our environment, the key to our success and continued survival, is under threat and it is all because of us.'

'Can you believe this?' Jacob breathed to Kira.

'I know,' she murmured. 'Mama was right all along. She'll be insufferable now.'

'The path we tread is leading in one direction,' Amira went on. 'Towards catastrophe. RanaTech scientists have assessed the situation, analysed the evidence, and they are all in agreement that this catastrophe will come much faster than initially thought. In fact, it will occur in less than a hundred years – within the lifetime of a child alive right now on this planet.'

'What catastrophe is that?' Jacob heard someone ask. He did not recognise the voice. His clouded mind was spinning.

'RanaTech scientists predict,' said Amira, 'that if we continue our current course, the Amazon rainforest will disappear within ten years, replaced by a dry savannah. All the ice in the Arctic will melt. Global warming will accelerate. Within thirty years, the oceans will have heated to such a degree that they will become acidic, destroying fish populations. Within fifty years, pollinating insects will become extinct and the planet's soil will be exhausted from overuse. Global food production will be in crisis. Before one hundred years have elapsed, large portions of the Earth will be uninhabitable. Human civilisation across the planet will collapse. That is to say nothing of the effect of rising temperatures on the human body. Vast swathes of humanity will have perished from heat death before we even reach that point. This is the fate that awaits millions upon millions of people unless we do something to stop it.'

Everyone stared at the holographic image of the burnt husk of the elephant, decaying on the scorched earth. The once magnificent and towering colossus was nothing more than a horrific jumble of rotting bones and skin.

'Nature will rebuild after we are gone,' said Amira. 'It always does. It rebuilt after the dinosaurs and it will rebuild after us. But that won't need to happen if we're the ones to rebuild it first. That's why I've brought you together. That's what Transcendent is all about. Using the laboratory onboard the Garden and the best equipment money can buy, you will develop strategies to end the destruction of our environment brought about by the human race and halt the catastrophe that is fast approaching. Be under no illusion. That catastrophe is nothing less than the end of the living world as you know it.'

'Why us?' Sakari asked. 'Out of everyone on the planet, why have you chosen us?'

'RanaTech has been scouring the globe for candidates and the four of you have been identified as some of the greatest young minds on this planet, in terms of sheer IQ. Moreover, each of you has dedicated years already to protecting our natural environment. Now that the four of you have made it through our tests of intelligence, resolve and comradeship, there is no one on this planet better suited to Transcendent.'

'What about Jacob and me?' Kira asked. 'We've never saved coral reefs or refrozen ice caps. We're nowhere near the same league as these two.'

'I beg to differ.' Amira shook her head. 'I've seen the video of Jacob demonstrating an atmospheric converter that successfully recycles carbon dioxide into fuel. RanaTech, with its infinite resources, has been trying to develop such a device for years and with no luck. You two managed to build it out of an electric microwave in your mother's garage. You have every right to be part of Transcendent alongside Sakari and Lulu.'

Kira and Lulu looked at each other and smiled nervously. Then they looked at Sakari. It took a few seconds but Sakari's anxious face broke into a small smile as well.

'OK,' said Sakari. 'I'm in.'

'You're . . .' Jacob faltered.

'What did you say?' Amira asked. She took one step closer and held her hand to her ear. 'Speak up, sweetie. I didn't hear you.'

'I said . . .' Jacob said quietly, 'I said, "You're lying."'

'Pardon me?'

Before he knew what he was doing, Jacob was on his feet and shouting. 'You're lying! Tell us about the Others!'

'The other who?' Amira replied, startled.

'The Others. The aliens. Aliens are coming and they're going to burn this planet to a crisp. That's the real threat and you know it. Are you working with them? Is that what this is? Is that why you've invented all of this about climate change or whatever?'

'Jacob,' Amira said slowly, as if speaking to a younger child. 'If I was in league with an advanced alien civilisation, I assure you I wouldn't be wasting time speaking to you.' She pointed at her cheeks. 'I would be finding out if they'd invented a blusher that actually blends with my skin tone.'

'What on Earth are you talking about, Jacob?' Eunata demanded.

Jacob ignored her. Adrenaline was coursing through him. His mother had been right. There was a sliver of ice in the heart of Amira Rana. She was lying about the Others and had fabricated a story about a climate catastrophe to bring Transcendent together. But why?

Jacob glared at Kira. He had expected her to stand up and accost Amira just as he had. Instead, she remained seated and avoided his gaze. A searing sense of betrayal burned inside him but there was no time to dwell on it. They were all in real danger. He forced his exhausted brain to work.

'I'm sorry,' Jacob said suddenly, holding his hands up in surrender. 'I'm so sorry, everyone. I've made a mistake. I've got no idea what I was talking about. I think . . . I think I'm just tired. Forgive me, Ms Rana, and thank you so much for the opportunity.'

Jacob marched towards Amira and put his arms around her in a brief hug. Then he stood back.

'Thank you again,' Jacob said solemnly, 'for the opportunity.'

Amira's shoulders were arched. She looked like a cat raising its hackles after being stroked by an unwelcome hand. Jacob turned back to Kira, Eunata, Sakari and Lulu, who were all staring at him and Amira with stunned expressions.

'I think I could do with some fresh air,' Jacob said pointedly. His eyes flashed at Kira. 'Would you mind coming with me?'

Kira hesitated.

'OK,' she said.

'Brilliant,' said Jacob. Before anyone could stop him, he had grabbed Kira by the hand and was leading her hurriedly to the steel door. He waited until it had slammed behind them before sprinting down the corridor to the lifts.

'What the hell are you doing?' Kira cried, hurrying after him.

'Come on, come on, come on,' Jacob said through gritted teeth, jabbing the button that called the lift. There was a *ding* and the lift doors drew open, spilling a yellow strip of light onto the floor and wall. As Kira followed Jacob inside, they heard thundering footsteps behind them. Jacob's fist pounded the button that closed the doors. Yang's furious face appeared through the rapidly closing gap.

'You're making a mistake, Jacob!' he bellowed fiercely.

The doors closed and he was gone. Jacob collapsed against the walls of the lift and they felt it catapult upwards.

'What the hell are you doing?' Kira repeated in exasperation.

'We need to get as far away from Amira Rana as possible,' Jacob panted. 'Mama was right. She's dangerous. Why would she tell us the human race is the enemy and not the Others? She's working with them. It's the only explanation.'

'You're not thinking straight!'

'I had to leave Mama, Sakari and Lulu behind but we'll figure that out later,' Jacob muttered, more to himself than to Kira. 'I could only get the two of us out of there without arousing too much suspicion. Yang must have already figured out what I've done. We'll have to come back for them somehow . . .'

'Jacob, you're not talking like yourself! Just stop! Just think!'

'No!' Jacob shouted. He was suddenly angry. '*You're* not talking like yourself! The Kira Flynn I know did everything she could to save a child from a bully! She took on a machete-wielding gang all by herself just to protect her family! What's happened to you?'

'That was different, Jacob. Things have changed.'

'Kira,' Jacob snarled. 'This is not different at all. Amira may be the biggest bully the world has ever seen. I've seen what the Others are going to do with my own eyes. If she's in league with them, we need to get as far away from her as possible and we need to find a way to stop her. And we need to eradicate the Others before they get a chance to burn the world.'

'Jacob—'

'You promised we'd stick together. Did you mean it?'

Kira looked up at the ceiling of the lift, her face twisted in frustration. Eventually, she sighed and looked back at her brother.

'I . . . I did.'

'Then trust me on this.'

There was another *ding* and the lift stopped. They had reached the marble entrance hall.

'What did you mean when you said Yang's already figured out what you've done?' Kira asked wearily.

'It's insane,' Jacob muttered to himself, shaking his head.

'What's insane? What did you do, Jacob?'

'No. It's insane that that sari of hers has pockets.'

'What do you mean?' Kira almost screamed at him.

'I mean,' Jacob grinned and pulled something from his back pocket, something small, glinting and dangling from his fingers, 'I just stole Amira Rana's car keys.'

CHAPTER TWENTY-THREE

'This is a bad idea,' muttered Kira.

They had found Amira's bright pink Aston Martin Rapide E parked outside the entrance to the Shard in front of Guy's Hospital. Jacob was in the driver's seat and rotating the steering wheel with manic intensity as he manoeuvred the car onto the road. Next to him, Kira desperately fastened her seatbelt. The car veered wildly before straightening. There was no roar of an engine, just the frantic whirr of an electric battery. Raindrops began to splash against the windscreen and run upwards in streams as the car accelerated alarmingly. Kira glanced at the wing mirror and watched the reflection of a monstrous, black car pull out of a garage door and follow them. The Jeep Cherokee was less than fifty feet behind. Even through the splatter of raindrops on the glass, there was no mistaking the huge form of Gustavo Yang, hunched behind the steering wheel.

'Jacob, Yang's behind us.'

'Not for long,' Jacob grunted.

He pressed his foot down even further on the pedal and the sheer force of acceleration glued Kira to the back of her seat. Almost as soon as the pedal had touched the floor, Jacob lifted his foot off and thrust the wheel to the right. The nose of the car swung right. The rear swung left. Jacob and Kira were tossed around, held in place only by their seatbelts. The Aston Martin drifted onto the crowded thoroughfare of Borough High Street, amid a flurry of outraged car horns.

'Sorry!' Jacob called over his shoulder.

'Jacob,' shouted Kira over the swish of tyres on the road. 'This is dangerous.'

'Help me find the button that turns on the windscreen wiper!' Jacob shouted back.

Rain was hammering the windscreen. The chaotic spray in front of them was lit in yellow by the headlights of the Aston Martin and red by the rear lights of the vehicles around them. Streams ran horizontally along the side windows. Fans of water sprayed from underneath black taxis and red double decker buses. The car swerved gracefully between them. Their murky shapes swam past, dangerously close on both sides. Kira scoured the black, carbon fibre dashboard. It was crowded with an overwhelming number of luminous, green instruments, emblazoned with symbols she did not understand.

'It's that one!' Kira pointed.

'No, it's that one!' Jacob pointed somewhere else.

'That one turns on the radio!'

'No, it opens the boot!'

Completely at random, Kira punched a button close to the steering wheel and a black, plastic arm immediately began sweeping across the windscreen, wiping away the rainwater and clearing the view. Kira twisted in her seat to look out of the rear window. She could no longer see the Cherokee behind them. Jacob put his foot down on the brake and the Aston Martin slowed abruptly to a crawl. Kira was thrown forward and twisted back to face the front.

Ahead of them, London Bridge straddled the steely Thames and disappeared into the swirling, grey cloud of smog. The junction connecting it with Borough High Street was heaving with a mesh of vehicles. Some drivers were out of their cars, standing with their doors open and clothes sodden in the rain. Horns honked. Yellow and red beams flashed in the downpour. The way was blocked.

'Oh, no,' said Kira, as she saw why.

A second, black Jeep Cherokee was obstructing the road at their end of London Bridge, parked with its side to the throng of traffic. Nothing was getting onto the bridge. The traffic was a flood, the Cherokee an immovable dam. And the Aston Martin was headed straight for it.

'They've got us, Jacob!' yelled Kira. 'Stop the car.'

'They've not got us yet.'

Jacob jerked the wheel to the right. The Aston Martin skirted the edge of the junction, around the traffic jam and mounted the pavement with a jolt. Jacob spun the wheel. Tyres skidded across wet paving slabs.

With mounting horror, Kira realised what Jacob was planning to do. On the right of the bridge was a narrow set of steps leading down to a promenade that ran alongside the Thames. Jacob slammed the accelerator completely to the floor. The car lunged forward. She dug her fingernails into black leather. The top of the steps rushed towards them and then the car was flying. Kira's stomach did a somersault. Sparks flew as both wing mirrors were torn away by the stone walls that closed in on both sides. The river loomed, grey and opaque. Then there was the squeal of rubber and metal on stone. Jacob and Kira were thrown violently around the inside of the car as it bounced on landing. A crumbling sign that read THE QUEEN'S WALK streaked past as Jacob struggled to regain control and then, before Kira could fully comprehend what he had done, the Aston Martin was hurtling along the narrow promenade. The wall overlooking the river on the left and the glass fronts of office buildings on the right were nothing but a blur.

Kira turned to her brother. 'Stop the car,' she said firmly.

'No,' said Jacob. He was moving the wheel no more than an inch to either side, squinting through the foggy windscreen. At its current speed, if the car were to veer by more than an arm's length, a crash would be fatal.

'I said, "Stop the car."'

'I'm not going to do that.'

'Fine,' said Kira. She unfastened her seatbelt with a click. It flew across her body.

'What are you going to do?' Jacob scoffed. 'Don't be an idiot. You made a promise. You said we were going to stick together and that's what we're going to do.'

'I can't do that anymore! The Others don't exist, Jacob! It's all nonsense spouted by some online conspiracy theorist!'

'What I saw is real!' Jacob bellowed. His knuckles were gripping the steering wheel so tightly, they were white. 'Everything has been leading to this! We have to stop Amira and the Others. It's what we've been preparing for our entire lives!'

'No, Jacob. I'm going to the Garden and I'm going to be part of Transcendent. That's what *I've* been preparing for my entire life.'

'Well, you're in the car now,' said Jacob bitterly, 'and you'll do whatever I do. You're terrified of being on your own, Kira. I know you. Things haven't changed *that* much.'

'You're right,' smiled Kira grimly. 'Things haven't changed that much. I'm still Kira Flynn, and I do as I please.'

She opened the passenger door, allowing the thundering wind to howl inside and lash them both with freezing rain.

'Ala!' Jacob shrieked in Swahili. He slammed his foot on the brake and the tyres skated across wet pavement.

It was too late. Kira had thrown herself from the moving car.

Her right shoulder hit the ground first and she felt both her shirt and skin tear. She rolled over as if she were tumbling down a steep hill. The wet paving stones were rock-hard fists that pummelled her over and over again. All the while, spinning around the edge of her field of vision was the pink shape of the car, narrowly avoiding flattening her head.

Kira finally clattered to a stop, lying, sprawled, on her back. She ignored the blazing pain and strained her body to twist her head to catch sight of the Aston Martin. The promenade had opened onto a wide area. The car was careering to the left, heading for the low stone wall that separated it from a drop of at least ten feet down to the lapping water of the Thames.

The deluge had stopped the brakes from working. Jacob had lost control.

'JACOB!' Kira bellowed, the rain battering her face.

There was the roar of an engine. A black Jeep Cherokee sprang from the Queen's Walk, narrowly avoiding Kira. She glimpsed the gigantic figure of Gustavo Yang wrenching furiously at the steering wheel. It was heading directly for the wall to get itself in front of the veering Aston Martin. In the seconds before the car could pitch itself over, Yang propelled the Cherokee between them.

The Aston Martin smashed into the side of the Cherokee like a pink battering ram. There was a deafening crunch of metal and splintering glass.

And then everything was quiet, apart from the slapping of rain on the paving stones and the surface of the Thames.

CHAPTER
TWENTY-FOUR

Kira's skin was numb to the chill of the rain. Only her right shoulder was hot from the small patch of red spreading on her shirt. She took a few shaky, painful steps. Her knees nearly buckled. There seemed to be hardly any damage to the rear end of the Aston Martin. The brake lights were still glowing a dim red as if in a vain attempt to avert the devastating collision that had already occurred. The rest of the car looked like a scrunched chocolate wrapper. The reinforced Cherokee had been crushed between the pink sports car and the promenade wall and there was a savage dent in its side. Shards of glass from the Cherokee's side windows had exploded outwards on impact and were scattered across the Aston Martin's bonnet. The two cars had become one in a mangled mash of metal. Steam rose in a haze. There was the hiss of hot machinery, sizzling in the rain.

Kira stumbled to the driver's door of the Aston

Martin, fumbled at the handle and wrenched it open. Jacob was slumped over the steering wheel, showered in white chips of glass from the shattered windscreen. Blood was streaming down the right side of his face from a gash on his forehead. He was not moving.

'No, no, no, no,' Kira murmured.

She managed to hook her arms underneath his shoulders and drag him from the car. Kira's legs gave way under her brother's weight and the two of them collapsed, splashing onto the wet paving stones. Jacob groaned hoarsely.

'Jacob!' Kira gasped, cradling him in her arms and gently slapping his face. 'Be all right. Please be all right. Just please be all right.'

Jacob's blue eyes flickered open. For a moment, they stared straight through Kira as if they did not see her. Then they grew dark and the only expression on Jacob's face was one of fury. He struggled out of Kira's arms.

'Jacob,' Kira almost sobbed. 'You need to let me help you. Just take my hand.'

'No,' he replied.

Jacob straightened for a moment, standing shakily, before his eyes rolled and he looked as if he were going to topple again. Kira lunged forward to support him.

'Jacob, take my hand,' she pleaded.

'DON'T TOUCH ME!' Jacob snarled with such ferocity that Kira took a step back.

The two of them stared at each other, breathing heavily. Jacob was swaying alarmingly. Kira still had her hands raised, as if in order to defend herself rather than to protect him.

Only now did Kira hear the sirens wailing faintly in the distance. At the same time, but closer, came the sound of splashing footsteps. Kira turned to see Eunata running and Amira walking briskly from another Cherokee that had emerged from a side street. The passenger and driver's door of the Cherokee were open. Amira's yellow sari trailed through the water behind her. Eunata wrapped her arm around Jacob's shoulder, allowing him to rest against her body. Jacob was a head taller than his mother. Her body buckled a little under his slumped weight but she held steady.

'The emergency services are on their way.' Amira spoke with an indifference that chilled Kira far more than the torrential rain, still thundering down upon them. 'It would be preferable if we are not here when they arrive. My people will be able to handle the admin.'

'The *admin*?' Kira exclaimed in disbelief. Her eyes wandered to the Cherokee, smashed between the Aston Martin and the promenade wall. 'What about Yang? We need to help—'

'My people will handle it,' repeated Amira. There was a hint of menace in her voice.

With one last, desperate look at the pulverised

Cherokee, Kira hurried to her mother to help carry Jacob. Amira paced through the water ahead of them, hair and sari fluttering behind her. As they reached the other car, the sirens were growing louder. No one spoke as they drove away, leaving the smoking wreckage behind.

CHAPTER
TWENTY-FIVE

Night had fallen by the time they arrived back at the Lounge. Billowing, black storm clouds and lashing rain rallied unrelentingly against the slanted windows. There was the occasional blue flash of lightning and low rumble of thunder. Sakari and Lulu were sitting together on a leather sofa when they entered. Kira and Eunata were supporting Jacob, who was trudging along with his head lolling to the side. Blood was still streaming down the side of his face. His eyes were rolling in his head. Kira could hear him mumbling something about steamed bananas.

'Scram,' said Amira to Sakari and Lulu, and they did. The two girls hurried past them to their rooms, glancing worriedly at Jacob as they went.

'Take him to his room. My medical team will see to him there.' Amira's demeanour was business-like. 'I'll need to speak to the RanaTech board of directors. You'll both be removed from Transcendent, certainly.'

Eunata led Jacob to the bedroom. He raised his head and spoke groggily. It was the first time he had said anything intelligible since Kira had dragged him from the crashed Aston Martin.

'Do what you want . . . I want . . . no part of this . . . going back to Uganda.'

Kira stared at Jacob. He stared back at her with a level gaze.

'You can do what you want,' he said again before allowing Eunata to lead him away.

'A word,' Amira said quietly as Kira stared after her departing mother and brother. When they had disappeared, Kira threw herself onto one of the leather sofas.

'I wouldn't worry about Jacob,' said Amira. 'My medical team will take good care of him, and nothing seems to be damaged beyond repair.'

'I'm not so sure about that,' said Kira.

'You know,' Amira sighed. 'My ex-wife told me I was crazy to recruit a bunch of thirteen-year-olds—'

'We're fourteen,' Kira interrupted.

'—and I should have listened!' Amira was suddenly angry. 'What was I thinking? Jennifer always said kids were spoiled, messy and more trouble than they're worth. I'm starting to think she was right about some things at least. You'll both be on the first plane back to Uganda tomorrow morning.'

'Please don't send me back to Uganda,' said Kira.

'I—what?' sputtered Amira.

'I don't belong in Uganda. I don't belong in London. Being part of Transcendent is the first time I've felt like I've belonged somewhere. It's the first time I've been around more people who are like me.'

Amira stared down at Kira. When she spoke, her manner and voice were strangely stilted. It was as if she were working muscles she had not stretched in a long time.

'I . . . I don't know if I can do that, Kira.'

'Please, Ms Rana.' Kira leaned forward. Her shoulder twinged and she clutched it. 'I'm sorry we wrecked your car.'

Amira shrugged. She turned to gaze out of the window.

'You wrecked one of my cars.'

There was a brief, blue glare of lightning and the Lounge was monochrome for a split second, long shadows thrown across the glass floor. Amira's back was to Kira as she gazed out of the darkened window.

'Truth be told, Kira, I see a little of myself in you. Your brilliance. Your independence. Kira. Amira. Even our names are spookily alike. And I too have always been . . . different.'

Amira paused for a long time.

'I'll persuade the board to allow you to remain part of Transcendent.'

'Thank you, Ms Rana.' Kira let out a sigh of relief.

'I won't be able to do the same for Jacob,' Amira went on, still not turning from the window. 'The board will want your heads for the mess you've made today and I'm going to have to give them something. Jacob will be removed from Transcendent. I'll make sure he's flown back to Uganda in comfort, if that's what he wishes. He'll be quite all right on his own, as will you. I should know. I've never needed anyone. I've been alone all my life.'

'Thank you, Ms Rana,' Kira said again as she stood up and limped towards her own bedroom. 'And I know the feeling. Trust me.'

Amira still did not turn from the window. She listened to Kira's limping footsteps. The sound of another set of footsteps joined them, walking quickly and angrily.

'Your brother is fine.' Amira heard Eunata's brisk voice. 'The medics have seen to him and he is resting now. Go to your room, clean your wounds and get some rest. I will deal with you in a moment.'

'Yes, Mama,' Kira said meekly.

Amira listened to Kira shuffling out of the Lounge and Eunata's footsteps coming closer. There was the sound of someone sitting down on a sofa near the window.

'Today,' said Eunata after a moment of silence, 'you spoke of something I have known to be true for most of my life. I have seen its truth with my own eyes. It is a truth that has been staring the world in the face for decades. The way we continue to mistreat our natural environment will end in calamity for millions upon millions of lives in the very near future.'

When Amira did not respond, Eunata continued.

'But I have seen the truth in your eyes too. It is always in the eyes. And I cannot figure out how you can speak about something so paramount to the survival of our planet and everyone on it, without even the faintest glimmer of care or interest.'

The edge of Amira's mouth curled into a smile. She still did not speak or turn around.

'So, what I suppose I really want to know is this,' Eunata went on. 'What is the plan, Amira? You have brought these children together. What for? What is the endgame here?'

'What's the endgame?' Amira sneered, finally turning from the window. 'Do you think Jacob's right? Do you really think I'm in league with an alien army and want to see the world blown up? I can't believe I have to say this. There is no evil scheme. There is no plan for world domination. There are no aliens!'

Amira prowled towards Eunata, back hunched and clawed hands gesticulating. It was the first time Eunata had seen her as anything less than stunningly beautiful.

'Do you really think I get anything out of Transcendent?' Amira cried. 'I'll tell you the truth if you really want to know. Transcendent is a joke. A publicity stunt. It makes it look like RanaTech is doing something to save the environment when, really, our technologies and global expansion are one of the biggest causes of its destruction! Whatever miraculous inventions these kids come up with, we'll just sell off to the highest bidder. That's all Transcendent is. A scam. It's not going to make a difference to climate change. It's not going to make a difference to anything. And if I wasn't contracted by the board to be the face of it, I'd have nothing to do with it at all. Do you understand? I don't care about Transcendent. That's it. I just don't care. I simply do not and never will care!'

There were flecks of spit on Amira's red lips as she spat out the last words through gritted, perfectly white teeth. She was standing over Eunata now, breathing heavily and slender shoulders heaving, so close that Eunata could smell her luxury perfume.

'The great Amira Rana,' Eunata smiled grimly. 'I've read all about you. You built RanaTech from the ground up in your father's garage in Delhi, and now look at you. Nothing more than a stooge for white men in suits. How did it come to this?'

'You know nothing about me.' Amira smiled bitterly. 'You know nothing of what it's like to be cast out by your family. My father took his belt to me when I asked to bring my first girlfriend to the house for chai and mithai. That's when I chose her over my family and now Jennifer and I are not . . . we're not even . . .'

Amira stood up straight, sniffing once.

'Transcendent is meant to save the world,' she said shakily, 'but what has the world ever done for me? Nothing can stop the damage caused by climate change. Everything's going to burn and I for one am going to be bringing a big bag of marshmallows.'

'You are wrong, Amira,' said Eunata calmly. 'First, I do know what it is like. Second, you may choose to believe there is nothing to stand for in this world but that means you will always stand for exactly that: nothing. I, on the other hand, choose to believe in my children. They will make Transcendent mean something.' Eunata stood up. 'But I was wrong too, Amira. You are not the villain of this story. No. Jacob and Kira have nothing to fear from you.'

Eunata walked away, leaving Amira standing there, alone.

'It is themselves they need to worry about.'

CHAPTER
TWENTY-SIX

Kira was already in bed when she heard a knock on her own door.

'Jacob?' she asked.

'No. It is your mama.'

'Oh.'

Eunata came inside and shut the door quietly. Kira's bedroom was identical to Jacob's, with three white walls, the fourth a slanted window. Eunata did not say anything for an uncomfortably long time. She eyed Kira closely as she walked over and sat on the end of her bed. Then she reached out and patted the small bulge in the duvet that signified the location of Kira's foot. A scrape on her ankle after her jump from the Aston Martin burned dully.

'Ow,' said Kira.

'That is exactly what you deserve for behaving so foolishly,' said Eunata. 'Yang is in Guy's Hospital and

I have been informed he is stable. He is lucky to be alive and you and your brother are lucky that you are not in prison. You have only Amira to thank for that.'

Kira simply nodded.

'Jacob wants to go back to Uganda,' Eunata said.

'I know.' Kira nodded. 'I'm not going with him. I'm going to the Garden.'

Eunata sighed. 'I would argue,' she said, 'but I think Transcendent is exactly what you deserve, too.'

She could not see Kira's mouth beneath the duvet, but the bunching of her daughter's freckled cheeks told her she was smiling.

'Do you understand, Kira, that if you go to the Garden, you will go alone?' Eunata asked. 'I can come with you to the launch facility but, from there, you will be on your own.'

'I won't be on my own, Mama. I'll be with Sakari and Lulu.'

Kira's face disappeared under the duvet completely. Eunata leaned forward to hear her daughter's muffled voice.

'We never belonged in Uganda. I thought it would be different in London but it's not. It's worse. The whispering, the staring, the comments . . . it's so much worse. I think it's always going to be that way for Jacob and me. We're not half Ugandan and half English. We're not half of anything. We're not mixed breeds.

We're completely Ugandan and completely English at the same time but it's like we're too light-skinned there and too dark-skinned here. We don't belong in either place. I don't think we'll properly belong anywhere on this planet.'

'Don't say that, mtoto.' Eunata gently pulled on the duvet to uncover her daughter's face. When Kira spoke, her bottom lip quivered and her voice shook.

'It's fine, Mama. If I'm never going to belong on this planet, I'll just leave. I'm going to the Garden to do what I do best and I'm going to do it with other people who are just like me. That's Sakari and Lulu.'

Eunata sighed again.

'I have never spoken about this with you and your brother, have I?' she said quietly, wiping the tears from Kira's cheeks with her fingers. 'Perhaps it has been a long time coming. When I chose to marry your baba, an Englishman, we were cast out by my own family in Kampala. But still, we were happy. We had each other.'

'But then Baba died,' Kira whispered.

'Yes.' Eunata took a deep breath and continued. 'On the slopes of Elgon. He slipped and fell. It was as simple as that. I was not even with him at the time. I was at home, looking after the pair of you.'

Kira removed her hand from underneath the duvet to hold her mother's. Eunata smiled softly.

'After the accident, I felt like I was alone too. Baba

had no family. My own family never wanted to speak to me again. For a long time, I was lost. It was like I was screaming in the dark. But, do you know what brought me back to the light? The two of you. The only time we can battle through the hardships and solve the problems of this world, Kira, is when we have someone fighting by our side. Do you understand what I am saying?'

'I do, Mama.' Kira wriggled to sit up straight, wiping her cheeks roughly so they were as red as her eyes.

'It is about hope, Kira,' said Eunata. 'Having people around you will always bring you hope, no matter what you are facing. I have never lost hope in anything in this world because the three of us were together.'

'Well, I've got my friends at Transcendent now, Mama.' Kira grinned. 'And if being a part of that means being apart from Jacob, then that's just the way the cookie crumbles.'

Eunata smiled sadly, leaned forward and hugged her daughter tightly.

'If that is truly how you feel, mtoto . . .'

It was hours later and the entire thirtieth floor of the Shard was in darkness. Rain was still pattering against the windows and there was the infrequent blue glare of lightning, followed by the low reverberation of thunder. Kira crept, barefoot, into the corridor and stopped outside Jacob's door. She raised her closed fist, hovering a few inches from it. Then stopped.

A muffled sound had given her pause. Kira lowered her fist from the door and placed her ear against it instead. There was definitely a sound, one that sounded like sniffling, coming from the other side of the door. It sounded like someone sobbing into a pillow in a way that was uncontrollable and yet quiet enough that no one else could hear.

Kira did not knock. She limped down the corridor and into her own bedroom, closing the door behind her.

CHAPTER
TWENTY-SEVEN

It took a few blissful seconds after Jacob woke for the memories of the previous day to flood back. When they did, he groaned. The chatter of excited voices and trundling of suitcases had woken him. Kira, Sakari and Lulu were leaving for Cornwall. They were leaving him behind. Jacob did not move from under the duvet but his eyes were wide open. He stared at the wall, unsure how long he remained there. That was, at least, until he heard a knock on the door.

'Kira?' he asked.

'No. It is your mama.'

'Oh.'

Eunata flung the door open. She stood in the corner of the room, arms folded. Her sleeves were rolled all the way past her elbows. Her eyes were wide, lips pursed and nostrils flared. Jacob did not sit up. He remained lying on his side, gazing at the painted, white wall.

'We are leaving,' said Eunata. 'I think the very least you could do after your foolish actions yesterday is speak to your sister before she goes. She is taking off in a rocket at noon tomorrow and who knows when you will see her again! At least say goodbye.'

'I'm not speaking to Kira.' Jacob still did not look at his mother. 'And I want nothing to do with Transcendent. I don't know what I believe is really happening anymore but what I do know is that I can't rely on Kira. She betrayed me and now she can do what she wants. I don't care. I'm going home.'

Eunata was silent for a moment.

'I am disappointed in you,' she said quietly. 'I do not know where this nonsense story of yours has come from. The only reason we have not spoken about it is because of the state you were in last night. I will be back in two days and, believe me, we will talk about it then.'

Eunata opened the door and was about to storm from the room when Jacob spoke again.

'How's Yang?' he asked.

She paused.

'He is stable and currently laid up in Guy's Hospital across the road if you feel like dragging yourself out of bed. If I were you, I would bring an extremely large bouquet.'

With that, Eunata closed the door and was gone. Immediately, stinging tears welled in the corners of

Jacob's eyes and he buried his screwed face into his pillow. He permitted himself one agonised sob before quickly swiping his RanaPhone from the bedside table. The white glare of the screen illuminated his face in the darkness under the duvet. Jacob began tapping furiously.

He needed answers and he knew exactly where to find them.

'And you?' Eunata demanded of Kira, who had been waiting with her suitcase just outside Jacob's door.

'He doesn't want anything to do with me,' Kira shrugged.

'Ridiculous.' Eunata shook her head as they made their way towards the lift, where Sakari and Lulu were waiting. 'If the two of you are not going to sort yourselves out, I need to take matters into my own hands. I am going to make a call.'

'Mr Yang has sustained severe bruising, multiple fractured ribs and a suspected punctured lung. We will take him for a chest X-ray this afternoon to confirm. Given the extent of Mr Yang's injuries, we asked him whether he would prefer to be changed into a more comfortable set of clothes. However, Mr Yang insisted *these* were his most comfortable clothes.'

'Yeah,' sighed Jacob. 'That sounds about right.'

Yang was sitting up in bed. Only his top half was

visible. The rest of him was covered with a thin, blue blanket. A black eye had blossomed spectacularly on the right side of his face as if to match the rest of his ensemble. Even in bed, Yang was still wearing his black bomber jacket. A gigantic pair of black, leather boots was placed neatly on the floor. Yang's bare feet were protruding from the end of the bed. His muscle-bound body looked like a pile of boulders beneath the blanket.

The violent storm of the previous day had blown itself out but the clouds outside were still a sullen grey. Rain trickled down the window. There was a dead fly upside down on the windowsill. The hospital room itself was small and harshly lit. Tubes attached to various parts of Yang snaked from under the blanket. Jacob was sitting in an uncomfortable chair by Yang's bed. There was an extravagant bouquet of tulips in a vase on the bedside table. The harsh smell of anaesthetic tickled Jacob's nostrils. There was the dull beep of a heart monitor.

A nurse was standing at the end of the bed and flicking through his notes. He was young, only a few years older than Jacob, and Jacob could tell he was nervous. The nurse's quivering fingers fumbled at the pages.

'Surgery may be necessary if a pneumothorax is confirmed,' continued the nurse, 'but I can let you know about that when we receive the X-ray results later today. As you can see, Mr Yang can sit up straight without too much discomfort.'

'He can speak for himself too,' Yang growled. The nurse's face turned pink and he left the room quickly. Yang heaved himself up and groaned. Jacob could hear his pain.

'Mr Yang,' Jacob said. 'I'm so sorry this happened to you. It's my fault. If you hadn't put yourself between me and the river, I'd be dead.'

'Jacob,' Yang began. His voice was low and rough, like the sound of a sack of gravel dragged across concrete. Jacob was not certain whether that was due to discomfort or anger, but when Jacob looked at him, he saw that even though Yang's face was pale and ravaged by pain, there remained a slight glint in his black eyes. 'You and your sister saved my life from the Blue Spider Gang a week ago. It was my pleasure to return the favour.'

Jacob put his face in his hands.

'Anyway, I can think of far worse ways to return that favour than a few weeks of hospital food,' Yang went on. 'Isn't the launch at noon tomorrow? You should be halfway to Cornwall by now.'

'I'm not going to the Garden,' said Jacob.

Ignoring the pain, Yang swivelled to face him, eyes wide with outrage.

'I know I've just been incredibly gracious about it,' Yang said, 'but I didn't go all the way to Uganda to fetch you and then almost get myself killed – twice – just so you could go home again. The world needs

Transcendent and Transcendent needs you. Kira needs you.'

'Kira doesn't need me,' said Jacob.

'She needed you when we were fighting the Blue Spider Gang,' said Yang. 'Why would she not need you now?'

'That was different!' Jacob's head writhed from side to side in exasperation. 'Kira's chosen her path. I've chosen mine.'

'How is it different?' Yang asked.

'IT JUST IS!' Jacob bellowed.

Jacob suddenly realised he was standing. His fists were clenched. His shoulders were heaving. Yang stared up at him, thin eyebrows raised. Jacob stomped from the room without saying another word. He slammed the door shut behind him as he strode along the corridor towards the exit. Yang remained as he was, staring at the door. Something vibrated on his chest and he winced. With some difficulty, he reached into his bomber jacket and pulled out his RanaPhone. The rectangular screen was aglow with the incoming call. Yang tapped the small, green telephone and held the RanaPhone painfully to his ear.

'Mrs Flynn? Always a pleasure. I'm feeling fine, thank you. I know. I've just seen him. No, he was a delight. Of course. What can I do for you?'

CHAPTER
TWENTY-EIGHT

Jacob stepped out of Guy's Hospital and onto St Thomas Street, wiping the tears from his eyes. He pulled his hood over his head and yanked the cords tight to shield himself from the biting cold, hiding his raw, reddened eyes under its shadow. Jacob had planned what he was going to do that morning. The second Eunata closed his bedroom door, he had turned on his RanaPhone and opened Double M's video page. He needed answers and he knew the world's foremost online conspiracy theorist and suspected spy inside RanaTech would give them to him.

Jacob had not been surprised at how quickly he had been able to determine Double M's precise location using a tracking app he had developed with Kira. What *had* surprised him was the discovery that Double M's address was not only in London but just one tube journey away. Jacob slipped his RanaPhone from his pocket and swiped at it with his thumb, ignoring the raindrops that splashed on the waterproof screen. He tapped a few more times. The location was somewhere in South London. Jacob thrust the RanaPhone back into his pocket and headed towards the tube station.

It was time for answers.

Emerging from Tooting Bec tube station, Jacob thought the high street was a galaxy away from where the Shard resided. It was almost similar to a street in Mbale or Jinja, if not for the grey sky overhead that confirmed he was still very much in London. The fronts of shops laid their wares of all kinds on the pavement, from lady's fingers to mutton rolls. It was still bitterly cold but, away from the city centre, the air was much clearer. Jacob could see all the way to each end of the street and smell the fragrant scents of fresh vegetables and spices. Over the tops of the slanted, slate rooftops, Jacob could see the dark, pointed shapes of skyscrapers jutting out of a grey smudge of smog on the horizon.

Holding his RanaPhone in front of him like a Geiger counter, Jacob meandered along the pavement. He accidentally knocked his shoulder into a middle-aged woman wearing a colourful head wrap. She cried out in indignation.

'Sorry, aunty,' he mumbled and ducked into the nearest side street.

Jacob was surprised that someone as high-profile as

Double M was based in a place such as this but, he supposed, it was useful to lie low in their line of work. Jacob imagined an underground bunker underneath an Indian supermarket, filled with high-tech equipment and walls plastered with newspaper clippings and criss-crossing red tape.

However, as Jacob navigated the maze of leafy, residential streets, he became more and more perplexed. Eventually, he found himself in a dense council estate: the Powell Estate, according to a fading sign. There was a row of wispy trees sprouting from gaps in the concrete. Grey blocks of flats towered on either side. There was the faint beat of Bollywood music from a loudspeaker. He could smell butter chicken cooking somewhere.

There was the rattle of rock on concrete and Jacob turned to see a boy, no older than ten, sitting on a low wall. The boy was wearing a black tracksuit with white stripes down the arms and legs. A pigeon perched itself on the wall next to the boy. Its ruffled feathers were as grey as the ground, buildings and sky. Beady, orange eyes examined the boy, who calmly picked up another rock and threw it. He missed and the bird fluttered into the air. The boy watched it disappear over the stained satellite dishes on the roof of the nearest block of flats before turning to stare back at Jacob, who found himself reminded of Spider.

Tearing his eyes away from the boy, Jacob looked

down at his RanaPhone. The place he was looking for was right in front of him: Enoch Tower. Jogging up fourteen flights of a stairwell, he emerged onto a balcony overlooking the central square. There was a row of doors along the balcony, which was cluttered with bicycles, garden chairs and plant pots. Clothes had been hung over the railing to dry. Jacob hurried along the balcony until he found number 143. Already beginning to think that his and Kira's tracking app had made a mistake and he was at the wrong location, Jacob took a deep breath and knocked.

There was immediately a loud clatter from within the flat. Jacob leaned forward so his ear was closer to the door but he jumped back quickly when he heard heavy footsteps approaching.

The door swung open abruptly. A man in his late twenties was standing in the narrow hallway. He was a large man and breathing heavily, as if the dash to the front door was more exercise than he had done in a long time. The man was wearing a black T-shirt with a chain around his neck and studs in both ears. Wiry stubble dotted his round face and he was eyeing Jacob suspiciously.

'Can I help you?' His voice was startlingly high-pitched.

'I'm looking for Double M,' said Jacob, eyeing the man back.

'Ah.' The man gave Jacob two thumbs up and turned theatrically to face the corridor, cupping a hand to his mouth. 'Double M! Double M! There's a young man here to see you! Oh, wait a minute. That's me. Double M. Otherwise known as Mike Mendonca. Nice to meet you.'

Mike Mendonca sarcastically extended a hand to Jacob who, more cautious than ever, hesitated before shaking. Mike's grip engulfed not just Jacob's hand but much of his wrist.

'If you'd care to follow me into my humble abode?'

Mike turned and lumbered down the corridor into a shadowy living room, evidently expecting Jacob to follow. Jacob remained with his feet planted squarely on the tattered doormat, wondering whether it would be a good idea to follow this strange man into a dark and enclosed space. Was this really Double M, who had laid bare so many international conspiracies and leaked evidence of an alien invasion from the biggest technology conglomerate in the world?

'You coming in or what, bro?' Mike called from the living room.

Jacob made up his mind. He followed Mike inside but made the deliberate decision to leave the front door open.

Mike's living room was almost as tight and confined as the corridor. There was no light on. The room was only illuminated by the harsh, white glare of an episode of *Doctor Who* playing on an enormous television. Shelf upon shelf of Blu-ray discs lined the shadowy walls. Jacob recognised the Star Wars poster he had in his own bedroom, except Mike's was framed. Mike himself was sitting on a black sofa. It was difficult, especially in the gloom, to see where the man ended and the sofa began. Between the sofa and the television was a low coffee table. Empty drink cans littered both it and the sticky carpet.

'Sorry, I can't offer you anything,' said Mike. 'I don't usually have guests.'

'I would never have thought,' said Jacob, looking around for a place to sit. There was none so he stayed where he was. 'I'm here to find out everything you know about the Others.'

'Everything I know is already online,' said Mike absently, his eyes on the TV. 'If you want to find out more, wait for tomorrow's video. I still need to think about content.'

'What do you mean?' Jacob asked, alarmed.

'If you want to maintain a good online presence,' Mike yawned, 'it's all about regular postage. Everyone knows that.'

'No, what do you mean, "You still need to think about content"?'

'You think it's easy, coming up with a backstory that

dense?' Mike's eyes swivelled to look at him. 'It takes time, bro! The creature design took me so long, I didn't leave the yard for a month! I even had to swerve on Crochet Club.'

'I don't believe this,' murmured Jacob. His head was spinning, and it was not because of the reek of energy drinks.

'It's every week at Tooting Library.' Mike frowned. 'What, you don't believe man can crochet?'

'The Others – you really made it all up?'

'Of course I made it all up. Most of the stuff on the Internet is made up. You think anyone actually looks like they do in their pictures?'

'But . . . but you've exposed some of the biggest scandals in the world! There was that oil company dumping waste in the Amazon rainforest! That princess caught selling black market arms! You're telling me you made all of it up?'

'No, of course not.' Mike shrugged. 'Sometimes, I steal things from other people. Do you know how many people get their update on current affairs from my videos rather than legitimate news sites? It's crazy. The trouble is, there's too much content out there. My views have been flagging recently, what with so much competition. I invented the Others story to keep things spicy. And you know what, bro? It worked! My numbers have skyrocketed!'

'The Others . . . really aren't real?'

Mike spoke to Jacob just as Amira had – as if Jacob were a small child.

'No. The Others aren't real.'

Jacob needed to sit down. Mike made no indication that he was prepared to make space for him on the sofa so he squatted where he was, holding his head in his hands.

'I thought Double M was a spy leaking information from inside RanaTech.'

'You thought I was a spy?' Mike's eyes turned from the television to look at Jacob again. He was smirking. 'A spy who opens their front door and says, "Can I help you?"'

Jacob looked up.

'Why, though? Why do you spend so much time posting lies on the Internet?'

Mike shrugged, looking at the television again.

'Because the real world is big and scary and, sometimes, a made-up world is the only one that makes sense.'

'But how could you make up something so horrific?'

'Well, for the design of the Others themselves, I lifted some elements from H. R. Giger's Xenomorph. There's a bit of M. R. James in there too but mostly it's because I don't like spiders.'

Jacob stood up quickly, shaking his head in incredulity.

'I don't believe this,' he said again.

'Seriously, it's the way they scuttle across the floor. It gives man the heebie-jeebies.'

'No,' Jacob said through gritted teeth. 'It's not that I don't believe you don't like spiders. I don't believe I've made a fool of myself in front of the wealthiest woman in the world by rambling about an imaginary alien invasion invented by a man in jogging bottoms. I almost killed someone in a high-speed car chase and now my sister is leaving the actual planet tomorrow lunchtime and I don't know when I'll ever see her again!'

Mike stared up at him, astonished.

'OK, bro, as backstories go, that one's a little far-fetched.'

'I'm leaving.' Jacob turned and strode from the living room.

'Make sure you get your sister to like and subscribe before she goes into space!' Mike shouted after him as Jacob slammed the door.

CHAPTER TWENTY-NINE

When Jacob returned to the Shard that afternoon, he undressed and collapsed into bed and did not move for more than twelve hours. His body was still but his head was a confused battlefield of rage, grief and embarrassment. Kira had promised to stand by his side but had betrayed him, running away with Sakari and Lulu to join Transcendent. He had been certain the Others had been real, a nefarious conspiracy with Amira pulling the strings, but it had all been a lie.

Rage. Grief. Embarrassment. Jacob did not know which would emerge victorious. All he knew was that he felt defeated. And he wanted to go home.

He was awoken the next morning by the pulsing buzz of a RanaPhone. In an attempt to pull on a T-shirt, he realised, in his bleary daze, that he was twisting his arm through a pair of dirty boxer shorts. *Surely*, he thought, *this is rock bottom.*

Tangled in his underwear and following the sound, Jacob rummaged through the sheets and found the RanaPhone buried underneath his pillow. He pulled the boxer shorts from his head and hurled them into the corner of his bedroom. He held up the RanaPhone in front of his face, blinking stupidly in its white light. The time read as a few minutes to eight o'clock. The launch was at noon. There were just over four hours until Kira was going to launch into space. Jacob tapped the small, green telephone.

'Yeah?'

'Still in bed, are we? At least I've got an excuse.' Yang's scowling face filled the screen.

'How are you feeling?' mumbled Jacob.

'My X-ray results came back yesterday afternoon. My lung is completely fine so I've been advised to stay in bed for a few weeks while my ribs heal. That's actually why I called. I was wondering if you could do me a favour. I've left my watch in my office.'

'Your watch? Isn't there a clock in your room?'

'My watch does more than tell the time,' said Yang.

Jacob understood. What Yang called a watch was his Oracle Mark I.

'Would you mind fetching it for me?' Yang asked. 'I'm getting tired of hospital TV and I've got a holographic recording of *The Best of the West End* at the Royal Albert Hall I've been meaning to rewatch.'

'I didn't know you were into show tunes,' Jacob frowned.

'Oh, yes. I've seen *The Lion King* three times.'

Jacob dressed and made his way unhurriedly from his bedroom to the lift. There was no need to rush. Eunata would be back from Cornwall the next day and then they would go back to Uganda together.

Yang's office was four floors below the Lounge. When Jacob emerged from the lift, he was suddenly amidst a throng of smartly dressed people hurrying past him in every direction. This floor had the same slanted windows as the Lounge but the ceiling was lower and, instead of leather sofas and decorative shrubbery, was filled with rows and rows of desks. The smoky mass of smog outside was growing paler under the rising sun. The people sitting at the desks were gazing blankly at paper-thin computer screens. There was the soft clatter of fingers on keyboards.

Yang's desk was not part of the open plan but behind a frosted glass door, stencilled with his job title, HEAD OF SECURITY. Jacob pushed the door open with the palm of his hand. No one questioned him as he slipped inside and closed the door behind him. The office itself was small and Jacob could barely stretch out both hands without touching the walls. He wondered how Yang, gigantic man that he was, squeezed inside it every day. The walls were painted white and undecorated, apart from one small, square canvas that was entirely painted black. There was a computer on the large walnut desk and nothing else, not even a speck of dust.

'No way has this guy seen *The Lion King* three times,' Jacob muttered.

He edged around the desk and rolled a gigantic, leather office chair out of the way. Underneath was a chest of drawers. Jacob pulled each of them out in turn. It was only when he opened the bottom one that he saw a small, glass disc on a black, leather strap, placed neatly on top of a stack of papers. Yang's Oracle.

As Jacob bent down and stretched his hand into the drawer, he heard the door of the office open and close. There was someone in there with him. Apprehensively, Jacob raised his head over the walnut desk to see who it was.

Doctor Arianna Shaw, the austere woman who had supervised the trials for Transcendent, was looming like a white gargoyle over the other side of the desk. Even with it between them, Jacob and Shaw were uncomfortably close. He could almost see up her nostrils, which were flaring as if there were a nasty smell in the room.

'Jacob Flynn,' she said. 'I've been expecting you.'

'But I was here first,' said Jacob, bemused.

Shaw looked down at her RanaTab, which had been clasped to her breast.

'I haven't got long this morning,' she remarked, hand scuttling across the screen, 'and I would quite like a seat.'

Jacob stared at Shaw awkwardly for a moment, not knowing how to respond to this, before realising that he was standing between her and Yang's chair.

'Oh, right,' he said and the two of them swapped places, shuffling past opposite ends of the desk. Shaw did not look up from the RanaTab as she sat down. Perched in Yang's enormous chair, the small woman looked like a child shrivelled in vinegar. Her feet in her pointed, white shoes did not touch the floor. At last, she looked up and squinted at him.

'Put that on the desk.'

'Put wha— oh.'

Jacob looked down and saw he was still clutching Yang's Oracle. He lay it flat on the polished wood between Shaw and himself. Shaw's hand scurried across the RanaTab even more furiously. The Oracle began to emit a high-pitched whine and glow with its eerie, white light. Seconds later, a hologram burst into being over the desk and filled the cramped office with a revolving, three-dimensional image of what looked like a sleek, white pencil. It took Jacob a moment to realise what he was actually looking at.

'Archangel 1 is a two-stage-to-orbit medium-lift launch vehicle that, at noon today,' Shaw looked at her own watch, 'which is in under four hours' time, will carry Kira and the other members of Transcendent to the Garden in low Earth orbit. Archangel 2, a second rocket, will launch a few hours later, bringing with it equipment and supplies.'

From the outside, the slowly revolving image appeared remarkably simple. Archangel 1 could have been designed by a child. It was assembled out of two sections or 'stages'. The first stage was a long, tubular section at the base of the rocket. The second stage was a smaller, bulbous section on top. If not for the fact that the hologram was slightly translucent and Jacob could see its nine engines, aluminium-lithium alloy tanks and absurdly complex jumble of inner workings and machinery, it would have been impossible to imagine the contraption in front of him being capable of blasting itself into space.

'It's magnificent,' Jacob breathed.

'It is,' replied Shaw. 'It's a shame you won't be on it. Why is that, may I ask? Why, as one of only five people on the planet selected for a program in which RanaTech has invested hundreds of hours and millions of pounds, have you suddenly decided it's . . . not for you?'

Jacob looked away from the rocket, not enjoying the accusatory tone of Shaw's voice.

'Transcendent's not what I thought it was.'

'And what did you think it was? Not, I presume, a daring initiative to unite the greatest minds of the young generation with the technology and resources to prevent the coming catastrophe caused by climate change and the destruction of our natural environment?'

'No,' said Jacob. 'I thought it was something to do with an alien invasion by a race of creatures called the Others.'

Shaw raised her eyebrows, pointed like arrow heads.

'Pardon me? Can you repeat that, please?'

'I thought it was something to do with an alien invasion by a race of creatures called the Others.'

'Thank you. I heard you the first time. I just wanted you to say that again so you could hear how utterly idiotic it sounds.'

Jacob let out an exasperated sigh.

'Are you trying to make me feel stupid?' he asked, struggling to keep his voice level. 'Because it's working. I'm already aware I've made a big mistake.'

'I'm certainly not trying to make you feel stupid,' said Shaw briskly. 'It's perfectly natural for us, as humans, to bury our heads in fantasy rather than accepting the responsibility that lies at our feet. That fantasy often manifests as the blaming of our own problems on . . . imaginary Others. It's something that's occurred throughout human history. You are not the first person to make that mistake and, I assure you,

you will not be the last. Case in point. I understand these Others of yours featured quite prominently in your Oracle Mark II simulation.'

'Yes.' Jacob shuddered.

Shaw's gnarled hand scampered across the RanaTab and the revolving image of Archangel 1 switched to high-resolution footage of Jacob's second trial. Jacob watched himself jerking in the pilot seat of the spaceplane, smoke and sparks billowing and cascading around him. Kira tumbled into the cockpit and threw herself into the seat next to him. Even though the hologram was silent, Jacob could see the holographic versions of himself and his sister bellowing at each other.

'The scenario used for your second trial was constructed using readings from the amygdala in your brain,' said Shaw. 'Put simply, it was the situation identified as the one to cause you the most possible distress.'

'Yes, my worst fear,' muttered Jacob. 'The Others.'

'Ah.'

Jacob's stomach clenched. The hologram had flicked to an image of an Other's face, leering out of the dark. Coarse hairs bristled on end. Small but sharp teeth oozed and glistened with alien saliva. Green eyes blazed with lividly black pupils.

'Everything inside the Oracle looked so real,' Jacob

muttered. 'It *felt* so real. I was convinced the Others really existed.'

'Didn't your mother ever tell you not to believe everything you see online?' Shaw asked.

Jacob did not answer. He was still gazing at the hairy face of the Other, forcing himself to remember the alien beast was not, and had never been, real.

'Here comes my point,' Shaw continued. 'Do you truly believe the scenario presented to you by the Oracle, your "worst fear" as you put it, was an attack by these "Others"?'

'What else could it have been?'

'Tell me what happened.'

'I was flying some sort of suborbital spaceplane. It was shot down by the Others and crash-landed. An Other attacked me. Actually, it did more than that. It nearly killed me. I had to fight it off.'

'What happened before that?'

'Well . . .' Jacob began.

He did not have to continue. The hologram projected from the Oracle on the desk was playing it out in front of him. Jacob watched as he and Kira charged out of the cockpit and into the corridor. They were screaming at each other. The holographic version of himself fell and cut his hand. The corridor shook as one of its walls was ripped away. Kira looked at Jacob and said something before she too was torn out of the corridor and flung out of sight. Watching it happen again made the non-holographic version of Jacob feel like his stomach and all his insides had been wrenched out of him, just like Kira had been from the plane.

'Kira,' he murmured. 'I lost Kira.'

'And there we have it,' Shaw said softly. 'That was the scenario the interface chose to present to you. Your worst fear was never the Others. The fact that the Others were part of the simulation is simply because the interface lifted them from your subconscious. Your actual worst fear, what drives you, what this has all been about from the very beginning, was never the Others. It was . . .'

'Losing my sister,' Jacob whispered.

'And,' Shaw glanced at her watch again, 'in what is now less than four hours, your sister will blast off in Archangel 1 and leave you behind. So, what are you going to do about it?'

Jacob dived forward and snatched Yang's Oracle from the polished surface of the desk, jamming it in his pocket. The hologram was extinguished instantly. Shaw blinked up at him in the suddenly darkened room.

'Thank you, Doctor Shaw,' Jacob said. 'I know exactly what I'm going to do.'

Jacob closed the door of Yang's office and sprinted to the stairs, taking them two at a time. Shaw did not smile but the wrinkles around her tightened mouth loosened slightly. She waited for the glass door to finish shuddering on its hinges before she reached inside her white blazer with thin, withered fingers and pulled out a RanaPhone. She tapped a few times and held it shakily to her ear.

'Yang?' Shaw croaked. 'I've done what you asked. I've spoken to the boy.'

'Thank you,' came the reply. 'Now we can only hope his mother will leave me alone.'

Yang had just placed his RanaPhone on the bedside table when Jacob burst into the hospital room with a rucksack thrown over his shoulder. Jacob was grinning. He hurled the Oracle and Yang caught it. It landed with a smack in his huge palm. The nurse was fiddling with the heart monitor, which continued its regular, monotonous beeping.

'I'm going to see Kira before the launch,' Jacob panted. 'I still don't want anything to do with Transcendent but I want to see her before she goes. We can't leave things the way we have.'

'That's excellent, Jacob,' said Yang as encouragingly as he could while sitting up in a hospital bed with a black eye swelling the right side of his face. 'But the launch is in three and a half hours. How are you going to get there in time?'

Jacob thought for a moment. He had not considered that.

'I'm going to get the train,' he said firmly.

'These days, the train won't get you there before tomorrow.' Yang rolled his eyes. 'I'll drive you.'

'I don't think that's advisable, Mr Yang.' The nurse straightened from the heart monitor.

'Try and stop me,' Yang growled. He hurled the thin blanket from the bed, already fully dressed in his black bomber jacket, shirt and trousers. His face contorted in a grimace of agony, he swung each tree trunk of a leg from the bed and slipped his bare feet into his black leather boots without touching the vinyl floor.

'Mr Yang!' The nurse flapped around him. 'You have multiple fractured ribs! If they do not heal properly, it could lead to internal injury to your lungs and build-up of fluid in your chest cavity!'

'Hakuna matata,' Yang groaned as he stood up.

'You *have* seen it!' Jacob exclaimed in thrilled amazement.

CHAPTER
THIRTY

There were three hours until the launch. Kira had not slept in over twenty-four.

The night of training at RanaTech Spaceflight's launch facility had been gruelling. There had been virtual simulations using the unnervingly realistic Oracle Mark II but also physical simulations, including several hours floating underwater in a gigantic swimming pool along with a submerged, life-sized model or 'mock-up' of the Garden. Kira was exhausted. Even so, Eunata had demanded to know how the three girls could possibly be expected to launch into space with so little training. Professor Kowalski, the sweating, balding man in a white coat who seemed to be overseeing proceedings, explained.

'Well, ma'am, adolescent bodies are simply more adaptable than adult bodies and are much more adept at handling the shock of the journey. The fact also remains that space travel is much more efficient than it was ten years ago. Of course, I would advise all three members of Transcendent to continue to take virtual training sessions onboard the Garden. For now, however, there is actually very little preparation needed.'

The three girls, Eunata and Kowalski were standing on the third floor of the Launch Control Centre. One of the walls was entirely glass and offered an impressive view of the launch facility. A patchwork of yellowing grass and grey concrete stretched to a hilly horizon. The air in Cornwall was cleaner than in London but the sky was the same ashen grey. A short distance away from the Launch Control Centre was a raised square. The launch pad. Next to it stood a two-hundred-foot steel fixed service structure. Attached to the top of the service structure by a narrow walkway and towering up from the launch pad was Archangel 1. Kira gazed at the gleaming, white rocket with mingled awe and terror.

At the same time, fragments of memories of watching a smaller model version shoot into a blue sky before exploding in a shower of flame and plastic tubing flashed in her mind like sunlight on steel. Kira cast them forcefully from her head.

Why was she not deliriously excited about what was about to happen? There was only a weighty feeling of intense dread, deep in the pit of her stomach, dragging her down like the anchor of a ship. Why? What was wrong? What was missing?

Without thinking about what she was doing, Kira pulled her RanaPhone from her back pocket, switched it on and scrolled through it until she found the contact, ORANGUTAN. It was when Kowalski called her name that she realised what she had done.

'Kira! Remember what I told you at the briefing. Mobile phones interfere with the equipment and need to be switched off. We will make our way to the launch area now. Archangel 1 launches in less than three hours' time.'

Kira dropped her RanaPhone back into her pocket. She looked at Sakari and Lulu and did her best to return their smiles of encouragement – but she understood now what was wrong. Transcendent was everything she had ever wanted but, if she left things the way she had with Jacob, there would always be something missing.

And now it was too late. In less than three hours, she was going to be catapulted into space and leave her brother behind.

CHAPTER
THIRTY-ONE

The cold light of the sun glared through gaps in the grey clouds that rushed over the Cherokee as it passed through Exeter on its way to Cornwall. Jacob was pleased to see fields for the first time since leaving Uganda but they were nowhere near as lush and vibrant as the ones he was used to. Thin patches of yellow grass clawed their way from stony and litter-strewn earth. Leafless trees waved their spindly fingers at the Cherokee as it thundered along the motorway. The majority of traffic in both directions were lorries, hauling shipping containers of goods in and out of London. The Cherokee careered from lane to lane to slip between the slower, more cumbersome vehicles, a speedboat overtaking ocean liners.

'There's only two and a half hours left till noon,' Yang said. 'Did you try calling them again?'

'They're not picking up their phones!' Jacob cried,

exasperated. 'I've called them both a hundred times. Can't you contact someone at RanaTech?'

'I've already said there's nothing I can do to stop the launch, Jacob. We can only hope we get there in time.'

Yang was clearly in a great deal of discomfort but doing his best to hide it. Every time he needed to yank the gear lever, he grunted in pain. Jacob could see beads of sweat collecting on his temple.

As the hours drew on, Yang's condition grew worse. It reached half past ten. An hour and a half until launch. Eleven o'clock. One hour till launch. When it was ten past eleven and the map on Yang's RanaPhone assured them there was still an hour's journey left, Yang gave in. He gasped suddenly and the Cherokee swerved. There was a squeal of tyres. A lorry driver behind them blew his horn angrily.

'I can't do this anymore,' Yang wheezed. 'I need to rest for a while.'

'No!' Jacob shouted, slapping his hand on the dashboard. 'There's only fifty minutes left! We're nearly there!'

'I can't do it, Jacob.'

'Can't I drive?'

'I don't think that's a good idea after what happened in London. Do you?'

Jacob looked desperately at Yang's huge bulk, crammed into the driver's seat. The man's entire form was shaking. He was pale, gaunt and blinking through the sweat that was pouring down his face.

'OK,' said Jacob. 'I'm sorry. We can pull over here.'

The Cherokee veered off the motorway and into the empty car park of a service station. One of the letters on the sign above the petrol station was missing and the window of the fast-food restaurant next-door was smashed. Lorries, dragging their battered shipping containers, roared past in both directions.

'I'm sorry,' panted Yang as he slowed the Cherokee to a jerky halt in one of the bays.

'Don't apologise,' said Jacob, trying his best not to sound frustrated. 'You're helping me even though I crashed a car into you and broke several of your ribs. I'm the one who owes you.'

'Well, now you mention it . . .' Yang managed a weak smile. 'I could really do with a cold banana milkshake.'

Jacob hurried back from the restaurant with the milkshakes and they sat for a while in the front of the Cherokee, slurping on the straws. All the time, Jacob's eyes were on the hills on the distant horizon and on the sun, blinking through the leaden clouds at nearly the height of its arc.

'Your mother was right, you know,' Yang said.

'What do you mean?' Jacob asked.

'She was right about the Blue Spider Gang. What happened in Uganda was RanaTech's fault. We blundered in and built a skyscraper on top of their city with no thought as to the consequences.'

'You blamed the gang for your own problem,' Jacob said.

'Yes,' nodded Yang. 'Just because they were different.'

'Mama always says we need to solve our problems together,' said Jacob, 'despite our differences.'

'She's a clever lady, your mama.'

'Yeah.'

Yang grunted and Jacob looked over. He had placed Yang's banana milkshake in a cup holder by the driver's seat. Yang was attempting to reach it but struggling. His hand was shaking, his face contorted in torment. He was able to lift his arms but not twist his body. With another grunt of frustration, he gave up and sat back in the leather seat, gasping for air.

'I got it,' said Jacob.

Jacob put his own milkshake down and picked up Yang's, lifting it to the man's quivering lips so he could drink. When Yang was finished, Jacob put the milkshake back in the cup holder.

'Thank you, Jacob,' said Yang, wiping his mouth.

'No problem, Gus,' said Jacob.

'You know,' said Yang. 'The ache's starting to go away. I think we can give it ten more minutes and I'll be good to go again. If we hurry it up, we should make it before—'

There was a light so blindingly bright, it sucked all the grey from the road and sky. The rumble of a hurricane reverberated through the very ground, causing shockwaves to ripple across the yellow grass and the Cherokee to shake beneath them. A piercing pain stabbed into Jacob's ears and he covered them with his hands. Through the windscreen, he saw what looked like a sleek, white pencil rising out of a billowing cloud of smoke and blazing light on the horizon. Jacob watched in horror as the pencil climbed higher, higher and higher, penetrating the upper atmosphere as effortlessly as a bullet fired up through water.

They were too late. Archangel 1 was on its way to the Garden, and so was Kira.

CHAPTER
THIRTY-TWO

'We should get moving, Jacob.'

Jacob said nothing. It had been fifteen minutes since Archangel 1 had disappeared beyond the clouds. It was as if the rocket launch had never happened. Lorries thundered up and down the motorway. A plastic bag rolled on the breeze like tumbleweed. Jacob was bent forward. His forehead was on the dashboard and his eyes were closed. Tears quivered on his cheeks just as his clenched fists quivered in his lap.

'We missed her,' Jacob said quietly. 'Who knows when I'll see her again after this.'

Yang sighed and placed his hands on the Cherokee's steering wheel.

'If I'd been faster,' he muttered, 'we could have made it in time.'

'No,' sniffed Jacob, leaning back and resting his head against the seat. 'This is all my fault. It couldn't have happened any other way. Let's just go back to London.'

Yang ignited the engine and slammed his foot on the accelerator. The Cherokee leaped out of the bay and he wrenched the steering wheel, sweeping the car back onto the motorway. However, Yang did not point the Cherokee back the way they had come but continued in the direction in which they had been heading, towards the RanaTech facility.

'What are you doing?' Jacob demanded. 'I told you I don't want to go any further. I'm not going anywhere near RanaTech if Kira's not there.'

'I think your mama would be happier if I brought you straight to her,' said Yang.

They drove for almost another hour. Aside from the rocket that had just blasted into the sky, it was hard to imagine that the rolling, desolate fields and dead trees were the location of a multi-million-pound launch facility. Eventually, they saw a large sign reading RANATECH SPACEFLIGHT. The Cherokee circled a roundabout and approached a security gate, with two sets of tall, barbed wire fences a few yards apart and stretching away in both directions. The Cherokee slowed next to the window of a hut, inside which a security guard was sitting and staring at his RanaPhone. He was wearing a white, sweaty collared shirt and a baseball cap with the RanaTech logo stitched onto it.

'Show him your pass,' said Yang.

When Jacob's only response was stubborn silence, Yang's black eyes threw him a dangerous glare. Jacob reached into his pocket and pulled out the Transcendent identification pass that Yang had handed to all the candidates during the briefing beneath the Shard. Jacob thrust the pass irritably at the guard, who inspected it, eyeing them both with suspicion. The guard picked up a telephone and muttered into it, so quietly that they could not hear. After a few minutes of sitting in front of the security gate, another black Jeep Cherokee, identical to the one Yang was driving, rolled into view on the other side. The gate shuddered open.

'Follow them.' The guard jerked a thumb and returned to his RanaPhone.

'Thank you,' said Yang.

The two Cherokees drove in procession into the RanaTech Spaceflight launch facility. The complex was flat with vast areas of grass and concrete that stretched into the distance in every direction. They drove for at least two miles, passing only a few low buildings before coming to a three-storey structure with a sign outside it reading LAUNCH CONTROL CENTRE. The two Cherokees parked, one in front of the other, and Jacob watched a RanaTech operative in a dark suit and sunglasses step out of the one in front. Jacob and Yang glanced at each other before getting out of their own Cherokee and following him into the building.

They walked through a spacious reception area and up a stairwell to the third floor, emerging onto a wide corridor. One of the walls was entirely glass. The sun was high in the sky now and Jacob could see its white glare where the grey clouds thinned overhead. Beams of light slanted down onto the flat patchwork that stretched all the way to a jagged horizon. Walking up to the window and pressing his hands and face against it, Jacob looked down at a raised, square area a short distance away. Next to it towered a two-hundred-foot steel fixed service structure. Jacob guessed he was looking at a launch pad, perhaps the one from which he had seen Archangel 1 launch an hour previously.

'What on Earth are you doing here?'

There was the sound of hurrying footsteps on the concrete floor and Jacob turned to see Amira Rana, dressed in a red and gold sari, and Professor Kowalski scurrying at her heels. Charging ahead of both of them was Eunata. Jacob's mother stopped a few feet away and glared at him with her hands on her hips. At the sight of her, however, all of Jacob's stubbornness melted away and he threw his arms around her, hugging her more tightly than he ever had in his life. He was so pleased to see her, he almost scooped her from the floor.

'Mama!' Jacob whispered in her ear. 'I'm sorry. I'm so, so, sorry for everything.'

'If you've come to drop off Kira's toothbrush,' Amira

said in her low drawl, finger pointed upwards, 'I'm afraid you're a little late.'

'I asked you what you are doing here,' said Eunata, releasing herself from her son and ignoring Amira.

'I came to see Kira before she went, Mama,' Jacob explained, 'but we were too late.'

Eunata nodded. Her cheeks were flushed due to the tightness of her son's grip. 'You came to stand with your sister despite your differences. I am proud of you.'

'It's no good now though, is it, Mama? Kira's gone and who knows when I'll see her again.'

'Kira has chosen her path, but what about you?' asked Eunata. 'There is one way you can see your sister again very soon. You know what that is.'

Jacob shook his head. He walked away from his mother and towards the window. Eunata, Amira, Yang and Kowalski stood together and watched him.

'I want no part of Transcendent, Mama,' said Jacob. 'Why not?'

'I was wrong about the Others,' said Jacob, smiling grimly. 'I admit that. I've never been more wrong about anything in my life. But that doesn't change the fact that Transcendent is not what I thought it was. It's not what I signed up for. I signed up to save the world.'

'What do you think Kira and your friends are going to be doing up there on the Garden?' Eunata asked scornfully. 'Did you listen to anything Amira said? Have you been listening to anything I have said to you your entire life? How many times have I told you? The natural world must be defended. Here is the greatest chance anyone will have to do just that and you are turning your back on it.'

'I know it's important, Mama, but the thing is—'

'You say you want to save the world!' Eunata nearly shouted. Her voice was shaking, as if she were on the verge of tears. 'What greater chance do you have than this? Think about what Amira said! Climate change caused by humanity's misuse of its environment is going to bring catastrophe to every person on this planet, no matter who they are, where they live or what they look like! It will bring the greatest disaster our civilisation has ever seen and it is going to happen sooner than any of us ever thought possible, within the lifetime of a child alive right now, Jacob!'

'Mama, I—'

'You cannot live in your fantasy world forever, Jacob! You say you want to save the world. Well, saving the world is not about jumping off rooftops, big car chases or space invasions. Saving the world does not just happen in books. In reality, everyone has the chance to save the world every single day. Here is your chance. Are you going to take it?'

Jacob said nothing. He looked out of the window, past the launch pad and at the shafts of sunlight, slanting down from the clouds rolling over the rugged hills and casting vast, swirling shadows on the yellowing grass.

'Quite a speech,' said Amira. There was a conflicted expression on her face, as if opposing sides of her personality were bubbling together in a volatile chemical mixture.

'I said it before and I'll say it again,' said Yang. 'Your mama is a clever lady.'

Jacob nodded, still gazing out of the window.

'Send me up,' he said quietly.

'What was that, Jacob?' Eunata asked.

'I said, "Send me up,"' said Jacob louder. He turned from the window to face Amira and Kowalski. 'I want to rejoin Transcendent. Is it possible?'

'How?' Amira cleared her throat, then added in her usual drawl, 'We don't have spare rockets lying around, you know.'

'There's always Archangel 2,' offered Kowalski. 'That launches in two hours.'

'There's an Archangel 2?' remarked Amira in mild surprise.

CHAPTER
THIRTY-THREE

Jacob was thrust back into the Cherokee and sped to the Operations and Checkout Building. There, he was made to shower, attached with an EKG and biosensor leads and given a Phenergan injection. All the time, Professor Kowalski was babbling away while Eunata watched on anxiously.

'Archangel 1 and 2 have been developed by RanaTech and are the first ever two-stage rockets to use biodiesel derived from a particular strain of algae as a propellant and are therefore completely carbon-neutral.'

Jacob was given a headset and dressed in a blue tracksuit with an excessive number of pockets and zips. JACOB FLYNN, TRANSCENDENT was stitched onto the chest. Scientists were bustling around Jacob, wiring him up and barking random pieces of information at him.

'The lack of gravity stretches the spine so don't be alarmed if you come back taller.'

'A condition called atrophy may mean your muscles and bones will weaken. You just don't need them in space.'

'All your bodily fluids will float to the top of your body. Don't panic if your legs become skinnier and your head puffs up a little.'

'For every action, there is an equal and opposite reaction,' Kowalski was saying as straps were tucked underneath Jacob's feet to hold his trousers in place.

'Isaac Newton's third law of motion,' Jacob panted, suddenly light-headed. He was in a daze, blissfully desensitised to the fact that he was getting closer and closer to something that should have been filling him with a horror unlike anything else he had ever imagined.

'Very good, Jacob. When the biodiesel enters the combustion chambers of the rocket, it's ignited which causes it to expand with lots of energy. This energy is forced down which, in turn, forces the rocket up. All you will need to do is sit still and hold tight. You don't need to control anything. The entire docking procedure is automated. It will take nine minutes for Archangel 2 to leave the Earth's atmosphere and it will dock autonomously with the Garden in less than two hours.'

Before Jacob knew what was happening, he was back in the Cherokee alongside Eunata and Kowalski and driving onto the launch complex.

He just about heard someone say, 'We are now entering the Blast Danger Area,' and then the Cherokee was going up the ramp towards the raised launchpad. Archangel 2 loomed. Jacob leaned forward, craning his neck. He was reminded of standing at the foot of the Shard and looking up. Next to the rocket was the equally tall, criss-crossing steel framework of the fixed service structure. Jacob knew the structure was connected to the capsule by a gantry two hundred feet from the ground but its sheer height, as well as the sunlight glaring through the gaps in the clouds, meant it was impossible to see. All Jacob could see of Archangel 2 was a monumental, white cylinder towering into the sky. Out of the open window, he could hear cascading water and steam gushing out of the rocket in harsh huffs and puffs. There was the unwieldy groan of metal as if it were a struggle to hold everything in place. The rocket was alive. Jacob still felt numb to the insanity of what was happening. He could see it and hear it. He just could not quite believe it.

'Do you need a bio break?' Kowalski asked as they got out of the Cherokee.

'What?' asked Jacob. His own voice sounded far away.

'Do you need to use the bathroom?'

'Only if I'm allowed to throw up.'

The three of them stepped into a lift, which rushed to the top of the fixed service structure. There seemed to be an empty pit where Jacob's stomach should have been. It was as if he had left it on the ground. They stepped out of the lift and Jacob suddenly realised that Kowalski was speaking to him. He was explaining that the gantry connecting the fixed service structure to the rocket was called the crew access arm. He also unhelpfully reminded Jacob that it would be the last place he would stand on Earth before stepping into the capsule that would carry him into space. Jacob looked at the view to distract himself.

'It's time for ingress,' came Kowalski's voice.

'What does that mean?'

'It means it's time to get in the rocket.'

The capsule was surprisingly spacious and reminded Jacob of the spaceplane cockpit inside the Oracle, except everything was white and clean. His seat was facing upwards so he was lying on his back with his feet in the air. People wearing black full-body suits were leaning over him and buckling him in so tightly that he found it difficult to breathe. He could move his head and arms but nothing else. There were small windows on either side but they were covered with dark material. There were no controls, only a tilted screen attached to the ceiling above his head. As the people in suits left the capsule, Jacob strained to turn his neck to the left to see Eunata and Kowalski, peering sideways at him through the circular hatch.

'You will hear the countdown to launch over the radio,' said Kowalski. 'There have been a few hiccups with our ground network so you may not be able to hear us for a while once you enter low Earth orbit. Don't worry about a thing, though, Jacob. The docking procedure is completely automated. Whatever happens on the ground, once the rocket has been launched, nothing can stop it from reaching the Garden.'

Kowalski stood back, allowing Eunata to lean through the hatch. His words had not filled Jacob with confidence.

'I will see you when you are back, mtoto,' whispered Eunata. 'I am so proud of you both. Remember that always.'

Jacob looked at his mother but did not say anything. He could not have said anything even if he had wanted to. Terror had tightened the muscles in his face and clamped his mouth shut. He just stared at her helplessly.

'It's time to go,' said Kowalski, using both arms to heave the hatch closed, causing Eunata to step back. Jacob caught one last look at his mother's face before it slammed shut. He heard the hatch seal and felt the air inside the capsule compress. Everything was silent for a long time. Then he heard a sharp crackle through his headset, making him jump.

'T-minus thirty.'

He had thirty minutes until he was going to be launched into space.

*

After being driven back to the Launch Control Centre, Kowalski led Eunata into a concrete room on the ground floor that looked like a vast auditorium, only instead of seats there were rows of desks and computers. Around a hundred scientists were sitting, whispering to each other and pointing at intricate charts and launch data. On giant screens hanging at the front of the room were multiple live shots of Archangel 2 at various angles. Eunata knew exactly where she was. She had seen it plenty of times in films. She was standing in Mission Control.

Amira was hovering by the front row of desks, conspicuous in her red and gold sari in the sea of men and women in white coats. She had her arms folded and looked as if she did not quite know, or care, what she was doing there.

Kowalski bent down to speak in hushed tones with an engineer at one of the computers. Eunata approached Amira while gazing up at the images of Archangel 2 with a mixture of awe and sadness. There were tears in Eunata's eyes. Steam puffed from the rocket's gleaming, white body as it towered into the sky. It already seemed to be piercing the clouds without even leaving the ground.

'He'll be fine, Eunata.' Amira glanced at her absently. 'They both will.'

'You had better hope so,' said Eunata, dabbing her

eyes. 'Otherwise you are going to wish you had been strapped to that rocket.'

Amira turned and looked at Eunata with a strange look on her face. It was as if something were occurring to her for the very first time.

Sitting inside the capsule, alone and in silence, the reality of Jacob's situation was also sinking in for the very first time.

'T-minus twenty.'

There was a big part of him, the part he would usually have listened to, that wanted to scream and cry, to tear at his buckles. He would explain to Amira that he had changed his mind. He would get back into that Cherokee and tell Yang to drive him away as fast as he could.

'T-minus ten. Displays are configured for launch.'

They would drive back to London and get on the first plane back to Uganda. He would get back under his bed covers and never leave them again.

'T-minus seven. Pre-valves are open.'

But that was just one part of Jacob and he did not listen to it. A small part of him answered with an even bigger voice. His family was his responsibility. His planet was his responsibility. Jacob could not turn back. There was work that needed doing.

'T-minus six. Engine chill has started.'

Now he had six minutes until he was going to be launched into space. How had twenty-four minutes passed so quickly? Time seemed to have warped, stretching itself thin like a chewed string of bubble gum.

'T-minus five. Fuel load is complete.'

Jacob heard something that turned his blood cold. He jerked in his seat, looking around in a panic. Something was rumbling far beneath him.

'T-minus three.'

What had happened to T-minus four?

'T-minus two.'

'T-minus one. We are go for launch.'

'T-minus ten seconds.'

'Nine.'

'Eight.'

'Seven.'

'Six.'

'Five.'

'Four.'

'Three.'

'Two.'

'One.'

'Zero.'

It started as a light tremor that grew rapidly into an all-consuming quake. Jacob heard the clamps holding the rocket releasing. It got worse. It felt as if a giant had grabbed hold of the capsule with both hands and was shaking it furiously. Jacob closed his eyes but it did not help. His teeth rattled. He could feel his brain vibrating inside his head. His eyeballs were being squeezed out of his skull like purée from a tube. The noise was getting louder and louder and there was a high-pitched whine inside his ears as the roar of the engines deafened him. The rocket was rising. The raw power of its thrust crushed Jacob into the back of his seat. G-force tugged at his flesh. He grasped two of the straps across his chest and held on to them for dear life, feeling as if the skin was going to be torn from his face. There was nothing he could do. Jacob was helpless. He could only sit there, strapped tightly on his back with his legs in the air, and allow all of this to happen to him. There was a thunderous *boom* and Jacob was thrown forward so violently that the straps cut into him. He panicked. Had something gone wrong? Had the engines cut out and he was about to be sent plummeting back to Earth? No. He remembered what he had been told. The first stage of the rocket had been ejected. There was another *boom* and Jacob was thrown forward again. The second stage had ignited. It was now just that small, bulbous section of the rocket carrying the capsule up and up and up at more than seventeen and a half thousand miles an hour. He was at max q, or maximum dynamic pressure, sitting on top of five hundred and fifty tonnes of explosive and hurtling up into the sky at almost thirty times the speed of sound. Searing, white sunlight exploded into the capsule. The window coverings had been ripped free. Jacob jammed his eyes shut again, blinded, so he did not see the sky turning gradually from blue to black. The cacophonous noise and cataclysmic quaking were worse than ever. Jacob did not know how much more his body could take. His heart was going to stop.

And then everything stopped.

Eunata's legs wobbled. Terrified butterflies fluttered inside her stomach at the roar of the rocket reverberating around the room. Even the bare image scorched off the screen. Archangel 2 had risen in a blaze of searing, white light, a pillar of fire all that was separating it from the planet's surface as it climbed higher and higher into the sky.

'Vehicle is supersonic,' said a scientist close to Eunata and Amira.

'Maximum dynamic pressure has been reached,' said another one next to them.

Archangel 2 was on all of the screens at a dizzying variety of angles. Eunata watched with her mouth hanging open and tears rolling down her cheeks. The light beneath it was burning just as brightly but she watched the surrounding sky slowly turn an ever-darker shade of blue. The long, white tube that made up most of the rocket fell away and then it was just the smaller, rotund section hurtling up and up. The fact that Eunata had already watched this happen to her daughter and now it was the turn of her son was so horrifyingly absurd that she did not know whether to laugh or scream. She just kept watching and the tears just kept falling.

'He actually did it,' said Amira in a peculiar voice. 'In the end, he actually took a stand.'

'He is not just standing.' Eunata managed a shaky smile. 'He is soaring. And it is not the end. This story is just beginning.'

'Stage separation is confirmed,' said someone.

'Second stage is following nominal trajectory,' said someone else.

Amira gazed up at the images of the round, white capsule hurtling higher and higher into the darkening sky. There were no tears on her cheeks but her hazel eyes were wide with that glint that Eunata could not decipher.

'This stupid planet must really have something going for it,' Amira murmured.

'More than you know,' Eunata wiped her eyes, 'and climate change is its biggest threat. *Nothing* will change that. But as long as powerful people like you start offering more than empty words, we might actually get around to saving it.'

'Saving the world.' Amira rolled the words around

in her mouth. 'That would certainly be a turn-up for the books. Perhaps you're right. Maybe this story is just beginning . . .'

Amira turned to Eunata and spoke softly so only she could hear.

'. . . but I do love a good twist.'

A loud thrum echoed around the concrete room as if a master switch had been flipped. All the screens turned black. There was a moment of shocked silence as every scientist stared blankly at their empty screens. The silence was deafening. The continuous humming of the countless computers was only noticeable now that it was gone. There was nothing. No sound. No picture on the screens. Nothing. Everything had been switched off.

Then people were on their feet, gesturing wildly amid a babble of panicked voices.

'We've lost contact with Archangel 2!'

'I have no camera view!'

'All communication with the Garden is down!'

Eunata stood still amongst the chaos. Her mouth was agape and unmoving. Even the tears had come to a halt halfway down her cheeks. She was a statue. Amira whipped around, hair and red and gold sari swished around her gesticulating body. Golden bangles rattled on her wrists.

'Kowalski! What's happening?' she shouted across the room.

'We don't know, ma'am! Our ground network has gone down completely. We've lost all signal and can't contact the rocket or the space station! This has never happened before! I . . . I don't know what's going on!'

'WELL, FIND OUT!' Amira hollered.

Eunata still did not move. At the very back of her mind, she noted that the only other time she had seen Amira crack her icy composure was during their argument at the Shard after Jacob and Kira's car crash. On that occasion, Eunata had thought she was seeing the real Amira for the very first time. Had it all been an act? Or was it something else? Questions whispered from a shadowy corner of Eunata's consciousness.

She stared up at the empty screens, looking for stars. Eunata knew that as soon as she would be able to glimpse the tiny, white specks of light, she would know the cameras were once again operational and that Jacob had made it. He had made it to outer space and would soon be reunited with Kira onboard the Garden. Eunata did nothing but stare up at the black, silent screens as Mission Control went on erupting around her.

'Come on, Henry, my love,' Eunata whispered. 'Give me some stars.'

But no stars ever came.

CHAPTER
THIRTY-FOUR

Jacob was dead. Or, at least, he thought he was.

The shuddering had been replaced by a serene stillness so sudden that Jacob's first thought was that his life had ended. But that was not true. He was still alive.

He felt queasy and light-headed. There was an eerie silence, apart from the ever-present ringing in Jacob's ears. The stillness was unnerving. After the shock of the launch, it was bizarre to feel as if he were not going anywhere at all. There was no sun streaming through the window anymore. It was incredibly dark outside.

'Woah,' Jacob breathed and jumped slightly. He was startled by the sound of his own voice. It was the first time he had spoken since leaving the planet.

That reminded him of something. Kowalski had been right. There was definitely a problem with the ground network. Jacob realised that his radio had been silent ever since the countdown. Something had gone wrong. There was no way of communicating with anyone on the planet below. And there was no way for them to communicate with Jacob. He was on his own.

Jacob's Captain Cosmic action figure floated past his face as if it were underwater. He stared at it, at the futuristic, crimson and gold spacesuit and the expression of smug determination. Jacob had forgotten he had shoved it inside one of the many pockets of his tracksuit back at the Operations and Checkout Building. He reached out with a finger and lightly tapped the action figure's foot. Jacob watched it spin into the corner of the capsule. With a jolt, he realised that if it were not for the belts criss-crossing his chest, he would be floating around the capsule too. Jacob was weightless. He strained his neck to get a good look out of the window but it was too small and in the wrong place.

He could just about glimpse the twinkle of stars.

Jacob reached up and jabbed at the screen above his head. It was completely black. At first, he thought it too was broken but then he realised it was offering a view of what was outside the capsule. The Earth was behind him and out of sight but what Jacob could see were stars – millions upon millions of them. Some glowed brighter than others and in infinitely different colours. What was constant and unchanging was the sheer blackness between them.

For the first time, Jacob felt a small surge of childish delight. He was in space!

Something new blinked into view. Whatever it was shone brighter than any star. It looked like a silvery tree, suspended in the emptiness of space and growing gradually larger as Archangel 2 approached.

The Garden.

Slowly, the space station filled the screen. It was enormous. What Jacob had thought was a tree trunk was actually what looked like the white tower of a crane. Running alongside it on either side were vast solar arrays – rectangles of glistening, black silicon, tilted to soak up the energy of the sun. The branches of the tree were actually silver modules and corridors, bolted together like links in an interconnected chain and stretching away from the main tower. The entire space station must have been four hundred feet from end to end, twice the size of the rocket that had carried Jacob to it. He stared in wonder at the Garden and its many branches, waving exaltedly in the breeze.

No, Jacob had to remind himself. There was no breeze. There was no sound, no air pressure, no oxygen and there was nothing natural about the Garden. It was a man-made intrusion, floating alone in the most hostile environment known to humankind. Staring at the silvery space station, a strange sensation of dread seeped slowly into Jacob as if injected by a thousand tiny needles. He was on his own. Except he was not. Somewhere out there was his sister, waiting for him.

A booster rocket fired and Archangel 2 seemed to pick up speed. It was heading for a docking port at the end of one of the many tree branches. Jacob squinted at the screen. He thought he could see the capsule of Archangel 1 docked with one of the branches on the far side of the space station. The black, gaping mouth of his own docking port approached. It looked as if it were going to swallow him whole. The gleaming rivets and silver panels of the Garden were all Jacob could see as the capsule neared. The RanaTech logo was printed in black on the side of one of the modules. There was the slightest of bumps and that was that. Jacob could not believe it. The impact was less than an aeroplane's landing gear connecting with a runway. After the hellish ordeal that had begun his journey into space, it had ended with no more force than two plastic boats knocking against each other in the bath.

Archangel 2 had docked with the Garden. Jacob had arrived.

It took a while to unbuckle all the straps that were tying him to his seat. There was no gravity. Everything had to be done slowly and gently. Tensing himself, Jacob climbed out of the seat and pushed himself away from it with the lightest of kicks. He soared across the capsule, grabbed the handle attached to the hatch and stayed there, bobbing up and down.

'Woah,' Jacob breathed again.

He pulled the handle out and turned it. The hatch swung open. Jacob climbed through the node connecting Archangel 2 to the Garden and found himself inside the first module, six feet wide and ten feet long. Each module was connected to the next, creating a twisting corridor which seemed to slowly writhe. Cold air washed over him, chilling him to the bone. It smelled harsh and metallic, produced artificially by air conditioners which whirred dully. Every inch of the walls was packed with equipment. Wires and pipes snaked between stacked cabinets and endless dials, gauges and switches. There was hardly any light, only the dull, blinking glow of machinery that cast the first and second module in an eerie haze. The twisting corridor disappeared into darkness after that.

There were handrails on the walls and ceiling and, for a few seconds, Jacob clung to one of them. He was not feeling well at all. He wanted to throw up. He was sweating. His back was hurting. Without gravity to hold them in place, his insides were floating weightlessly inside him. He desperately needed to go to the toilet. Jacob tried to push all of that out of his head. He hooked a few fingers onto the handrail and used them to propel himself headfirst into the gloom, thinking about what he would do or say when he finally saw Kira again.

He did not have to wait long to find out. Jacob had floated barely a few feet when there was a piercing scream and his sister exploded from the darkness before him. Kira's eyes were wide and bulging, her hair dishevelled. Her grabbing hands latched onto the chest of Jacob's tracksuit and tore him from the handrail. The two of them, entwined and catapulted by Kira's momentum, were hurled back into the closed door of the hatch. Jacob's shoulder collided with the metal surface.

'What are you doing, Kira?' he gasped, shoulder smarting.

Kira scrabbled at him with clawing hands. Her electric blue eyes were so close to Jacob's face that their unabated horror filled his vision.

'You were right, Jacob! You were right!' she shrieked into his ear. 'We need to get out!'

'What are you talking about?'

There was another piercing scream but this one was unlike anything emitted by any human. This was something he had heard before. It was the screech of fingernails being dragged down a blackboard.

As Jacob floated there, clutching his sister, he was suddenly aware that his warm and wet insides, suspended weightlessly inside his body and so easily punctured, had turned to icy slush. A shiver trickled like cold water down his elongated spine.

'No,' he whispered.

He stared over Kira's shoulder. Two pinpricks of poisonous, green light appeared in the blackness that seethed just metres beyond.

'No,' Jacob whispered again. 'They're not real. They're not real. *This isn't real.*'

The two lights grew larger. Closer. The creature slowly emerged, an Other far bigger than and unlike any Jacob had seen before. Its gargantuan form, more than two metres tall and with the same wiry, black hair standing in coarse spikes all over it, engulfed the corridor from floor to ceiling. Blazing, green eyes and livid, black pupils fixed upon them with inhuman hatred. In the absence of gravity, the creature too was floating nightmarishly towards them, breath rasping. Glistening, grey fingers curled and uncurled with chipped, black fingernails slicing closer to Jacob and Kira with every second.

The Other screamed and so did they.

JACOB AND KIRA WILL RETURN IN BOOK TWO.

ACKNOWLEDGEMENTS

Thanks must go first to my agent, Kemi Ogunsanwo of The Good Literary Agency, for her unwavering dedication and support. Kemi has the uncanny ability to always be right about everything. Whatever she asks, whether it's to write two sequels or order dessert, I've learned to just do it the first time around. It saves everybody time.

I would also like to thank my two editors, Katie Lawrence and, previously, Polly Lyall-Grant, as well as everyone else at Hachette Children's Group.

Tom and Carla Gill founded Play Action International, formerly East African Playgrounds, which carries out great work constructing playgrounds and other programmes allowing children their right to play, positively impacting their education, development, and wellbeing. The charity also gave me the opportunity to travel the southern regions of Uganda, particularly Jinja and Lake Bunyonyi, for three weeks in 2015, a trip that provided much of the inspiration and research for this book.

My mum, Lorna, grandma Eunata, aunty Tessie and uncles Ian and Errol were also exceedingly helpful in telling me all about their Ugandan upbringing.

Finally, I would like to extend my gratitude to Gerard McKeown, my English teacher at The John Fisher School in Croydon, for instilling in myself and so many others an eternal passion for storytelling, as well as subordinate clauses, that paid off and then some.

© Shotbyjo

Patrick Gallagher is a primary school teacher from South London with roots in Goa in India and Donegal in Ireland. He studied English and American Literature with Creative Writing in both Kent and Maynooth and is a keen artist and violinist in his spare time.

Like lots of Goans of that generation, Patrick's mother was born and raised in Uganda and the time he himself has spent there inspired the spectacular backdrop to *Transcendent*.

Jacob and Kira's story has been years in the making. It draws not only on Patrick's experience of dual heritage but every science-fiction and adventure story he devoured as a child, every *Doctor Who* episode and *Spider-Man* cartoon, every comic or short story he scribbled on scrap paper, every daydream on long car journeys.

To Patrick's class and every other child reading *Transcendent*, he would like to say this: if you love writing stories, keep going.

You never know. You might just never stop.